PRAISE FOR FREYA BARKER

Freya Barker writes a mean romance, I tell you! A REAL romance, with real characters and real conflict.

~*Author M. Lynne Cunning*

I've said it before and I'll say it again and again, Freya Barker is one of the BEST storytellers out there.

~*Turning Pages At MidnightBook Blog*

God, Freya Barker gets me every time I read one of her books. She's a master at creating a beautiful story that you lose yourself in the moment you start reading.

~*Britt Red Hatter Book Blog*

Freya Barker has woven a delicate balance of honest emotions and well-formed characters into a tale that is as unique as it is gripping.

~*Ginger Scott, bestselling young and new adult author and Goodreads Choice Awards finalist*

Such a truly beautiful story! The writing is gorgeous, the scenery is beautiful...

~*Author Tia Louise*

From Dust by Freya Barker is one of those special books. One of those whose plotline and characters remain with you for days after you finished it.

~*Jeri's Book Attic*

No amount of words could describe how this story made me feel, I think this is one I will remember forever, absolutely freaking awesome is not even close to how I felt about it.

~Lilian's Book Blog

Still Air was insightful, eye-opening, and I paused numerous times to think about my relationships with my own children. Anytime a book can evoke a myriad of emotions while teaching life lessons you'll continue to carry with you, it's a 5-star read.

~ Bestselling Author CP Smith

In my opinion, there is nothing better than a Freya Barker book. With her final installment in her Portland, ME series, Still Air, she does not disappoint. From start to finish I was completely captivated by Pam, Dino, and the entire Portland family.

~ Author RB Hilliard

The one thing you can always be sure of with Freya's writing is that it will pull on ALL of your emotions; it's expressive, meaningful, sarcastic, so very true to life, real, hard-hitting and heartbreaking at times and, as is the case with this series especially, the story is at points raw, painful and occasionally fugly BUT it is also sweet, hopeful, uplifting, humorous and heart-warming.

~ Book Loving Pixies

ALSO BY FREYA BARKER

La Plata County FBI
ROCK POINT SERIES 4

10-CODE

FREYA BARKER

ISBN: 978-1-988733-37-1

Cover Design:
RE&D - Margreet Asselbergs

Editing:
Karen Hrdlicka

Proofing:
Joanne Thompson

Interior Design
CP SMITH

DEDICATION

To the amazing women who introduced me to Durango, Colorado, where this series is based.
Linda and Delia,
thank you for your hospitality, your time, your friendship and your love.
You are the reason I developed such a great passion for beautiful Colorado and all it has to offer.

10-CODE

CHAPTER 1

MARYA

"I've changed my mind."

I look to my side where Liam is slouched in the passenger seat of my ancient Jeep Cherokee. We just dropped off his brothers at my mom's place. They hadn't been too excited with the prospect of sitting in the bleachers at their brother's first soccer game of the season at eight thirty on a Saturday morning. Since I'm not comfortable leaving an eight and a thirteen-year-old unsupervised, their grandma's place had been their only option.

Let me tell you, getting my three boys out of bed at six on a weekend, so we can hit the soccer field in bloody Bloomfield fifteen minutes before game time, as instructed, is no mean feat. Theo, my oldest, had to be enticed with a soaked sponge over his face. It did the trick, got him out of bed, but with a foul temper. Harry, I couldn't even wake up, and I spent ten valuable minutes wrangling him in clothes without his cooperation. I had to carry him to my car and again into my mom's house, where I dumped him on the couch. He may only be eight, but that's still a ton of deadweight to lug around.

Liam, my middle child, was a little easier, seeing as he'd been excited about his first game, but apparently that shine is wearing off.

"Suck it up, buttercup," I tell him. "Out of the eight games on the schedule, you only have two early ones, the rest are at a more civilized hour. You'll get used to it. You worked hard to make this team, don't tell me you're giving up before you even get started." I bite back a reminder that I'd taken on a second job with a cleaning service so I could afford getting him enrolled, which was more than my regular tight budget could handle.

He mumbles something I can't quite make out and his posture still spells his displeasure, but he doesn't make a fuss.

I'll take it. He's been moody as of late. That is, moodier than normal. Of all my kids, Liam is the one who was most affected when Jeremy bailed five years ago. He was six at the time and idolized his father, so he felt that betrayal deepest.

Theo was eight and had been too aware of what was happening in our sham of a marriage. He just seemed relieved the constant tension we lived under at the time was over.

At three, Harry had been blissfully oblivious, perfectly content to be wherever I was.

But Liam, he felt it deep. It's one of the reasons I worked hard to make his dream of joining the soccer league come true. The other two have not expressed any interest in organized sports, but Liam craved it. I thought he might benefit from the team bonding, not to mention the male influence of a coach. He doesn't get much male exposure, other than his brothers. His teacher is a woman and then there's his grandma and me, and we've turned avoiding men into an art form.

"Eat your Pop-Tart, kid. You're gonna need the energy," I urge him.

My lofty plans to make the kids egg sandwiches for breakfast flew out the window this morning, and I barely managed to throw a few quick things in plastic a bag for Liam. Parenting fail. Luckily, Mom can be trusted to take care of the other two with something far more nutritional.

I know by the tearing of the wrapper he's doing as asked, and I wish I'd thought to throw an extra one in the bag for me. My stomach is rumbling. No coffee and an empty stomach make the prospect of sitting on the hard bleachers for a couple of hours even less appealing. I hope to God there's a coffee shop nearby, so I can pop out and grab myself a little reinforcement.

The hour-drive is otherwise quiet, since Liam seems to have dozed off beside me. By the time we pull into the parking lot of the Chamblee Soccer Complex, I can see from the volume of cars we're probably one of the last to arrive. Shit.

"Grab your gear, we're going to have to hustle."

Apparently the nap has done my boy well, since he doesn't argue and pulls his bag from the back seat before setting off for the field on a steady jog. I follow behind at a much more sedate pace.

Parents and families fill the small bleachers on the sideline, and I scan the benches to look for an empty spot when my eyes land on a familiar face and the impressive body it belongs to.

Dylan Barnes. A hard man to miss; not that I've been trying.

Since my friend, Kerry, who owns the bookstore slash coffee shop I manage, met and married his boss, Damian Gomez, Dylan's been in to grab a coffee from time to time. Dylan is an agent with the La Plata County FBI field office and looks at least as imposing as his title implies.

Aside from the fact I've sworn off men completely, he's probably ten years too young for me anyway. It doesn't mean I can't look, which I do every opportunity I get.

I'm surprised to see him here, and briefly wonder if he's one of the coaches, when I see a boy about Liam's age jog up and toss a baseball cap at him. His spitting image: same dark floppy hair, same dimpled smile, same melty chocolate eyes. Holy shit.

I realize I'm still standing at the foot of the bleachers, gawking at Dylan with his obvious son, and notice more than a few faces turned in my direction.

The flush I feel on my pale cheeks burns into a full blush when Dylan turns to look at me as well. Not only that, the only open space seems to be on the bench beside him.

Where's the goddamn coffee when you need it?

DYLAN

"Dad, can you hang on to that? Coach says we can't wear baseball caps on the soccer field."

I catch the cap he tosses my way and bite down a grin. I told him that five minutes ago when he ran off, eager to join in the warm-up starting on the field. Max is at the age where I'm no longer recipient of his blind faith, but apparently his coach is.

"He says I can have the right-winger spot," Max says with a toothy grin. Last year he played defense and wasn't too enamored with that. He prefers being in the thick of the play, getting more opportunities to score.

"Good stuff, buddy. Just make sure you listen to Coach and don't hog the ball.

"I won't, Dad."

He runs off and I catch a glimpse of a woman standing ten feet away, staring at me. It takes me a minute to place her. The oversized hoodie, ripped jeans, and hair in a sloppy bun are not her usual look when I drop in at Kerry's Korner for a coffee on my way to work. It's usually a stern ponytail, reading glasses on a chain, nondescript work clothes, and sensible shoes.

Marya Berger sure as fuck looks a lot more approachable this way.

I know the woman's story, I was in Denver at the time, but I heard when I came back. She'd fallen victim to some sleezeball, who was using her to get to Kerry. The guy didn't succeed, but Marya got hurt pretty badly in the process.

I throw her a smile and pat the empty space beside me. When she doesn't move, I call out.

"Marya—come sit."

I watch as she takes a few hesitant steps closer and points at the coffee in my hand. "I'm gonna need one of those," she shares. "Where'd you get it?"

"Sonya's Diner. It's just up 2nd Street, left on Ash, and…you know what, I could use a top up myself. You sit down, I'll go grab us some coffees. You stay here and keep our spots." I get up and indicate for her to sit down.

"It's okay, I—"

"Marya, sit down," I cut her off. "I'll be no more than five minutes. What do you take in yours?"

She looks like she's going to protest again but then shakes her head sharply and plonks down on the bench. "Cream, one sugar."

"Large?"

She lifts her face and slowly raises an eyebrow.

"Large it is. Anything else?"

"Yeah, something to eat. Anything." She digs through her purse as she mutters, "A muffin or a

Danish, I don't care. I'm starving. Please?" She pulls out a twenty-dollar bill, offering it to me but I wave her off.

"Be right back." Without giving her another chance to protest, I turn on my heel and head for the parking lot.

When I get back ten minutes later with a tray of coffee and a paper bag with food, she's still sitting in the same spot, her eyes peeled on the soccer field where the game has just started. She looks up when I sit down next to her.

"So who's your kid?" I ask, handing her a coffee.

"Tall, dirty blond hair, his socks already slouching around his ankles. That would be Liam."

I scan the field and pinpoint the boy she describes. "A forward," I note.

"Yeah, that's what he told me, but I have to admit, I'm not sure what that means." She looks down when I start pulling containers from the bag. "What on earth? That's no muffin."

"Nope. Can't start a day on a muffin, so I got us a decent breakfast." I hand her plastic cutlery and a container with scrambled eggs, bacon, and home fries. "You're not a vegetarian are you?"

Her eyes squint at me. "Raising three boys and looking like this?" she points out, indicating her pleasantly rounded body. For emphasis she shoves half a strip of bacon in her mouth. I grin and dive into my own. "Your boy?" She points at the field where Max is dodging around the defense on the sideline, the ball glued to his foot.

"Max," I confirm. "Winger." Things get tense when Max feeds the ball to Marya's boy, who lands a solid kick, but the ball misses the crossbar by a hair. "Nice shot," I mumble.

"I'll take your word for it," she counters, making me grin again.

She surprises me. Very different from the stuffy and slightly grumpy librarian persona she displays in the bookstore. I already knew she was pretty, but I didn't know she was funny to boot. I'm liking this more relaxed version of Marya a fuckofalot better.

We finish breakfast in silence, taking in the game, before she speaks up.

"Thanks, I needed that. Feeling almost human now."

"Good." I grab her empty container, along with my own, toss them into the garbage next to the bleachers, and return to my seat beside her. "Where are your other two boys?"

She glances over before her eyes drift back to the field. "My mom's. They weren't too hip on getting up at this ungodly hour to watch their brother run around a soccer field."

"How old are they?" I ask, figuring her son, Liam, would be about the same age as Max who turns eleven in five weeks.

"Harry is eight, Liam eleven, and Theo is thirteen. Don't know what I was thinking having one after the other," she grumbles cutely. "Hormones are hitting my household hard, and the prospect of another ten years of that is giving me nightmares."

I chuckle at the horrified look on her face.

Yeah, I definitely like her much better like this.

"Their dad any help?" I probe.

"Ha!" she barks out loudly. "Haven't seen or heard from him in five years. Not that he was any help before, mind you. Too busy plotting his desertion with his new pregnant plaything." She glances over, takes in my shocked look, and shrugs apologetically. "Sorry. Too much, I know."

"I asked," I remind her.

"Not for my life story."

"It was hardly that," I assure her. "But insightful all the same." I lean closer and bump her shoulder with mine. "Besides, sounds like we have more in common than our sons playing on the same team."

She looks at me curiously. "Yeah? How so?"

"Six years ago, my ex walked out on us without as much as a glance back," I share.

"For real? She walked out on her own child?" She shakes her head sharply. "I just don't get some people. I mean, Jeremy was an ass, and I really shouldn't be surprised he bailed, but a mother abandoning her baby? That is just mind-boggling to me."

I stifle a smile at the vehemence in her tone and the angry set of her jaw. I don't bother pointing out that a father abandoning three children is no less incomprehensible. At least to me.

Loud cheers go up around us, drawing my

attention to the field where I just catch Max high-fiving Marya's son, who apparently scored. On my feet in a flash, I stick my fingers in my mouth and whistle my approval. Max's head instantly swivels in my direction, a big grin on his face, and the other boy follows suit, his smile more subdued.

"What just happened?" Marya asks in a soft voice as I sit back down beside her.

"Your kid just scored a goal."

Her face breaks open in a bright smile. "For real?" She turns to the field, where the boys are already resuming the game, jumps up and cups her hands around her mouth. *"Yay, Liam! You rock!"* she yells, just as the crowd settles down again. Her son whips around before ducking his head quickly, a look of mortification on his face. Oblivious to the attention she's drawn, she drops back down in her seat, the smile still on her face. "Righteous," she whispers.

Oh yeah, I'm liking this Marya. Seriously fucking cute.

When the game is over—the Chargers win with that single goal—Liam and Max walk over like they've been buds forever.

"Great job, boys," I tell them. Liam looks up with a cautious grin.

"Proud of you, kidlet." Marya ruffles his hair, and he hides a smile as he ducks her touch.

"Dad, Liam is WillIAm103 in my *Fortnite* group," Max announces breathlessly.

Like his dad, my son likes his PS4 games, *Fortnite*

being his top favorite. Instead of forbidding him to play the game, I decided to join him. Better to monitor what he's up to and who he interacts with, than to have him play it on the sly without any supervision. WillIAm103 is the handle of one of the kids he sometimes plays with online.

"No kidding? Cool to meet you, Liam. I'm Max's dad." I stick my hand out, which the boy hesitantly takes.

"Is that the game you and your brother spend most of your time playing downstairs?" Marya asks her son.

"Yeah." The bored tone of his voice doesn't match the sharp side-look he darts her way.

"Dad is 10-CODE," Max babbles on happily, sharing my handle with his new friend. I assume he's already shared his: BitMax1.

"Max, maybe you wanna say hello to Liam's mom first?"

My kid is borderline ADHD, which means he rarely takes a breath to think. My reminder registers in the bashful look he shoots my way before turning to Marya.

"Hey, Liam's mom," he says, sticking out his grubby hand. It doesn't seem to bother Marya as she grabs onto it. "Marya," she corrects. "Nice to meet you, Max." She lets him go. "So I'm guessing you guys didn't know you were playing on the same team?"

"Nope." This from Max. "I've seen him around at

school, but I'm in the fifth grade and Liam is in sixth. I never even knew he was WillIAm103."

"Go figure," Marya says on a smile.

"That's what I said." Max grins back. "Hey, you guys wanna go get a burger? There's this awesome diner Dad always takes me to after the game."

"Bud," I caution him in a soft voice. Like I said, he leaps before he looks.

"I mean, if that's okay?" He turns his trademarked look of innocence my way. Little late, Kiddo.

I'm about to answer when Marya jumps in. "Not this time," she quickly responds with an awkward smile at me. "We have to go pick up Liam's brothers at their grandma's before they decimate her fridge again. Maybe some other time?"

"Cool," is Max's response. "Hey," he turns to Liam as they start walking. "I didn't know you had brothers. Wicked. I don't have brothers or sisters."

Liam, who remained quiet throughout most of the exchange, seems to have no issue talking to Max as they make their way over to the parking lot. Marya and I follow behind.

"He's a talker," she notes.

"That he is."

"My youngest is like that. Came out flapping his lips. Not a moody bone in his body, unlike his older brothers."

"Yup. That's Max," I confirm, watching as the boys stop beside a beat-up Jeep. Presumably hers. I find I'm not quite ready to let her go so easily.

"Look…" I stop her with a hand on her arm. "Not sure what next week'll look like—my work can be a bit unpredictable, which means it's possible my mom and stepdad show up with Max—but if I'm at the game, why don't we try for that burger then?" I can tell before she even opens her mouth she's going to blow me off, so I quickly add, "It's just a burger, the kids'll love it, and they have seriously fucking good milkshakes too."

A battle wages on her face, before she finally settles on resigned. "Okay. I guess we can do just burgers."

"Great. Look forward to it."

"I do…" She hesitates and then says, "I'll see you later," before joining the boys by her car.

I call out to Max, who comes bounding to my side as I unlock my new Ford Bronco. Casting one last look over my shoulder, I just see Marya's round ass disappear in her Jeep before hopping behind the wheel myself.

I barely hear Max's chatter on the way to Sonya's Diner, my mind is on that sentence the pretty brunette left unfinished. *I do too.*

CHAPTER 2

MARYA

"Mom! He's killing me!"

I take a deep breath at the sound of my youngest screaming at the top of his lungs. Thank God we live in a small, detached house, otherwise I'd have the cops at my door daily for violating the noise ordinance.

"What the hell is going on now?" I stomp my way down the stairs into the basement, where my boys have their pad.

These last few weeks I've been rethinking my decision to ban all gaming from their bedrooms, in favor of turning the rec room downstairs into their PS4 lair. It was Mom's idea last Christmas to set each of them up in their own semi-private area with beanbags and separate secondhand gaming systems. An advance on their inheritance, she'd claimed, but I knew that was a load of bull. Mom's not much better off than I am in the financial department. It took some convincing before I caved to that extravagance, but when the boys' fights over the single system we had at the time almost turned bloody, I gave in.

The only brand-new purchases had been the beanbags and the paint, but the refurbished game consoles and office dividers Mom was able to snag at bargain prices, and the total revamp of the rec room cost less than eight hundred dollars. Still a whack, but as Mom argued, she'd have spent about two hundred on each of the kids for Christmas anyway, so she had it in her budget.

The peace it created had been bliss until a few weeks ago—about the time Liam started moping around—when the frequency of conflicts picked up again. The fighting is usually between him and Harry. Theo seems unaffected; he just tunes everyone out with the help of his sound-cancelling headphones.

"Enough!" I bark when I catch sight of Liam hauling back to punch his brother in the face. "What on earth has gotten into you?" I grab Liam's arm and pull him off his younger brother, who already sports the mark of a successfully landed fist on his cheekbone.

"He just came at me," Harry hurries to explain. "I didn't do nothing." I'm not buying his innocence for a second, but that doesn't excuse the scene I walked in on.

"I'm talking to your brother," I shut him up.

At first Liam struggles, still seething and focused

on his brother, until I clamp my hands on his shoulders and turn him so I'm the only person he sees.

"Don't make me ask again," I threaten.

"He's an idiot," Liam hisses, dropping his eyes to the ground.

"Christ, kid. You're all idiots from time to time; you don't see me pummeling the snot out of you. That's a piss-poor excuse and you know it." I give him a little shake.

"Harry called Liam a pussy," Theo, pulling off his headphones, contributes. Apparently my oldest had been paying attention after all.

My eyes fly to my youngest, but my hands keep hold of Liam. "First of all, we don't use words like that in my house. You know it and it's gonna cost you. Why would you call your brother that?"

Harry throws Theo a dirty look, but knows better than to do any more than that. Theo would wipe the floor with him. He's not just tall, but at thirteen, he's already filling out. "You're a snitch," my baby hisses at his older brother.

"I'm good with that, since you're a liar and a pain in the ass," Theo fires back.

"All right! That's enough," I order. "Harry, up to your room. I'll deal with you in a minute, and you'd better not give me lip," I add, when I see the stubborn look on his face. "Or I'll double your punishment." I wait for him to stomp up the stairs before I turn to Liam. "You know better, kid. Whaling on your baby brother because he cussed you out is not acceptable.

Ever. Do you get me?" He glares at me, but when I wait him out he eventually gives me a jerky nod. "Sticks and stones, buddy. Remember that. Now, I want you in your room as well, and you'd be smart to stay away from your brother. You hear me?" Another jerky nod. "I'll be up shortly." With that I let him go and he follows his younger brother, without the stomping.

Then I turn to Theo.

"Wanna clue me in?"

Theo glances over at the stairs before his eyes return to me. "Liam plays online with some friends and Harry's been bugging him to be included. Harry's pissed because Liam won't let him and has been poking at him all morning."

"Any idea why he won't let him play?"

He shrugs his shoulders and focuses on his screen, dismissing me. "I'm not a mind reader."

My firstborn is a smart-ass, but I'll let that slide, since I have my hands full with his siblings.

"Turn off their systems when it's time to go, yeah?"

He flicks me a quick glance. "Sure, Mom."

Then I haul my ass upstairs, so I can tell my other boys there'll be no gaming for a week.

It's promising to be a fun Sunday night dinner at my mother's.

"Gimme him."

I wiggle my fingers at the cutest one-year-old in

the world.

Kerry, who just walked into the bookstore with baby Dante perched on her hip, grins at me. "Have at it, but he comes with a full diaper, so that's yours too."

"That doesn't scare me." The little boy stretches his arms toward me and I pluck him off his mother and snuggle him close. "Whoa, little dude. How can something so cute and adorable produce the stink of an open sewer?"

Kerry snickers as I reach out a free hand for the diaper bag and take Dante to the small office in the back of the store.

I adore this boy. All smiles and happy babbles, I've never seen him in a bad mood. I'm hit with a wave of nostalgia, remembering my own babies at this age. I adored every minute of them being sweet and cuddly. They're not that anymore, except perhaps Harry, who still snuggles with me on the couch every now and then.

I soak up Dante's gurgles and dimpled smiles while I can, since the mood at home this past week has been subzero. After last Sunday's blowup, both younger boys were banned from their PlayStation, and have made sure I know how unhappy they are. I hate to admit it, but I'll be glad when this week is over.

"There you go, sweet cheeks," I mumble at the baby, tucking him back into his onesie and bib overalls. "Now you smell as edible as you look." For good measure I blow a raspberry in his neck and he dives his little fingers in my hair, pulling hard as he giggles.

"Gah!"

I can hear Kerry talking to a customer when I walk back into the store, but I don't know who until I round the large bookcase and see Dylan leaning on the counter, smiling down at her.

Of course, it would have to be him.

I managed to quash any and all thoughts of him this past week out of self-preservation. I don't get why I always have to be attracted to men who are assholes, deadbeats, or way the hell out of my league. Dylan Barnes being case in point. The man is too young, too fit, too nice, and too good-looking. Did I mention young?

I know this, and still I slow my pace as I take stock of my appearance. Especially in contrast to Kerry, who always looks fabulous with her bohemian clothes and kick-ass hair. My work wardrobe consists of bland monochromatic thrift store purchases, because there's no extra money when you have three growing boys. The hair pulled back in a ponytail may not be flattering, but it's practical. Except now—thanks to Dante—it lilts sideways and a chunk of hair hangs over my face, and the baby is chewing on the collar of my dress shirt, dripping drool down my front. I make a lovely picture, not that it should matter because I've sworn off men anyway.

Lifting my chin a notch, I approach the counter.

"Gah!" Dante gurgles when he spots Dylan, and promptly abandons my collar as he virtually launches himself out of my arms.

The man is quick, catching Dante just as he slips from my hold.

"Easy, kiddo," he mumbles at him, tucking him close to his chest, and I feel my resolve melt at the gentle smile he directs at the baby. Then his eyes lift up and the corner of his mouth twitches as he takes in my disheveled state.

Just fabulous.

"Hey." My voice comes out breathy, and I catch Kerry's curious glance when I try to blow the chunk of hair Dante dislodged out of my face as I straighten my shirt.

"Marya," he rumbles in greeting.

"Looking for coffee?" I ask, turning to the fancy machine Kerry invested in a few years ago, without waiting for an answer. "Americano, black?"

"Sure."

Kerry leans her butt against the counter beside the espresso machine, and I feel her glare on me. I ignore her and focus on Dylan's coffee. Anything to keep my eyes occupied and my hands busy.

"I actually popped in to let you know I'll be out of town for the next few days, so I won't make the Chargers' game."

I almost drop the small coffee filter but recover quickly. "Oh, okay," I mutter, wondering if the elastic holding up these synthetic navy pants is bunching up in the back. My ass doesn't need the added bulk.

"My mother will be bringing Max," he continues,

and I risk a glance at Kerry while his coffee brews. The expression on her face tells me, the moment Dylan is out the door, I will be grilled. "So I hope you don't mind a rain check on that burger?"

"Don't worry about it." I wave my hand dismissively before pouring the coffee into a carryout cup and finally turning to face him.

Despite Dante's little fist pummeling his face, his eyes are on me and his expression is serious. "Not worried," he clarifies. "Pissed. I was looking forward to it, but now I have to wait another week."

Alrighty then.

An awkward three-way shuffle over the counter ensues when I try to hand him his cup without spilling, and he tries to hand the baby off to Kerry. We eventually manage without dropping coffee or Dante, and I watch him saunter to the door where he turns around.

"See you next week and tell Liam good luck tomorrow." I mutely nod in response. "Later, Kerry," he adds, with a quick glance her way before he's out the door.

I can sense when Kerry turns her attention on me, and I reluctantly meet her eyes, bracing for what I know will be the third degree.

She doesn't make me wait long.

"What the hell was that?"

DYLAN

"Got all your stuff?"

I have to wave a hand in Max's face before he clues in I'm talking to him. He pauses the game and pulls his headgear off. "What?"

"We've gotta get going, bud. Do you have everything you need?"

He gets up to shut off his PlayStation and the TV before walking over to me. "I'm ready."

"Don't want to bring that?"

I point at his discarded headphones with mic.

"Don't need it," he says, which surprises me. Mom and Clint got him the same gaming system so he could play at their place, but he always drags his gear along.

I should've been on the road a while ago, so I don't have time to probe the wistful look on his face as he passes me. He grabs his backpack in the hallway, swings it over his shoulder, and tags his overnight bag. I pick up my duffel and his sports bag before following him out the door.

"Son," Clint rumbles with a nod at me when he opens the door to us. He barely manages to ruffle Max's hair, who slips by him and into the kitchen, where I'm sure Mom is waiting.

My mother and stepdad moved from Cedar Tree to Durango almost two years ago, when I was assigned the La Plata County FBI field office, mostly for Max's sake. They took on the bulk of his rearing since his mother took off and I joined the FBI, and I'll forever be grateful. I wouldn't be where I am if not for their support after I cleared a not so stellar patch in my life.

My biological father died before I was even born,

and Mom raised me on her own. Max was already two before Clint came into her life. He's a good man: salt of the earth and completely devoted to Ma. She deserves nothing less after putting her life on hold for me.

Theirs is as much a home for Max as mine is, and for a single father in a career that's anything but nine-to-five, it's a huge bonus. Especially when I'm given last-minute notice I'm expected to report to the field office in Grand Junction for a task force meeting at eight tomorrow morning. Since there are no direct flights, it's faster to drive the four hours through the mountains it'll take me to get there. I just don't particularly want to do it in the dark, which is why I'm eager to get going.

"That his stuff for tomorrow?" Clint asks when I step inside and drop Max's sports duffel in the hall.

"Yeah. His game is at eleven thirty at the Farmington Complex, but he should be there fifteen to twenty minutes before game time for his warm-up."

"We'll get him there."

"Sorry to dump this on you. I just got this assignment this afternoon."

Clint drops one of his massive paws on my shoulder and grins. "Not like it's a hardship, Son. He's a good kid and having him here makes your ma happy, which in turn means good things for me."

I roll my eyes and shove past him, trying not to grin at his teasing chuckle. Like I said, he's a good man and worships my mother. Hard to find issue with that.

"Those boots better be clean." She's already wagging her finger in my face before I have a chance to say hello. "That hellion of yours already dragged his dirt onto my floors."

I ignore her grumbles—that's just her way—and wrap her up in a hug. "Thanks for doing this, Ma."

"Pfssht." She dismisses me with a wave of her hand and pulls from my hold. "I made soup and quesadillas. You're not getting on the road on an empty stomach."

"I don't have time," I tell her regretfully.

"Knew you were gonna say that," she says, grabbing a travel mug and a cooler bag and handing them over. "Potato leek soup you can drink, and I've wrapped up a bunch of quesadillas so you can eat on the road."

I lean down and kiss her cheek. "Thanks, Ma."

"Max!" she yells. "Your dad's leaving!"

His feet come stomping down the stairs and he slides across the floor on his socks, slamming into my midriff. "Bye, Dad." He grins up at me, his arms around my waist.

"Couple of days, bud. I'll call you, okay?"

"Yeah."

"Listen to your coach and play like you did last week, you hear?"

"I will, Dad."

I kiss the top of his head and let him go. "Good."

"Dad?" he calls after me when I get to the door.

"Yeah, Max?"

"Get the bad guys before they get you, okay?"

He's told me this each time I've left on an assignment, ever since I ended up in the hospital with a gunshot wound to my shoulder last year.

"I will, buddy. Love you."

"Love you too, Dad."

Those words I tuck away when I walk out the door and get in my Bronco, and the entire way to Grand Junction I hope I can make good on my promise to get back home to my boy unharmed.

CHAPTER 3

MARYA

I don't want to examine too closely why anticipation
for my son's soccer game has my stomach in knots.

But it does.

We're on time today, judging by the parking lot.
Last Saturday—Liam's second game—we'd been late
again when Harry hit his head on the edge of the coffee
table in a wrestling match with his oldest brother, just
as we were about to leave. Blood flowed copiously
from the relatively small cut over his eyebrow, and
it had taken me fifteen minutes I didn't have to spare
to calm him down, clean him up, and butterfly the
heck out of his injury, before I managed to wrangle
the boys into the Jeep.

I swear I should've stopped after my second ended
up a boy as well.

This morning I took no chances and had the boys

sit on opposite sides of the living room until I was ready to head out.

"Can I head over to the playground?" Harry asks, skipping beside me as we walk over to the field.

I look over to where a bunch of kids are already dangling from monkey bars and defying gravity on the swings. "If Theo goes with you, but I'm just gonna say, if either of you get injured there'll be no first aid until halftime."

"Come on," Harry punches his big brother, yelling over his shoulder as he takes off on a jog. "Bet I can swing higher than you."

"Fat chance," Theo mumbles, before he runs after his baby brother.

I watch after them with a sigh. If I could cover those kids in bubble wrap I would. In the past thirteen years, I've seen too many bloody noses, knee scrapes, concussions, black eyes, fat lips, cuts, and even a few broken bones. I'm over it.

"Good luck, kid," I call after Liam, who never slowed down his march to the field. There's no reaction. Still moody, even though both he and his younger brother got their gaming privileges back. I'm blaming it on hormones. *Mercy.*

My eyes drift to the bleachers. Plenty of room, but no Dylan. Instead, I spot his mother and stepfather, who Max excitedly introduced last weekend. I'd already met Beth, in the bookstore, but had no idea she was Dylan's mother. Clint, his stepdad, seemed a nice guy, and I spent a few minutes chatting with them after the game. Still, I try not to acknowledge the letdown I'm feeling at the lack of Dylan as disappointment. I should know better.

"Marya! Over here!" Beth calls out, and I climb up the bleachers to sit down beside her.

"Good morning."

"Mornin'," Clint returns, but his eyes on the field where the boys are warming up.

"Dylan's held up with this case, he couldn't make it back in time," Beth voluntarily shares, and I glance over catching her scrutinizing me. "Wasn't sure why he asked me to share that with you, but seeing your face when you spotted us here instead'a him, I figure I've got a good idea."

"Beth," Clint's warning rumble falls on deaf ears.

"My Dylan, he had a bitch for a wife and has buried himself in work and raising Max ever since she took off. Time he had some fun."

"Bean," Clint tries again. "Quit your meddlin'."

"I'm not meddling," she fires back. "Just friendly conversation."

"You're as subtle as an earthquake, woman."

"Whatever." She dismisses her husband by turning her back on him, focusing her attention on me. "I'm just saying; it's clear you're not the only one who would've preferred it to be my boy sittin' here."

Oh my. Last week it had been Kerry, who—after grilling me on Dylan—spent twenty minutes trying to convince me what a good guy he is. Now I have his mother trying to play Cupid. I'm going to have to nip this in the bud.

"There's a simple explanation," I start, causing Beth to raise her eyebrows questioningly. "Max invited Liam for an after-game burger a couple of weeks ago, and I'm sure Dylan doesn't want to disappoint the boys."

"Mmm hmm…"

"Really," I try to be convincing, but that clearly falls way short.

"Sorry, sweetheart," Clint apologizes over his wife's shoulder. "The woman's got something stuck in her head, it ain't easy to dislodge. Got plenty of experience with that. Best just to ignore that. Oomph…" He suddenly doubles over when Beth spears him with a swift elbow.

"Ignore that," she mumbles under her breath before straightening in her seat, as if nothing happened, and watches the start of the game.

From my vantage point, I can check on my boys in the playground. Harry is dangling upside down from a jungle gym and Theo is sitting on a swing, playing on his phone.

Yes, I'd caved. For his thirteenth birthday I got him a phone, turning into a teen and all, but he also pays part of the cell phone bill with money he makes delivering the paper and mowing the lawn for a few of our neighbors. Until the other boys can find a way to contribute, they'll have to wait to get one.

The boys only show up once, during halftime, complaining they're starving. I warned them before we left the house to stick a granola bar in their pockets, but they didn't, so now they can go hungry.

"You're tough," Beth points out when the kids slink off, realizing their mom's not going to budge.

I shrug my shoulders. "I warned them there was no concession stand. I suggested they bring something from home and they didn't. Not like they weren't warned. Besides, there's no way they're hungry after the stacks of pancakes and panful of bacon they tore through this morning. They'll live."

Clint chuckles but Beth is back to scrutinizing me. "You do this on your own," she concludes before asking, "How long has it been?"

Funny how I know exactly what she wants to know. "Little over five years. I know I can be strict on some things, but there's no other way to be. It's three to one, and I don't hold firm, I may as well throw in the towel."

Beth opens her mouth to respond, when my phone rings in my pocket and I fish it out. Unknown number. I lift a finger in apology as I get up and climb down the bleachers, answering the call.

"Hello?"

The voice on the other end has my blood freeze in my veins. "It's me." When I don't respond, mainly because my voice is stuck in my throat, he adds, "Jeremy." He sounds disgruntled, and that turns the ice in my veins to boiling lava.

"I got that," I snap. "What I don't get is why, after five years of blissful silence, you suddenly feel the need to connect. Especially since I have nothing to say to you, and there is nothing I can even imagine would interest me coming from your mouth."

"Still with the attitude, I see."

This acerbic tone is more familiar and I feel it slicing the top layer of my skin. There was a time those cuts would wound to the bone, but not anymore.

I suck in a breath before responding, "Unless you have anything of value to convey—"

"I wanna see the boys."

"You're kidding, right?" comes flying out of my mouth at higher than conversational volume, but I don't even notice the eyes turning on me with curiosity. "Suddenly you want to see the boys? I can't believe you'd have the gall to even think this is something I would allow."

"I'm their father," he says stubbornly.

"No. That's where you're wrong. You were their father, but now you're nothing more than a sperm donor. That's what happens when you disappear for *five years!*"

"Marya…"

"Don't call me that. Don't call me anything. In fact, don't call me at all."

"You don't want to make this harder than in needs to be."

I bark out a bitter laugh at that threat. "You're kidding, right? Harder? For your information, anything you think you can do to me now is a cakewalk compared to what you've already done."

With that I end the call, shove the phone back in my pocket, tilt my eyes to the sky, and take in a lungful of air.

Sonofabitch.

"Guessing that was one blast from the past you woulda gladly passed up on," Clint's deep rumble sounds behind me, just as I feel a large hand settle in the small of my back.

"You wouldn't be wrong." I turn to find his warm, concerned eyes on me.

"You okay?"

I glance over his shoulder to catch Beth's intense look among the many curious ones. Guess I drew an audience. *Shit.* "I'm good," I quickly reassure Clint, even though I'm far from good. I'm almost vibrating; I'm so livid. Still, I plaster on a smile, give him a little nod, and climb back up to my spot beside Beth, who remains surprisingly silent.

It's not until the final whistle blows that she leans over and presses something in my hand.

"My number and Dylan's number. Any more calls from that fucktard, you use one of them."

"Beth, I'm sure—"

"Promise me."

"I'll be—"

"Promise," she repeats firmly, folding my fingers over the card in my palm.

I watch my boys jog over from the playground and wait by the gate to the field for their brother, and that's when fear, tucked away somewhere deep in my chest, slowly unfurls its tentacles.

"I promise."

DYLAN

I had foresight.

Like the first early game when she was late, looking harried for lack of caffeine and nutrition, Marya looks much the same, hurrying after a running Liam toward the field. This time, however, I'm prepared, having made a quick stop at Sonya's to pick up reinforcements.

Clint pulled me aside the moment I came to pick Max up the day before yesterday. Filled me in on what happened at the soccer field last weekend, when he and Ma witnessed Marya take a distressing call they concluded was from her ex. Apparently not an amicable parting of ways, and he said Marya was clearly rattled by the call.

If Clint hadn't mentioned the fact Ma gave her my number—as well as hers—in case of emergency, along with the tidbit of wisdom an independent woman like Marya may not be impressed to have me step in and take over, I might've done something rash.

Instead I held back and, more or less patiently, waited for today to make sure with my own eyes she's okay.

Her eyes find me and widen when I hold up the coffee cup and brown paper bag for her. There's no hesitance this time as she dives in the seat beside me, making a grab for her coffee.

"Bless you," she manages to mumble before putting her lips to the carryout cup and gulping down the still hot coffee.

I don't bother holding back the grin when she eyes the bag in my hand.

"Pancakes this time," I offer, handing her one of the Styrofoam containers.

"I will worship at your feet."

I try not to fidget in my seat when my cock wakes up at the visual her words bring up. The soft moans as she digs into her food are not helping either.

"I'm guessing you're not a morning person," I suggest, trying for a distraction. This catches me a squint of her pretty honey-colored eyes.

"I am *so* a morning person," she argues. "Unlike my sons, who like to sleep like the dead on weekends. I couldn't get my oldest out of bed at all, so Mom had to rush over to my place while I chased Liam around to get ready." A deep sigh escapes her lips. "Some days I wish there were two of me."

A sentiment I get. I often wish I could be two place at the same time, one of them being at home with and for Max. I love what I do, but it would be so much easier if I didn't have to hustle Max around whenever I'm needed on the job.

It's been a long almost two weeks, since I got called in on this case that turned out to be a little more involved than I'd been told. Half that time I spent surveilling a strip club, where a known arms dealer liked to do business. In order to blend in, I had to contend with more pussy being shoved in my face in the past two weeks than I'd seen in all my adult years before.

I got some ribbing from some of the other guys, calling me a lucky bastard for having caught that particular assignment, but all I'd been able to think about was the only pussy I'd be interested in examining close up.

The job came to a conclusion three days ago, when the guy we were after finally showed up at the KitKat Club. We were able to catch him red-handed trying to sell twelve cases of military-grade assault rifles, two grenade launchers, and twenty-five anti-personnel mines to a local militia group. I don't even want to think what those rednecks had in mind with that kind of armory on home turf.

The bust did not go without a hitch and bullets went flying, one catching a CBI guy in the gut, but last report was he's recovering well.

Still, I got the bad guys and got home to my boy unharmed.

"Everything okay?"

Marya's soft inquiry surprises me. She is watching me closely, the plastic fork with her next bite suspended in front of her mouth.

"It's all good." I shoot her what I hope is a convincing smile, before opening my own container and digging in.

"I get you can't talk about your super-secret spy

work, but I'm a good listener. You know, if you needed to unload. Or something." I glance sideways and watch her tuck a hank of hair behind her ear as she presses her lips together. She's nervous, and just caught herself rambling. It's cute.

"We usually leave the super-secret spy work for the CIA," I tease, bumping her shoulder. "And I don't want to spoil the best meal I've had in two weeks."

She looks down at her pancakes before turning a smile on me. "They are really good. Thank you."

"Food's good. Company is better," I tell her, stuffing another piece of pancake in my mouth. I keep my focus on the field where the ref drops the ball in the circle for kick-off, but I can feel her eyes on me.

After a lengthy pause I hear her softly say, "Agreed," and I grin around my next bite.

Definitely liking this Marya better.

CHAPTER 4

DYLAN

"What does 10-CODE mean?"

I lower the burger I was just about to take a bite from and look up at Liam. It's the first thing he's said to me since we got to the diner.

It had taken a bit to convince Marya to come. She'd tried to use the excuse she wasn't dressed to go out to a restaurant—a load of bull if you ask me, she looks just fine as she is—but when I pointed out Sonya's is hardly some fine restaurant, she finally conceded.

Max had been elated and Liam didn't seem opposed to the idea either, which is how we ended up at the diner, baskets with burgers and fries covering the table.

"It's a radio code," I answer him. "It's used by law enforcement officers to communicate without words."

"Are you a law enforcement officer?"

"Dad's an FBI agent," Max proudly responds before I can.

His buddy's eyes grow big. "Like Uncle Damian?"

"He's my boss."

I watch as Liam seems to process that information. "Isn't it easier just to use words?" he comes back with.

"Not always. Code can be faster, which is handy when you find yourself in an emergency. Sometimes we use it when we're not alone and don't want the other person to know what we're saying."

"10-4 means message received," Max shares, eager to impart with his knowledge. "Dad taught me. 10-0 means be careful, and 10-78 is when you need help, right, Dad?"

"You bet, kid."

"Cool," Liam mutters, diving back into his fries.

I glance over at Marya, who is observing the interaction with mild amusement. I catch her eye and she grins full out, mouthing, *"You have a new fan."*

I wink and take a bite of my burger.

It's when the waitress drops the bill—ending in a brief tug of war with Marya, which I win—Max pipes up.

"You should come to my birthday!" he announces with a big grin at Liam. "It's gonna be so cool. We're gonna dig for gold!"

"Pan for gold, Max," I correct him automatically, while mentally assessing if there's enough space in my four-door Bronco to fit another kid in.

"Whatever," he dismisses me before turning back

to his buddy. "We're gonna go down in the mining tunnels, and we get to wear helmets with lights and everything. It's gonna be awesome."

While Max rambles on about the plans for his birthday in two weeks, I decide to take Clint and Ma up on their offer to drive to Silverton so they can take some kids too.

"I'm sorry," Marya whispers, putting her hand on my forearm.

"For what?"

"Well, uh…"

I lean across the table and share, in a low voice, "My son may not think before he speaks, but this time his idea is a good one. Come. Bring the other two boys as well; they'll get a kick out of it. You've already met Clint and Ma."

"Oh, I don't know."

"Have you ever been?" I ask, changing tactics.

"Well, no, not yet, but—"

"The boys?"

"No, but—"

"Perfect. We planned it for a weekend when the team has a bye." I plow right over her again, hiding my grin at her disgruntled look. "Ma took me when I was twelve, and I remember that trip to this day. It's a pretty unique experience. Your boys will love it."

"Look, I don't even know my work schedule yet for that weekend. Kerry sometimes needs me to cover for a half day." Her protest is not very convincing, especially not when she glances at her son beside her.

Liam is grinning wide, listening to Max's excited babble, and Marya is looking at him like she's witnessing a miracle. "I'll check with Kerry," she mumbles without taking her eyes off the boy.

I grab her hand and give it a little squeeze. "Fair enough," I concede, but I do it smiling. I have a feeling Liam's enthusiasm will go a long way to making up her mind.

The boys run ahead of us to her Jeep and my truck, parked side by side in the parking lot. I tag Marya's elbow and hold her back, turning her to me. "You have my number?" The top of her head comes to my chin and she has to look up. Her eyes are guarded.

"Your mom gave me a card with both your numbers. I put it in the console in my car."

"Right. Give me your number." I pull my phone from my pocket. "I want you to call me after you talk to Kerry."

"Then why do you need my number?" she snaps, tilting her head in challenge.

"So I don't ignore you when you call and I don't recognize the number," I fire back.

"You make a habit of that? Ignoring your calls?"

"I do if I'm in the middle of something, unless it's someone on my team, my parents, or the school. I know it's you calling, I'll pick up too."

She rolls her eyes but rattles off her number anyway. I store it under her name, dial it, and watch as she fishes her ringing phone from her pocket.

"Save it."

"Bossy," she mutters, as she adds me to her contacts. I pointedly ignore her comment.

"I'll pop in for coffee this week," I tell her when we start walking to the cars, which causes her to stop again.

"Look…" She appears a little uncomfortable as she faces me. "Thank you for lunch, but I'm not…I mean I don't really get…" She stops talking, takes in a deep breath and starts again, "I'll just put this out there, but I'm not really interested in dating. You're a great guy. Super nice and all, but aside from the fact I'm much too old for you, I've sworn off men."

"Now there's a challenge," I tease her, tugging on that chunk of hair that keeps falling in her face.

"Dylan…"

"Relax, Sweetheart. We just had a friendly lunch with the kids, me popping in for coffee is nothing new, and the trip to Silverton will be chaperoned by a gaggle of kids and my parents. If I make a move, I can assure you it won't be with the kids or Mom and Clint in attendance."

She seems stumped for words, and before she has a chance to find them I tap her nose, throw her a wink, and aim for my Bronco.

I lied.

I'm totally making a move.

MARYA

It's been weeks—months even—since I've seen Liam

this animated.

"Mom?"

"Yeah?"

"We can go, right?"

The eager anticipation on his face is impossible to resist. "Yeah, Bub. I have to check my schedule with Aunt Kerry, so don't say anything to your brothers just yet, but even if I won't be able to take the time off, you can go." It'll be outside my budget, but I can see if I can pick up a few extra cleaning shifts to make up for it.

"Cool," he mumbles, trying hard to sound nonchalant, but failing miserably when I just catch his grin break through as he turns to look out the window.

I have to admit, I'm kind of excited at the prospect as well. We don't often get to do fun stuff as a family, and this is something the boys and I will all enjoy. Besides, I like Beth and Clint, so I don't have to worry just having Dylan to talk to.

Oh yeah, I didn't buy his little speech for a minute. I haven't been out of the dating game long enough to forget what it looks and sounds like when a man is determined to get in your pants. I haven't the faintest idea why Dylan seems to have his mind set on me. I shouldn't even be on his radar.

Maybe he's looking for a sure thing and hopes targeting an older woman—one who is far removed from the general beauty standards and has been around the bend a time or two with the dents and bruises that come with that—will mean a quick and easy capitulation. In which case, he's barking up the wrong tree. I'm determined to stick to my guns.

I pull up to Mom's place, a small two-bedroom bungalow near the hospital in a tidy neighborhood housing mostly senior citizens. She's lived here for four years and loves it.

After Jeremy left us, I had no way to maintain the large house he'd insisted on renting. There just never seemed to be enough money to save for a down payment, with my ex drifting in and out of jobs he'd claim would be the answer to our problems. He'd been a firm believer that if you lived and acted accomplished; success would come to you. He took his clothes and the much too expensive and brand-new, leased Infinity JX with him, leaving me with the ancient Jeep, a part-time job, and a monthly rent I couldn't afford.

We ended up at my mother's house, the old place on Lawrence Avenue I was raised in. She had the space, with three small bedrooms, a master, two baths, and a finished basement. Harrison was just a toddler, so he and I shared a room. Living with Mom gave me a chance to get a job without needing to worry about childcare that first year. It helped me get back on my feet.

A year later, Mom indicated she was ready to downsize, wanted the boys and I to stay in the house, and bought the small bungalow. Now I pay off the mortgage left on the house and my name was added to the deed.

"Well?" Mom addresses Liam when we walk in.

"Won," he says with a little smug smile.

"Of course you did." The smile gets a little bigger. "Next week I'm coming to see you play. Those lazy brothers of yours will have to deal." Mom ruffles his hair and gives him a little shove in the direction of the kitchen. "Cinnamon rolls on the counter, and leave two for your mom and me," she calls after him. "There should be four on that plate, Liam!" She turns to me with a smirk. "I've had to threaten those other two with corporal punishment if they got close to that plate."

"I bet." I grin at her, leaning in to kiss her cheek. "Got any coffee?"

She huffs. "Is the Pope Catholic? How many cups have you had though?"

"Mom…"

"High blood pressure is nothing to mess with, missy," she scolds me. "You told me yourself the doctor said no more than two a day."

"I know, Mom. It's only on the weekend I need that occasional jolt to get through the day." She's been on my case ever since I had my last physical, and the doctor gave me a stern talking to about keeping my weight in check and watching my blood pressure. I get it, my Aunt Ida, who lives in Silverton, had a heart attack a few years ago. It scared the shit out of Mom.

I'm pretty sure my hypertension is stress-related, but I keep that to myself.

"Half a cup," she concedes, leading the way into

the kitchen.

I'm glad to see Liam left two pastries as instructed, although where the rest disappeared to so fast, I don't know. The kid just had a massive cheeseburger and fries. I spot him sitting on the steps to the small yard, where Theo is trying to lift Harry up to grab a Frisbee that got stuck in the tree.

"Careful!" I call out on instinct. They should give me frequent flyer miles at Mercy Hospital for the number of times I end up with one of the kids in the emergency department. I don't want to end my weekend with another visit there. It's a miracle Child Protective Services hasn't been notified about all the injuries my boys sustain.

"Momma, look at me!" Harry yells, waving enthusiastically and I see him teetering in Theo's hold.

"Careful!" I yell again, but it's already too late, the two of them are going down.

"*Shit.*" I jump down the steps but when I get to the boys, they're rolling in the grass, giggling their asses off. "You guys, you're gonna give me heart attack one of these days."

"Don't joke about that," Mom yells out of the kitchen door.

"Not joking!"

Before I have a chance to check to make sure Harry hasn't broken anything, he's wrapped his skinny arms around my hips. "Hey, Mom."

"Hey, kid. You behave for Grandma?"

"I licked the bowl of icing," he shares, leaning his

head back to beam his gap-toothed smile up at me.

"Lucky." I grin down at him. "But it doesn't answer my question, did you behave?"

"Yup." His eyes dart to the door, which probably means he got into some trouble.

"Mmmhmm."

Suddenly he lets me go. "Mom? Can we have a dog? That'd be so cool. We could walk him and everything."

"Right. I already know who'll be doing the feeding, the cleaning, and the walking, buddy, and it isn't gonna be you. So the answer is still no."

He opens his mouth to complain when my phone rings in my pocket. I quickly lift a finger in his face to quiet him, before walking around the side of the house, pulling my cell from my pocket.

No 'unknown number,' but still one I don't recognize.

"Hello?"

"Do not hang up." *Fucking Jeremy.* "Last chance, Marya. I want to see the boys. If you insist on being difficult, you'll hear from my lawyer."

"If you think threatening me will help your case, you are delusional. I have a threat for you: push this, push me, and I *will* press charges for domestic violence."

"I'd like to see you try," he taunts me. "Who the fuck you think is gonna believe you after all these years?"

"Fuck off, Jeremy."

With that I hang up, my hands shaking as I block the last incoming number, and stuff the phone in my pocket. I take a few deep breaths before returning to the yard, where Liam has now joined his brothers, tossing a Frisbee around.

"Forget the coffee," I tell Mom when I step into the kitchen. "I need a stiff drink."

She throws me a scrutinizing look, turns to the cupboard above the fridge, and pulls down the Baileys. "It's all I've got."

"It'll do."

"Care to tell me?" she asks, handing me the drink.

I swallow half of it back, wincing slightly at the sweet taste, before lifting my eyes to her.

"Jeremy."

"That was him?" She looks confused. I didn't tell her he called the first time. I hadn't wanted her to get upset. "What the hell?"

I take a deep breath. "He first called last week, telling me he wanted to see the boys. I told him off and hung up on him. That was him again, just now. Looks like he's not going to go away."

"Son of a bitch," Mom mumbles. She grabs another glass, fills it to the brim with Baileys, and tosses the whole thing back.

CHAPTER 5

DYLAN

"You going for coffee?"

I stop outside Damian's office and stick my head around the door.

"Yeah, you want anything?" I ask him.

"Come in for a minute, and close the door."

I do ask he asks, and sit down across from his desk. "What's up?"

"That's three times this week."

His face is impassive but his eyes are keen, so I don't even bother pretending not to know what he's talking about. My hackles are up.

"And?"

"My wife is her friend."

"Yeah, and?"

Damian leans forward, elbows on his desk. "Right. I see you're not in the mood to listen, but I'm going to say this anyway. I'm not sure what it is you think you're doing, and I know you weren't around when things went down with her, but we're talking about a woman who has been played and knocked around enough."

I can feel my nostrils flare when I release the breath I've been holding, along with my temper. I match Damian leaning forward over his desk, getting in his face and measuring my words. "When have you known me to toy with a woman? Any woman? Ever?"

It takes a moment for the fierce intensity to leave my boss's face. He sits back in his chair and runs a hand through his hair. "Jesus, kid."

That term rubs me the wrong way. "Hardly a kid," I bite off. "Old enough to know what I want."

"She's a single mom in her early forties with at least ten years on you."

"Eight, to be exact," I correct him. "And for the record; I'm a single parent too."

Another brush of his hand goes through the hair streaked with silver. "Shit." His eyes come up. "You mess with her, hurt her in anyway, that's going to make my wife very unhappy, which in turn will make me extremely unhappy."

"So noted. Now, if that was all?" Pissed, I shove the chair back and get up, swallowing down my anger.

"Yeah," he mumbles, but when I start walking out of the office he stops me, adding, "Large Americano—black—and grab me one of those brownies if she has any left."

"Right."

I can't quite shake my anger until I push open the door of Kerry's Korner and see the brief flash of worry on Marya's face, before she hides it behind a sunny smile.

"Your standard order?"

"I'm hauling back coffee for everyone. Damian wants a large—"

"I've got it. I know everyone's order by now. Jasper and Luna too?"

"Please."

Knowing it'll take her a few minutes; I walk over to the couch under the window and pick up the discarded newspaper. I'm flipping through the pages without registering much; I'm too busy sneaking peeks. Something is off with her. I noticed earlier in the week that she seemed a little jumpy, hiding it quickly each time.

"Everything all right?"

She looks away from the espresso machine and glances at me. "Yep. Fine. Why do you ask?"

"You've just seemed a little...preoccupied. Like something has you spooked."

I see it then, a quick flash of uneasiness, before the mask drops back in place.

"I may be a little tired, that's all. I've worked three nights in a row, I'm short on sleep."

"Don't you close at five?" I get up and make my way back to the counter, leaning an elbow on the stainless steel.

"Oh, the store? Yes, but I'm talking about my other job."

I observe her a little more closely and notice dark circles under her eyes and a tightness around her mouth I haven't seen before. I hadn't known about the second job, but given what Ma shared with me about her ex being a deadbeat, it doesn't surprise me she'd need the extra income to provide for herself and three kids.

Still, I don't think fatigue is what makes her jumpy.

"What's your other job?"

"I work for Corporate Cleaners. Cleaning offices after hours." She lifts her chin, almost in challenge.

"How many nights a week?"

"Usually just one, maybe two, but lately I've done three." She shrugs, tapping the grinds out of the filter. "I'm lucky I have Mom to look after the boys."

I'm about to ask why she upped her shifts, when the penny drops. "Liam's soccer."

It doesn't take much to read from the expression on her face, I got it in one.

"Just for extras."

I'm not rich by any stretch of the imagination, but I make a decent income. I can afford to live without big financial concerns, don't have to consider every penny I spend, and Max sure doesn't lack for anything. I remember money was always scarce growing up, though. Ma was on her feet all day long, six days a week at the diner in Cedar Tree, and whenever it was close to my birthday or Christmas; she'd work double shifts whenever she could get them.

With three boys, I imagine there will always be extras that need funding. Max's birthday invitation last Saturday comes to mind and I wonder whether part of Marya's initial hesitation was financial concern. *Shit.* I should've thought of that.

"Have you had a chance to talk to Kerry yet? About Silverton on the twenty-eighth?"

She pulls out a cardboard tray and starts tucking the cups in. "Just this morning. She says she won't need me."

"Good. I'm glad you and the boys'll be able to make it. We'll hammer out the details next week. You don't have to worry about anything except wearing clothes that can stand to get dirty; everything else is taken care of. Ma's bringing a trunkful of junk food and pop, so the boys will be good and wired, and I'm taking care of the tickets, so all you have to do is be ready."

"That's easy enough. I haven't even told the kids yet." She grins. "Liam knows of course, but I've sworn him to secrecy until I knew for sure. The boys'll be excited."

"So will Max," I share. And then I share some more. "I'm pretty excited myself."

Her eyes briefly meet mine before she shoves the tray over the counter.

"That's fifteen sixteen, please."

I pull out my wallet when I suddenly remember. "Shit, Damian said something about brownies."

"Never fails," Marya mumbles under her breath as she moves to the glass-domed tray on the other end of the counter.

"What was that?"

"Damian," she says, lifting the dome. "He knows I bring in fresh brownies on Thursdays."

"You baked those?"

"First thing in the morning," she confirms, holding up tongs.

"In that case give me five."

"Five?" She looks pointedly at the tray with four coffees.

"Two for me," I clarify with a grin, and see a hint of pink hit her cheeks. I watch as she packs them in a small box, and adds them to my order.

"Twenty-three ninety-one, please."

"I can't believe you bake. I wonder if..." I purposely let my words trail off as I pull the money from my wallet and hand it to her.

"Wonder what?"

"Never mind." I wave her off, grabbing the tray and the box. "You're busy enough as it is." I start to turn to the door when her hand snakes out and grabs hold of my wrist.

"What is it?" she insists.

"Oh, okay. I usually get Max one of those premade cakes from the City Market, but what if I bought you the ingredients?" I am so going to hell for this. "Would you consider baking him a proper birthday cake? It would absolutely make his day."

Her face lights up. "I'd love to. I do my boys' cakes every year. But you don't have to get the ingredients, I'll take care of—"

"No way," I cut her off, setting down my purchases and pulling my wallet out again, slapping two twenties on the counter. "I pay for the ingredients and no argument."

I snatch up the tray and the box and make a beeline for the door.

"Wait!" she calls after me. "I don't even know what he likes."

"I'll text you later," I return before slipping out the door.

I'm grinning ear to ear when I get behind the wheel.

I'm not only going to hell, my mother is going to ream me a new one when I tell her she's not making Max's cake this year.

MARYA

The kids should be home soon.

I'm being ridiculous. I've sat here at the kitchen counter for the past half hour with the phone in my hand, Dylan's contact information open.

He said he'd text me, but my phone's been quiet since yesterday. Then I thought maybe he'd drop by the bookstore this morning, but he didn't.

I'm sitting here wondering if I've lost the last of my marbles. How did I get from keeping my distance to being impatient for a glimpse or a word?

The door flies open and my boys come barging in, dropping their backpacks where they land.

"Hey, Mom!"

"Guys, pick up those bags right now and take them up to your room," I direct the kids. "Then get your butts down here and bring your dirty laundry."

There are a lot of days I wish for carpeted stairs, today being one of them. It sounds like a herd of stampeding buffalo through my house.

After Mom moved out, I pulled up the old, dusty pink carpet to expose the nice hardwood floors throughout the house and I've occasionally questioned the wisdom of that. I always intended to sand and refinish them, but never got around to it. So instead of gleaming, they look scraped and dented. Probably for the better anyway. I'll wait until the kids have passed their loud and destructive phase before sinking time and effort into it.

Despite the age of the house, and aside from the small closed off entryway, the main floor has an open feel: one big living and dining space, and only a long counter separating the kitchen. I like it, makes it easier to keep an eye on the kids while I cook, the flip side of that being there's little privacy. I will occasionally escape into the small laundry room off the kitchen if I don't want to kids to overhear or interrupt, and I briefly contemplate slipping in there to try and call Dylan.

"Mom?" Harry yells, already thundering his way back downstairs. "Can we order pizza for dinner?"

Resolutely, I put my phone facedown on the counter and get up to grab the overflowing basket from my youngest. The amounts of laundry these boys produce every week is overwhelming and takes me most of my weekend to get through.

Pizza is a luxury I let them indulge in only on my biweekly payday, which happens to be today. I swear my youngest keeps track. "We'll see." Harry already pumps his fist in victory before he sits down at the counter.

Liam is the last one to come down. I take his basket, shove it in the laundry room with the others and wait until he's taken a seat.

"You wanna tell them about next week, Liam?"

His eyes shoot up at me, a surprised grin on his face. "We can go?"

"Looks like it."

While he enthusiastically shares with his brothers, I pull the brochures I printed out at work this morning from my purse and hand one to each of the boys. Even Theo, who is the most laid-back of the bunch, lets out a whoop.

"Just to be clear," I finally manage to get a word in edgewise. "Your homework better be done every day, there'll be no fighting, and I don't want any lip from you two…" I point first at Theo and then Harry, "… about getting up tomorrow morning to come to your brother's soccer game."

"What time?" Theo asks, and I send him a scathing look.

"Seriously, kid? You're considering passing up on this depending on what time you have to get up? Don't think I won't cut you out and leave you with Grandma while your brothers and I go have fun, because I will."

He looks a little sheepish and mumbles, "Never mind."

"Good call, Bub."

———

It's after homework, pizza, and a rerun of *Iron Man* the kids and I piled on the couch to watch—them be-cause…Marvel, and me because…Robert Downing Jr.—with popcorn, our Friday night family fun.

The kids are in bed and I'm just straightening up the kitchen before turning in myself when my phone, still facedown on the counter, vibrates against the surface.

Dylan: Sorry for the late hour. You awake?

I was pretty proud of myself for not checking my phone all night, thinking I nipped this unhealthy attraction in the bud. However, the immediate butterflies his message sets loose in my stomach proves otherwise. *Shit.*

Me: Yes

It takes me several minutes to formulate my

response. Typing, erasing, typing some more, only to backspace the whole thing again, and this is what I end up with. Ugh.

I startle when the phone rings in my hand, quickly answering.

"Hello?"

"It's been a crazy two days." The sound of his chuckle so close to my ear has goosebumps pop up on my skin. There's something intimate about the lazy drawl in his voice, as if talking to me at the end of his day is a common occurrence.

"How so?" My own voice sounds a little hoarse, and I quickly clear my throat.

"A new development in a case that kept me busy into late last night, so Max stayed at his grandparents. I didn't see him until I picked him up from school this afternoon, and then we had homework to deal with, went to get groceries, cooked dinner, and we ended up both passing out on the couch watching some TV. I just put him to bed, but he woke up long enough to announce he likes red velvet or chocolate."

"Life can get crazy when you parent alone." I catch myself smiling, even though I know he can't see me. With the phone at my ear, I make my way around the house, flicking off lights and making sure doors are locked before I head up the stairs.

"That's for sure."

"And by the way, I can do red velvet and chocolate."

"Really? That's awesome."

"Other than soccer and gaming, is there anything

else he really likes? A book, a show, a movie—anything I could use for inspiration?"

"You need inspiration for a cake?" He sounds incredulous, which strikes me as funny.

"You do if you plan on decorating said cake."

"I see. Well, he's a big fan of Marvel."

I flop down on my bed, smiling. "The boys and I just finished watching *Iron Man*."

"Really? The original?"

"Are you seriously asking that? Of course." There is that chuckle again in my ear.

"*Iron Man* is cool, but Max is sold on *Deadpool*. That's his favorite Marvel movie."

"So violent, though." I shudder remembering some of the bloody scenes. "I thought it would be more like the other movies, otherwise I would probably have thought twice about letting the boys watch it."

"I get that, but I figure it's better to let them watch when you're around than to see it at a friend's house without supervision."

"I guess." I stifle a yawn, my week catching up with me.

"I'm sorry, I'm keeping you from your bed."

"Not exactly," I confess. "I'm already there."

There's dead silence on the other end and I realize that for someone trying to keep their distance, I may have shared more than I should've. Suddenly self-conscious, I start to ramble.

"I mean, I haven't changed or brushed my teeth yet, but I'm in my bedroom, lying on my bed." I snap my mouth shut. It's like I have no filter. I'm only making this worse, but I can't seem to help myself. "I don't usually sleep in my clothes—except maybe when it gets so cold outside I can't get the house warm—but normally I don't wear clothes to bed. I mean I wear something, of course, with kids around and all that, but—"

"Marya, stop talking," he finally rumbles.

I wince, mortified. *Jesus*, I'm a tease—a cock tease. I totally fail at keeping my distance.

"Sorry," I whisper. "I was just…"

Being an idiot?

"As informative as this conversation has been," Dylan says, humor in his voice. "I'm going to hang up now before this goes places I know we're not ready to go. I'll see you tomorrow at the game."

My head is stuck on those *places* he's talking about, but I still manage to echo my goodbye.

"Yeah, see you tomorrow."

The moment I hear dead air, I drop my phone on the mattress, roll over and shove my face in the pillows, and let go of a frustrated groan.

I am so fucked.

CHAPTER 6

DYLAN

She brought her family.

I watch as Marya approaches, a lanky boy I assume is her oldest, dragging his heels by her side, while behind her an older, gray-haired woman has a much younger boy by the hand. The resemblance tells me this is her mother, and the young boy looks the spitting image of his older brother. The same dark hair as their mother, unlike Liam, who is blond. He's already joined his team on the field.

"Morning," I greet them, standing up when she stops in front of me, a little tentatively.

"Morning," she echoes, before turning to her mother. "Mom, this is Dylan Barnes, he works with Damian." To me she says, "My mom, Lydia Stewart, and my boys, Harrison and Theodor. Boys, this is Max's father."

I shake hands with her mother and both boys, when the youngest pipes up, "Do you think we'll find gold?"

I'm guessing Marya told her boys about next weekend and I grin at him. "Anything is possible. I've been there before and never have, but I've heard stories of people going home luckier than me."

"You get to keep it?" the older one, Theo, asks.

"Yup. You find it, you keep it."

"Rad," he mutters.

"Mom, can we go to the playground?"

"Sure, but stick with your brother, okay?"

Harry nods, punches his brother in the arm and starts running in the direction of the small park on the far side of the field, the other boy chasing him.

"Have you seen Liam play before?" I ask Lydia when we sit down.

"I have, but not in an actual game."

I see questions in the woman's eyes, which have little to do with her grandson or the game on the field, and I read her concern, but I have no answers to give. Not yet anyway. I know what I want, but I'm not sure I can have it, that'll be up to her daughter.

Twenty minutes into the game my phone rings. It's the office.

"Excuse me." I get up and walk away from the bleachers to take the call. "What's up?"

"Sorry, Barnes," Jasper answers. "Any way you can get to the office? David Aiken just dropped in and wants to meet with us all."

"Out of the blue?"

David Aiken is the big honcho at the FBI's Denver office who Damian reports to.

"Yup. Had me call everyone in, he's holed up in Damian's office for now."

"Not getting a good vibe from this," I share.

"You're not the only one. Anyway, I know you've got Max to sort out, I can stall for an hour or so."

"I'll need it. I'm in Aztec at his game. I'll have to call in some help." My eyes drift to Marya, who is looking at me with concern in her eyes. The stress I feel must be visible. "An hour," I repeat before hanging up.

"Everything okay?" she asks when I return.

"Got called into the office for an emergency meeting in an hour. I'm going to have to pull Max and drop him at Ma's."

"Don't do that. We can take him back with us, drop him at your mother's."

I open my mouth to object, but I change my mind at the last minute. This is not familiar to me, but the offer of help feels fucking great. It's always been me and Ma or Clint in emergencies.

"You sure?"

She smiles as she nods, and I can feel the warmth of it in my gut.

Fully aware of her mother sitting on the other side of her, I lean in and limit myself to kissing her cheek. "I owe you big time," I whisper against her ear.

Ten minutes later, after a quick chat at the fence

with Max and a call to warn Ma, I'm on my way back to Durango, the knot in my stomach at what awaits me there getting tighter with every mile.

***

"You're kidding?"

I look up to find Luna glaring at Aiken.

"Luna," Damian warns, drawing her attention.

"I'm sorry, but this is bullshit. We're already spread pretty thin, and now we're supposed to babysit fresh trainees?"

"Actually, they'll have graduated their training, so technically they're fresh agents," David offers sardonically. "Besides, as you said, you have been spread thin and since it's not currently in the budget to assign another experienced agent, this will provide you with an added body, without digging into your wallet. Quantico is picking up the tab for this."

It's clear Luna is resistant, and I can understand why, working together with a team requires trust, and that's not easy to give for Luna. It took me over a year to get to a point where she saw me as a full member of the team. Bringing someone in for three-month stints at a time is hardly enough to build the kind of trust required, but everyone has to start somewhere.

Damian and Jasper seem only mildly annoyed. I agree it's going to mess with the nice balance we have in our office, but David's right, it's a cheap addition of manpower. In addition to that, it will make me no longer the junior agent in the office, which is something I look forward to.

I'm not going to say that out loud, though. Not with Luna up in arms. I like my balls attached to my body.

"Why a small field office like ours?" she questions. "Wouldn't it make more sense to have them in a place that has more constant action? Bigger? Like, say, Denver?"

I bite down a chuckle and glance at David, but he just seems equally amused at Luna's sarcasm.

"In a larger office, they'd see maybe twenty-five percent of the casework. Here they'd not only be exposed to the full view, but can see how the different levels of an investigation work together. For an office this small, you have a uniquely complete set of skills represented between the four of you."

Luna rolls her eyes. "Now he starts with the compliments," she mutters.

"He's right," I finally speak up, catching her heated look. "I learned more in a month here than in all the time I spent in Denver. Having a chance to work all angles of a case has given me a much better understanding. Made me a better agent."

"I still don't like it."

"I'm not breaking out the champagne either, Luna," Jasper adds, "but you've gotta admit it makes sense."

"Right. Now that we have that out of the way, let's have a look at the first candidate coming your way. She's a former officer for the Denver PD and has just graduated Quantico. She'll be here a week from Monday. Her name is Toni Linden."

And just like that, the knot in my stomach is back.

MARYA

It's a tight fit, but we managed to cram all four kids in the back seat of my Jeep.

I'd promised my boys burgers for lunch and Max was in enthusiastic agreement when I suggested we stop at Sonya's. Lunch had been an extended and rambunctious affair, during which Liam seemed to grow more and more quiet. We finally asked for the bill, which I had to fight Mom for. I lost.

On our way back to Durango, I check Liam in my rearview mirror and notice him looking almost uncomfortable, staring out the window, while the other three chat about next week's mining trip and their PS4 games.

"Everything okay, Liam?" I ask, thinking maybe he's bummed they lost the game. "You guys played a good game. Can't win them all, right?"

His eyes catch mine in the mirror and my breath sticks in my throat when I see a flash of anguish on his face before he quickly turns away. Something is going on with my middle child.

I find Mom looking at me with an eyebrow raised, but I surreptitiously shake my head. It'll have to wait until later, but I intend to ask if she's noticed anything.

"Why don't I come over and make my famous mac and cheese for you guys tonight?" Mom asks after we drop Max at his grandparents.

The loud cheers from the back seat are deafening, but when I shoot another quick glance in the mirror, I note to my relief that Liam seems as excited as the other two. The boys are not the only ones who love Mom's mac and cheese. I do too. She uses four different cheeses, adds sautéed onions and bits of ham, and it comes out of the oven with this crunchy golden crust I could eat all day long. It may be a gazillion calories a serving, but it's the best kind of comfort food I know.

After a quick detour to the grocery store, so Mom can get her ingredients, we pull into the driveway. The boys are out of the car, before I even shift it in park. Stupid, since I have the key to the front door so they have to wait anyway.

The moment I get the door open, the stampede is on and within minutes the kids have disbursed. Liam upstairs for a shower—thank God I don't have to chase after him like I do with the other two when it comes to hygiene—and the other two straight to the basement.

"What's with that boy lately?" Mom asks as we put groceries away.

I put my finger to my lips and walk over to the stairwell to listen for the shower running. "What have you noticed?" I answer her question with one of my own.

"He's been moody, almost listless at times, except when his brothers piss him off, then he's a ball of rage. I was relieved to see his enthusiasm on the field today. Thought maybe he turned a corner, but that was short-lived."

I run my hands over my face. So much for hoping my maternal antennae were perhaps a bit oversensitive. "Something is wrong," I admit out loud and it makes me wince. "I kept thinking it was a bad day, or maybe a bad week, but it's gotten to a point where aside from a few momentary glimpses of the generally good-natured kid I know him to be, I almost don't recognize him." I slap my hands over my mouth to stifle the sob wrenched from my gut.

Instantly my mother's arms are around me, and like when I was a little girl, her embrace allows me to let go and trust it all to her—no words required.

It's been a lot lately and my emotions feel like they've hit the spin cycle.

I used to be like Teflon, shit would slide off me barely leaving a trace. After the evaporation of my marriage, the assault a few years ago, and the years under constant stress trying to rebuild a life for me and the boys, the layers have worn thin. With my ex's sudden reappearance and Liam's slide out of reach, I'm gouging the bottom.

"Oh, honey…" Mom coos in my hair. She gives me an extra squeeze before setting me back. "We'll figure it out. Why don't you go splash some water on your face before the boys catch you, and we'll talk?"

She's right. The last thing I need is the kids walking in on their mother losing her shit. I scoot into the powder room and a few minutes later, after freshening up and getting myself back in hand, I walk out finding Mom waiting with a pot of tea.

"I could use a coffee," I suggest, earning a sharp maternal glare.

"That's the last thing you need right now," she decrees and I give up when she shoves a hot mug of tea in my hands. I take a sip and sit down at the kitchen counter. "You know, it wouldn't surprise me if that unconscionable bastard is somehow responsible for Liam's funk." I don't need to ask to know she's talking about Jeremy. She'd be the first to lay responsibility for global warming at my ex's feet if she could. She hates him that much for what he's done to the boys and me.

"I don't see how that would be possible. If he'd actually approached him, the other kids would've been around. He's not on the approved list at the kids' school and the boys are always together before and after. They're never out on their own."

Mom shrugs. "I still wouldn't put it past him," she grumbles. "By the way, have you heard anything else this week?"

"From Jeremy? No. Nothing. I'm kinda hoping he's lost interest."

"And I'm hoping I'll win the next Powerball, but we both know that ain't happening either." She dives into the fridge, pulling out some of the ingredients for dinner before she pins me with a stern look. "All I can say is brace. I have a feeling that scumsucker is not done wreaking havoc yet."

"Who's a scumsucker, Grandma?" Harry walks into the kitchen, his eyes big on his grandmother.

"You wouldn't know him," she recovers quickly. "He's not a very nice man, but you shouldn't be using words like that, Harrison Berger." She wags an admonishing finger in his face and I suppress a snort at the incredulous look on Harry's face.

"But you said it first."

"In sixty years, when you're my age, you get to say it too—not before."

He regards her with an assessing stare before coming to the conclusion that contradicting the maker of the world-famous mac and cheese, might not be a good idea. "How long 'til dinner?" he asks instead. "I'm hungry."

"Grandma's barely started, and you just had a burger a couple of hours ago," I point out.

"So? I'm hungry," he repeats.

What I should do is tell him he can wait, but I know that will only mean he'll be in my ear until he's fed. "Fine," I capitulate. "There's a bag of pretzels in the pantry, you can share that with your brothers."

"I want Oreos."

"And I want a week's vacation on a Caribbean island," I fire back. "You're not eating cookies. If you're hungry, you'll eat pretzels, otherwise wait for dinner."

I'm not quite sure what it is he mumbles under his breath as he stomps over to the pantry, but I'm thinking that's probably a good thing.

Jesus, I thought I had time before my baby came down with a case of attitude; it's infectious. Three growing boys—why didn't anyone stop me? At this rate, I'll be slurping Baileys for breakfast before the year is out.

"*Help,*" I mouth at Mom when Harry disappears downstairs with the bag of pretzels. She just turns back to the grater and grins.

"You know I'd love to grill you on that handsome man this morning, but it'll have to wait. I notice Liam hasn't come down yet, you may want to check on him?"

A quick glance at the clock shows me he's been up there for a good half hour. More than long enough. Suddenly worried, I rush up the stairs. I don't hear the shower, so he's done in there. I knock on his bedroom door.

"Liam? Are you okay?"

When there's no answer, I push the door open to find him facedown on his bed, still wrapped in a towel. He appears to be sleeping, or at least is doing his best to make me think so.

The white-knuckled hold of his hand on the pillow is a dead giveaway.

CHAPTER 7

DYLAN

"You excited, Max?" I ask my son, who is bouncing on his stool.

"Yes," he answers emphatically. "When's Grammy gonna be here?"

"She's on her way, Kiddo. Hang tight."

Easy to say, but for Max, who's almost coming out of his skin with excitement for his birthday party, the wait is sheer torture.

He doesn't even know Marya is on her way with the boys too. I would've picked her up, but she insisted on coming here, claiming it made more sense since, that way I didn't have to worry about dropping her and the kids home again after.

I didn't see her all week. On purpose.

The news last Saturday had thrown me for a loop. Toni Linden and I have a history I would've preferred to leave in the past, and hearing I'd have to be working with her starting Monday wasn't exactly welcome.

Karma can be a raving bitch at times, and it looks like her eye's on me.

The timing sucks, just as I was starting to feel Marya open up to me. At this point, I'm sure she's still skittish enough she'll take any excuse to run full speed in the opposite direction. The arrival of an ex-girlfriend on the scene, one I'd be working with for the coming three months, is a definite kink in my cable.

Call me a coward, but last night when Marya texted, asking if I was all right after not hearing from me all week, I was tempted to ignore it. I couldn't though, not with Max's birthday today and the commitments already made; not to mention the guilt I was already feeling. Instead of texting her back, I called because I'd missed the sound of her voice.

Call me crazy, but I don't want the connection I feel with her—however new—to be spoiled by the aftermath of poor mistakes I may have made in the past.

Yet after talking with her, even just discussing mundane arrangements for today, I knew I wouldn't be able to maintain the self-imposed distance. So this morning, sitting across the island from my virtually vibrating son, I feel my own excitement building.

I grab our breakfast dishes and am just about to quickly wash them by hand when the doorbell rings. Before I even have a chance to wipe my hands, Max is already opening the front door.

We live in a moderate townhouse in a neighborhood with predominantly families. It's a fairly new subdivision, maybe twenty years old. I bought the house without much thought, other than it had to be relatively close to Max's school, and it had to be available on short notice. This place fit those requirements.

Although I like the open concept—I can see from the kitchen straight through to the front door, where Ma and Clint are greeting Max—the place itself has little character. It's convenient, and it fits us, that's about it. Still, with my son's excited chatter and the people filing in—apparently Marya was right behind my parents—it feels like a home.

"Quick, hide this in the fridge," Marya, who slipped past the huddle, hisses, handing me a large cake box.

"Can I see?"

"Later." Her saucy wink almost has me cover her barely-there smile with my mouth.

Yeah. Fuck distance.

Max's three other friends are dropped off fifteen minutes later, and it takes another ten to get driving arrangements sorted. I don't care who drives with who, as long as Marya's ass is in the seat beside me.

Clint has an extra bench in the back, so Max and his four buddies pile in the back of his ride, and Marya with her other two boys come with me.

Harry, her youngest, chatters excitedly when we

set out, his older brother mostly grunting in response, while Marya sits quietly beside me. About twenty minutes into the drive, the back seat falls silent, and I check in the mirror to see both boys slumped over, fast asleep.

"Friday night is our movie night," Marya explains, casting a glance over her shoulder at the boys. "Last night was a *Lord of the Rings* marathon." She stifles a yawn. "I would have put them to bed earlier, but I fell asleep on the couch. Woke up at one thirty and they were still at it."

I toss her a grin. "Happens in our house too. I'm away quite a bit, and then when I get home, Max is all geared up when all I want to do is sleep."

"Yeah. Liam is an early bird, like me, but his brothers like to sleep in."

"Like their father?" I carefully probe, feeling her eyes on me.

"Yes," she answers after a brief pause. "He never got out of his college habits of hitting the weekends hard. Not even after the kids were born." She lets out a derisive huff before adding under her breath, "I guess banging whoever his squeeze at the time was wore him out."

"Yikes." I steal a quick glance in the mirror to make sure the boys are still out. "So not just the one?"

This time she actually laughs. "God no. Apparently, there'd been numerous indiscretions over the years."

"And you had no idea."

"I was run ragged looking after the kids. In

hindsight, I probably didn't want to examine his frequent late nights and absences too closely, for fear of what I might discover." I don't like hearing the self-recrimination in her voice.

"You were in love," I offer, reaching over to give her knee a squeeze. "You focus on the best in the people you love. I know I did for far too long."

"I was in love with the family we had created," she corrects me. "It just took me too long to figure out Jeremy was never a part of that." She glances over her shoulder at the boys again. "It's always been me and the boys."

"No one you've been tempted to add into the mix over the years?" Her head snaps back and the look she flashes me feels hot on my skin. I almost start to fidget in my seat when she finally responds.

"A few times, but I don't think men exist who'd be willing to take on the whole package. Me, maybe, but three growing boys? Hell no."

"Don't be so quick to lump us all on the same pile," I say softly, reaching over again. This time I take her wrist, move her hand to rest under mine on the center console palm up, and slip my fingers between hers. For a moment, it feels like she might pull away, but then her fingers curl warmly around mine.

I haven't been this excited about holding a girl's hand since elementary school. I thought that had been a huge stride forward in getting my hand up Ginnie Markham's shirt—she was cursed with a D-cup by fifth grade—but Marya's fingers entwined with mine is arguably bigger.

Her reservations around me are not exactly a secret. She hasn't had much reason to trust men in general, and I also know she's giving our age difference far more weight than it deserves. Lastly, she's looking out for her kids, which is only an added attraction for me. She's a good mother. A conscientious one who works herself to the bone to ensure they have all they need.

What she doesn't know is that if she gives me half a chance, I would prove to her I'm not out to hurt her, I don't give a flying fuck that she is a little older than me, and I would rather stab myself in the eye than do anything to upset her boys.

Her warm palm against mine is a start.

A very fucking great one.

MARYA

"It's too big!"

I look over at Harry. The helmet he'd been handed is sliding off his head, almost covering his eyes.

"Here," Dylan pipes up before I have a chance to respond. "I'll see if they have one that fits better." He takes the helmet from Harry and disappears back into the small building.

We've all been outfitted with hard hats and yellow slickers, waiting to get on the mine train to get us down the shaft. All but Clint and Beth, who opted to wait aboveground for us.

The kids are all huddled together, talking excitedly, and I catch Liam with a grin on his face. I let that sink into my skin.

The boys didn't wake up until the road we were on turned to gravel. Up until that time, Dylan had not let go of my hand.

I'm not sure what possessed me to wrap my fingers around his, other than it felt good—*real*—when I'd been so conflicted after his pointed absence all week. There'd been no ambiguity in his words, or in his hand seeking out mine for that matter. Whatever had kept him away this week apparently had little or nothing to do with me.

"Here you go, kid," Dylan says, walking up to Harry and handing him another helmet. "Try that one." Harry throws him a grateful grin when this one seems to fit better.

"Thank you," I mouth at Dylan when he turns my way, thinking he didn't waste any time showing he meant what he said.

The wink that only enhances the heat in his dark brown eyes sends a tingle down my back. I don't even know I'm catching my bottom lip in my teeth until he drops his gaze to my mouth and his nostrils flare ever so slightly.

"All aboard!"

The guide's loud announcement breaks the spell, and the next minute we're herding excited kids into the small train carts.

The cacophony of children's voices bounces off

the wet rock of the mine shaft, until the guide calls their attention to some abandoned gear and tools along the way, settling into a historic overview geared specifically to the boys' age-group. Even Harry, whose voice can usually be heard above all, is listening to every word.

Tales of the three brothers who claimed the mine almost a hundred and fifty years ago, digging for the rich gold veins they believed hidden inside the mountain rock, keep the kids entertained until the train comes to a stop. A quick sidebar with the guide has him leading the pack down a tunnel, with Dylan and I bringing up the rear to catch any stragglers.

I try to focus on the tour, but am acutely aware of Dylan's much longer strides beside me. Every so often his fingers brush mine, and I lose track of what our guide is saying.

The boys are soaking it up, their excitement cranked up when the guide stops at a display that includes an old-fashioned detonator. He's about to launch into an explanation when I'm suddenly grabbed back by the arm and pulled into a narrow tunnel branching off the main one.

"Hey…"

That's all I manage before I find myself quite literally pressed between a rock and a hard place: the damp tunnel wall and Dylan's solid mass.

"Oof…" barely escapes my lips before the sound is swallowed by Dylan's mouth claiming mine.

There is nothing tentative about this kiss. It's a

no-holds-barred, balls-to-the-wall display of barely contained hunger. A kiss that has my fingers twisting in the longish hair at the back of his neck, and my tongue eagerly participating in a wild tangle with his.

One of his hands skims under the rain slicker to the small of my back, and slips under the waistband of my jeans. His long fingers dig into the meat of my bare ass, pressing me flush against the hard ridge of his erection, and I almost climb the thick thigh he wedges between my legs.

Geezus, holy mother of balls.

I've never quite understood the appeal of dry-humping, until meeting the firm bulge of Dylan's femoral muscle.

I'm lost to sensation, not even a fraction of rational thought involved in the mindless grinding, tasting, clasping of bodies. So when Dylan pulls away from me, emitting a tortured groan, it takes a few seconds for reality to penetrate.

Water dripping on my head and the damp, slightly musty smell remind me where I am.

"Shit, the kids," I mutter, wiping pointlessly at the wet strands stuck to my forehead.

"Yeah," is Dylan's drawled response. I lift my eyes to find a gleam in his, despite the lack of light in the tunnel. "I couldn't wait. Fuck." He runs a hand through his own damp mop of hair. "Shoulda waited," he mumbles. "Now I won't be able to get the taste of you—the feel of you—out of my mind."

"There you are." We jump apart hearing the guide's

voice behind us.

"Sorry, we got lost," Dylan replies as he turns, grabbing my hand. He pulls me along behind him, muttering, "To be continued," to me over his shoulder.

Still dazed, I can't quite decide the rest of the afternoon whether to take those words as a threat or a promise.

"That's amazing."

I turn at Dylan's awed tone to find him staring at the cake over my shoulder. I'm pretty proud of myself. Four hours of coloring and molding fondant over the three-layer sculpted cake until it resembled Deadpool's mask in the early hours yesterday morning, resulted in a fairly decent representation. Enough, clearly, to impress Dylan.

I'd found some soccer ball birthday candles on Amazon last week and ordered them for next day delivery.

"Do you have matches?"

"Yeah, hang on."

I can feel him moving away. The earlier tension still crackles between us, and I'm afraid even the slightest brush will ignite us. That's why I'd virtually hugged the passenger side door on the way home, actively keeping the boys' excited replay of the afternoon going as a distraction.

I glance over at Beth, who's been clearing away the remnants of the pizza we ordered on the way back.

Her eyes have been closely monitoring any and all interaction between her son and me from the moment we came back up from the mine. It's as if she could sense something changed between us. Even now, her expression is knowing, a slight uptilt at the corner of her mouth and one eyebrow a fraction higher than the other.

Thirty-three years of mothering and she's clearly not lost the ability to tell when her son is up to something.

She holds my gaze and a smile forms when I feel a hand land heavy on my shoulder, startling me.

"Here." Dylan hands me a box of matches.

It takes me three tries to get one lit with my shaking hands, almost feeling his breath at the back of my head. "Why don't you grab some plates?" I snap, irritated with my body for giving so much away. I ignore Beth's snicker and focus on getting all eleven candles lit.

"I'll hit the lights and bring down the plates," Dylan announces. "You carry the cake."

"But it's your—"

"You baked it, you carry it."

He's gone down the basement steps before I have a chance to respond.

"No changing that boy's mind once he figures out what he wants. No use fighting him," Beth shares sagely, before she too disappears to the basement.

Taking in a deep breath, I pick up the cake and carefully follow them down the stairs.

"Awesoooome!" Max yells when he catches sight of me.

He dives into the task of blowing out his candles the moment I set the platter on the coffee table, but it's not until Dylan flicks the lights back on that he gets a good look at the cake. The other boys crowd around him and I soak up the oohs and aahs with a smile. More buzz from the boys when I start slicing, exposing the alternate red velvet and dark chocolate layers filled with buttercream frosting and cherry compote.

I hand the first piece to the birthday boy, who doesn't waste a minute to shove a bite in his face. With his mouth full, he looks at his grandma and the hair stands up on my arms. It's like I know it's coming.

"Better than yours, Grammy," Max announces, crumbs flying from his lips.

CHAPTER 8

DYLAN

"Max, let's go!"

I was expecting this. Because of Max's party on Saturday, all our normal weekend chores had fallen on yesterday, and Max had already been dragging his feet. This morning even more so, but I have no time to play games. I have to get to the office.

"Max!"

"Coming!" he finally yells back, his footsteps pounding down the stairs. His backpack is slung over his shoulder and I quickly stuff the lunch I made him inside.

"Dad?"

"Grab a coat, kid. It's chilly today," I direct him, yanking my own jacket off the coatrack.

"Dad?"

"Max. Coat."

The eye-roll is nothing new, but at least he tags the lined flannel jacket Ma got him. "But I need to tell you something."

"Tell me in the car, okay?"

I don't mind mornings, but I prefer quiet ones. A challenge with Max, since he likes to fill silence with the sound of his voice. I'm ready to let his usual verbal stream slide off me when I climb behind the wheel, but when he starts talking I'm immediately alert.

"Remember you told me that if ever I felt uncomfortable, I should tell you?"

"Absolutely," I don't hesitate answering, looking at my son's face, pinched with worry.

"There's this kid in my *Fortnite* group who's been weird."

Since the spring, I've allowed Max to play the game online, with a bunch of warnings and restrictions. In the beginning, I would play with him, feeling out some of the kids he'd play with, but the last few months I haven't had much time. Still, he knows not to give his own name, our phone number, or address, and that if ever anyone makes him feel uncomfortable, to let me know right away.

"Weird how?" I ask, backing out of the driveway.

"I dunno, just weird."

"You're gonna have to be more specific than that, Max."

"It's just…he's been asking questions. First it was about sports and pets and other things. If I play any, do I have a dog, if I like my school—stuff like that.

Then he wanted to know if I had a girlfriend, and when I said no, he asked if maybe I liked boys better." My blood chills. It sounds like an almost textbook approach for a predator. "That made me feel weird, so I avoided him for a while, but last night when I got on, he was there and wished me a happy belated birthday." I stop at a light and glance over at him. He's tense and I can see the worry in his face. "But, Dad, I never told him my birth date, I promise."

I ignore the urge to grill him with questions—he already seems freaked enough—and instead reach out to ruffle his hair. "I believe you, Kiddo. Maybe stay off the Internet for a while, yeah?" I make a mental note to disconnect Wi-Fi the first chance I get.

"Sure," he mutters, looking forward but worry still clear on his face.

"Hey…" I draw his attention and force what I hope is a calm smile. "Your old man will take care of it, okay?" I'm rewarded with a little smile in return.

"Yeah, Dad."

I stop at the school's drop-off zone and turn to him. "Just stay close to your buds. Okay, Max? You know the drill; we've been over it before. And if you're not sure, or something feels off, call me."

Being away from home for work regularly, I bought Max a basic cell phone for his ninth birthday. A lot of folks might consider that too young, but it was both for my own peace of mind and his. I programmed it with a handful of numbers: mine, Ma and Clint's, his other grandma's, and the office phone. He's only used it a handful of times, mostly when I was on assignment and he needed to connect for one reason or another.

In my job, I encounter a lot of the bad side of humanity, so I'd started him young instilling basic safety rules. A precaution that paid off, given he came to me with his concerns.

Despite the fact I stopped kissing him in front of his school at his request a few years ago, I tag him behind his neck and pull him in an embrace, pressing my lips to his forehead. He doesn't struggle, just holds on until I let go. "Love you, Kiddo."

"Love you too, Dad," he mumbles getting out of the truck.

Ignoring the impatient honks of waiting parents behind me, I watch as he catches up with a buddy on the sidewalk and walks into the school. Only then do I pull away from the curb, my mind spinning as I aim for the office.

Preoccupied with what Max shared, I hadn't mentally prepared for what is waiting for me when I walk into the office.

Toni Linden.

She's changed little these past couple of years. Still packs a punch with that gorgeous California girl look. Long, sleek, blonde and blue-eyed. She used to look hot in uniform, and I guess some might still consider her hot in her FBI getup: white dress shirt and navy pants suit. A bit of a cliché, especially in our mostly relaxed field office, because it's rare to find any of us in a suit, unless we know we've got brass coming.

Her smile is bright when she sees me come in, but it oddly has no impact other than to make me slightly uncomfortable.

"Agent Linden, we meet again." I stick out my hand, hoping to cut off any unwanted familiarities. My word choice may not have been the best, since Jasper glances at me curiously over his computer screen. "Agent Linden and I had opportunity to work together on a case," I explain. "Although, she was Officer Linden at the time."

"Dylan…" she starts, smiling at Jasper before she catches herself. "I mean Agent Barnes is in part what inspired me to switch to federal law enforcement."

"Is that so?" Jas drawls, and I shoot him a warning glance.

"I have something disturbing come up I may need your help with." My words work as an adequate distraction since Jasper's face morphs into Bureau mode. Then I outline my talk with Max earlier. He's already pounding keys before I've even finished talking.

Jasper Greene is our resident technical whiz and cyber intelligence specialist. I'm no slouch, but I don't hold a candle to the information he's able to unearth with the help of his computer.

"*Fortnite*? Fuck. Write down his handle and password." Jasper shoves a pad in my direction and I sit, jotting down what he asks.

"I'm in the same group. I'll give you mine as well," I inform him, adding my 10-CODE handle and password.

"Good. Have you disconnected your router yet?"

"Was going to do that first chance."

"Go do it now, and bring it back with you, I'm gonna to need it."

"I get the feeling I'm missing something," I observe, getting a sense of urgency from Jasper that makes me uneasy. The look he throws me only makes it stronger.

"Likely nothing more than coincidence, but twenty minutes before you came in, we received an Amber Alert notification. Twelve-year-old boy missing from Flora Vista. I spoke with the SAC in Farmington, who mentioned the kid was seen going up to his room last night, but wasn't in his bed this morning. It wasn't even slept in. The game system in his bedroom was still on. He'd been in the middle of a game when he disappeared."

"Jesus." The chill in my veins turns to ice. I almost shrug off the warm hand that lands on my shoulder.

"We should go." Toni's gentle voice startles me. I'd almost forgotten she was there.

"We?"

"I'm supposed to shadow you my first two weeks," she clarifies when I push up, dislodging her hand from my shoulder.

"On a job. This is personal," I bite off, making her wince.

"Like hell," Jasper interjects. "We're treating this as an investigation. Toni goes."

Damian walks in just as I open my mouth to object, and quickly gauges the tension in the office.

"What's going on?"

"You go," Jasper reiterates before turning to our boss. "I'll fill you in."

I don't wait for her, but on the way out of the office I snatch the keys to one of the FBI Expeditions in the parking lot. For some reason, I don't want her ass in my new Bronco.

There's something about her being here that irks me, but I don't have the time or the inclination to examine it. I have bigger fish to fry.

MARYA

"I swear I just want to grab him by the ears and shake some sense into him."

Kerry throws me a sympathetic smile.

We're sitting on the floor, surrounded by boxes of books that just came in this morning. Normally a fun job to unpack all the new releases and sorting them on the shelves—which is why Kerry came in to help—but my head isn't in the game.

Saturday had been a great day as far as the kids were concerned. All three had a good time in Silverton and seemed to get along fine afterward as well.

For me the day had been a tad overwhelming. First of all the interesting developments with Dylan, the hand-holding, the smiles, and finally the hunger of his kiss when he accosted me in the tunnel. But even after, at his place. The almost palpable chemistry between him and me, and the fact his mother seemed to pick up on that, had put me in a fight or flight mode.

To top it all off, Max made that comment about the cake, and as grateful as I was he liked it so much, I was mortified at what he said. I was also furious at Dylan for lying to me, telling me he'd usually grab a store-bought cake. He's a guy and maybe doesn't understand how territorial women can get about their baking, but that doesn't negate the fact he lied.

Not only that, he made me look bad. Had I known his mother normally did the baking, there's no way I would've made that cake. Now it looked like I was trying to steal her thunder.

Even though Beth assured me several times she didn't mind in the least, and was in total agreement with her grandson, I couldn't shake feeling embarrassed. Although I did give her the recipe for the layers when she asked, admitting she could bake, but didn't have a creative bone in her body and sucked at decorating.

Then Sunday had started with another altercation between Liam and his younger brother, this one luckily without fists, but with brutally harsh words. I don't even know what the fight was about—and it doesn't really matter—but when Harry told me what Liam had said, I saw red.

"Kids say stupid shit in anger," Kerry offers. "They don't mean half of it."

"I know, but telling his baby brother the only reason their dad left us was because he never wanted another kid, is unbelievably cruel."

Kerry winces. "Yikes. It's so hard to wrap my head around him saying something like that. He's never struck me as a mean kid. Did you ask him why?"

"Of course I asked him, but all I got back was attitude. He claimed not to understand what was so wrong about telling the truth. Apparently he'd overheard his dad and me fighting, and Jeremy had yelled that we never should've had another baby."

"*Geezus,*" she hisses. "That poor kid."

"Which one?" I ask, and she looks up at me with an eyebrow raised.

"Both. It was cruel for Liam to throw that at his brother, but can you imagine being a kid and hearing something like that? Not only that, but then holding on to it for five years?" I flinched. All these years, I thought I'd done such a good job shielding the boys from all the ugly shit both before, and after, the dissolution of our marriage. Turns out I hadn't been so successful. "Did you end up finding out what caused the argument?"

"Yeah, Harry's game system had frozen so he got on his brother's while he was in the shower. Liam wasn't happy when he found out. I ended up punishing him by unplugging his PS4 and tossing it in my bedroom closet."

"Good for you."

"Maybe, but I don't know who's hurting more," I confess. "He hasn't spoken to me since."

Kerry reaches over and gives my arm a squeeze.

"He'll get over it."

"I hope so."

Half an hour later, we've lined up the last of the new books on the shelves and stand side by side admiring them. "I'm going to have to take a few home," Kerry mumbles, taking a selection off the shelf.

"I know, I was just thinking the same thing." I grab for the latest Anna Bishop Barker book. A new favorite of mine.

"I've barely seen Damian the last couple of days with that Amber Alert still active," she says, leading the way to the coffee counter.

"Those poor parents," I commiserate. "I can't even imagine what they must be going through."

I'd assumed it was the news of the missing kid from Vista Flora, just over the New Mexico border, that had kept Dylan busy. I haven't heard from him since we left his place Saturday night.

"I know. I keep hoping he somehow got lost and someone will find him soon, but it's already been seventy-two hours. The guys have been working around the clock, but apparently they have very few leads."

While Kerry breaks down the boxes, I grind some beans for a fresh cup of coffee. Blood pressure be damned. "I need some reinforcement. Want one?"

"Yeah. I could use one too." Kerry throws me a grateful look.

"It just makes me sick. The thought of that young boy out there, living through God only knows what.

And knowing the longer it takes; the less likely it is they find him alive. If that were one of mine—"

Kerry's hand grabs my wrist firmly.

"Don't say that. Don't even think it."

My head has barely hit my pillow tonight when a ping from my phone on the nightstand announces a message.

Dylan: Checking in if you're ok. Been a crazy week. Again.

Me: I'm good. Amber Alert? So sad.

The phone suddenly rings in my hand.

"Were you sleeping?" Dylan's tone is gruff with exhaustion.

"Not yet. Kerry tells me you guys have been at it nonstop. You sound tired."

"I am. Unfortunately, home to sleep tonight. Not that I expect I'll get much."

It takes a second for the weight of his words to settle in. When they do, a painful knot forms in my chest and tears well in my eyes. "Oh, no…"

"Yeah," he confirms in a pained voice. "Woulda gone a month without sleep for just the hope of a different outcome."

"I bet," I whisper, sniffling softly.

"Shit, I'm sorry, honey. That was stupid of me. I

just wanted to hear your voice…I…I shouldn't have called. I'll let you—"

"Don't hang up," I interrupt him. "Just talk to me."

"I can't. Not about the case, there's too much…It's an ongoing investigation."

"Not about that," I clarify. "Talk to me about anything else."

"Max is still at Ma's. I almost went to pick him up, just so I could hold him close all night to get that image out of my head, but it was already late."

I hum my understanding, doing my best to mask the sob trying to break free. I can't even imagine the things he sees in his line of work. Suddenly his thirty-three years don't seem so young anymore.

"Have you eaten anything?" the mother in me asks, making him chuckle.

"I actually ate a huge piece of leftover cake before I rolled into bed," he admits, a hint of a smile in his voice

"Hardly a nutritionally balanced meal."

"Maybe not, but I thought it might feed my craving." His meaning isn't subtle, and I know he's not talking about his sweet tooth. "But it wasn't enough."

"Dylan…"

A heavy silence follows, which he breaks by yawning loudly.

"You should try to get some sleep," I urge him gently.

"I don't want to hang up," he whispers, stifling

another yawn.

"Then we won't. Just close your eyes."

It takes a few minutes before I can hear his breathing even out, and I know he's fallen asleep.

I wait another ten to make sure before I end the call.

It's already getting light out when I drift off myself.

CHAPTER 9

DYLAN

"Go home."

I look up from the piles of data on my desk I've been digging through for any hints of a lead, to see Damian looming over my desk.

"I'll head out soon, I'm just finishing these—"

"Barnes," he says sternly. "I know this one hit close to home, but you've had how many hours of sleep since Monday? We'll catch the bastard who put Seth Mayer in that ditch, but it won't help if you collapse on the job. Shut down that computer, go pick up your boy, and go home."

I take in the copy of the coroner's report I've been squinting at for the past two hours without registering the words. "Fine."

"You too, Linden," I hear him say to Toni. I'd almost forgotten she was there.

"Yes, sir."

"Both of you take the weekend. The Farmington office is lead on this, we're just along for the ride. See you Monday." With that he turns on his heel and walks out the door.

As much as I hate to admit it, he's right. Not knowing whether the boy was dead or alive, we barely stopped to take a breath. After finding his poor broken body yesterday morning, sadly speed became less of a concern and a sharp mind was priority. Six hours of sleep in four days does not equate a sharp mind.

Closing the files on my desk, I get up and shrug on my jacket, waiting for Toni to grab her things so I can turn off the lights and lock up the office.

I was surprised I slept at all when I woke up this morning, my cell phone still in my hand. At some point Marya must've hung up and I wonder if she'd managed to get to sleep herself. I texted a quick *thank you*, and a few hours later got back *you're welcome*.

"Why don't we have a quick dinner?" Toni suggests, following me down the stairs and out the door to the parking lot. "We still have some catching up to do."

I grind to a halt, turning to her in disbelief. "You're shitting me, right?" The look on her face tells me she's not kidding. *Un-fucking-believable.* I've spent the past days trying to ignore the uneasy feeling that Toni's arrival in Durango is not exactly by chance. Wasn't hard to do since the case claimed everyone's attention. "Look," I try for a more modified tone.

"I'm not sure what you want. We had a brief thing in Denver, which—as I explained up front—could be nothing more than casual. You knew, you agreed, and then you went and…"

"I know, I know," she pleads, putting a hand on my chest and I immediately step out of reach. "I was desperate, I see that now. It was stupid."

Stupid isn't exactly the term I would've chosen, but I'm not about to argue that point. "Why are you here, Toni?" I ask her instead. "Why are you suddenly FBI and here in Durango?"

Her face instantly turns impassive, a careless shrug lifting her shoulders. "Like I said, you inspired me. It seemed like the right career choice for me. Then this opportunity came along, and I jumped at it. I didn't know—"

I shake my head sharply. "You played me for dumb once, don't do it again," I warn her. "Whatever game you think you're playing here is not going to work."

Without giving her a chance to respond, I aim for my truck, eager to get out of here.

Max's excitement at seeing me walk into Ma's house has me shake off any lingering anger. He comes charging at me, plowing into me hard.

"Geeze, kid. Easy on your old man, okay?" I grumble, grabbing him under his armpits and hauling him up my body, like I used to do when he was half the size. It takes some effort—he's getting big—but

I welcome his weight as his limbs wrap around me, clinging tight.

"Did you catch the bad guy, Dad?" He lifts his head from my neck, a solemn look on his face.

"Not yet," I tell him honestly, giving his body a reassuring squeeze before lowering him to the ground. "But we will. Now how about you and me pick up some junk food on the way home, and veg out on the couch with a movie?"

"Yeah!" He grins and pumps his fist. I'm lucky it doesn't take much to put that smile on my boy's face.

"Sorry," Ma says from the kitchen when Max sprints off to grab his things from upstairs. "There was no way to shield him without keeping him out of school."

Although Max has a general idea what the kind of job I have entails, I keep details from him as best I can. With a case like this—involving a kid his own age, which I'm sure has been all over the media—there's no way to control what information he's exposed to.

"No way to keep something like this from him, Ma."

"Has he told you he knows that boy?"

My body jerks involuntarily. "Seth Mayer?"

Mom nods. "Saw his picture in the paper this morning and told me he knows him from soccer. Played against him a few weeks ago."

"You're kidding me." I'm already dialing when Max comes down the stairs, carrying his things. "Give me a sec, okay? I'm just gonna step outside to make a quick call. Go say bye to Grammy and Gramps."

"Dylan?" I hear Jasper's voice on the line as I step out on the front porch.

"Yeah. Listen, I just found out Seth Mayer plays soccer in the same league as Max. Did I miss this?"

"Hold on." I hear tapping on a keyboard, but I don't have to wait long. "It's not in the report."

"Shit. Apparently Max saw his picture in the paper this morning and mentioned it to my mother."

"I'll give the boys in Farmington a call. Maybe they missed it."

"Thanks, man." I turn around when the front door opens and Max sticks his head outside to see if I'm ready. "I've gotta get going. I promised the kid junk food."

Jasper chuckles. "I crave the day I can make my kid happy with junk food," he shares, being a new father to his four-month-old daughter. "The only thing Maisy gets excited about is her mom's boob."

"TMI, brother," I quickly shut him down. "I'll catch you later." I can still hear him laughing when I end the call.

Max and I raid the snack aisle at the City Market, stock up on root beer—for Max—and a couple of bottles of a local IPA—for me—and hit the couch the moment we get home.

I don't give a flying fuck we're watching *Deadpool* for the seventy-ninth time. Ryan Reynolds is still funny as shit, and I have my boy safely tucked under my arm.

When I wake up a little after midnight—wrappers and empty chip bags littering the coffee table, the DVD logo bouncing over the screen, and Max's weight heavy against me, fast asleep—I turn off the TV, snag the quilt from the back of the couch, and stretch out with my kid tucked firmly against me.

Fuck brushing teeth.

MARYA

I watch as Liam runs ahead while I grab the bag and tray of coffee, and lock the Jeep.

Dylan's truck is parked a few spots over, so I know he's already here. I don't know if he got my text in time, since I didn't hear back, which might mean we both got breakfast.

I spot him as I get nearer to the bleachers, pacing back and forth on the far side, phone to his ear. His back is turned. There's plenty of room, so I take a seat two rows up, setting the bag and tray next to me and letting my eyes drift to the field.

This morning had been hectic. We dropped Theo off at a school buddy's house, where he's supposed to be working on a project and sleep over tonight. Mom offered to take Harry with her to see my aunt Ida in Silverton, mainly to give me some one-on-one time with Liam, and my youngest went willingly. Excitedly even, probably thinking he could con Mom into taking him back to the mine. He hadn't stopped talking about the place all week. Poor Mom, I have a feeling she might regret her offer by the time the weekend is over.

My middle one is the only kid who didn't leave the house happy this morning. He's not excited about spending the weekend with me; that much is clear.

Other than the odd yes or no, he's been able to maintain his angry silence. It's killing me, but I'm not budging; that PS4 will stay on the shelf in my closet until he changes his attitude.

I watch as the coach calls my son over to the sidelines, puts a hand on Liam's shoulder and leans down, obviously talking to him. Liam nods in response and jogs back to his position on the field.

I glance over at Dylan, his back still turned but he's stopped pacing, standing still with a hand clasping the back of his neck. As I watch, he turns his head and his eyes come straight to me, lifting his chin in greeting. A whistle sounds, drawing my attention to the field, and the start of the game.

It's not long before I notice Dylan approach. He sits down beside me, close enough the length of his muscular thigh is pressed against mine.

"You brought breakfast."

"Sonya's version of a Sausage McMuffin."

Dylan digs into the paper bag I'm offering. "Perfect. I'm starved. I didn't have a chance to pick anything up, I've been on the phone for the past half hour."

"Work?" I hand him his coffee before taking a sip of my own.

"Mmm." He leans in placing his mouth right by my ear. "New lead." I try not to shiver when his lips brush the shell before he straightens up.

"Good news," I mumble, hiding behind my coffee cup.

"Last night was my second decent sleep this week," he volunteers, nudging me with his elbow and I feel my cheeks warm. "First one I was in bed listening to you breathe, last night I had Max tucked against me."

I turn to look at him when I see something from the corner of my eye that has my heart stop in my throat, and I swing my head back.

On the far side of the field, leaning over the fence, is a painfully familiar figure casually taking in the game. Hot rage flows like lava through my veins.

"Oh, fuck no!" I don't realize I yell out loud, and surge off the bench, setting off in a dead run, my eyes never wavering from my target.

I'm just rounding the corner of the field, when an arm snakes around my waist and I'm being lifted off my feet.

"Easy does it, tiger," Dylan's voice sounds behind me as I struggle in his hold. I don't know if that's what has Jeremy turn his head toward us, but noting the smirk on his face when his eyes lock with mine, I figure he's toying with me. It's what he likes to do.

"Let me go," I grind out between clenched teeth, trying to pry Dylan's arms away.

"Not a chance. Not until you explain who the fuck that is, and why he has you hell-bent to get your hands on him."

"Jeremy. My ex," I bite off, letting myself go limp in Dylan's hold. He's immovable.

"The fuck? The guy, who hasn't seen his kids in fucking years, shows up at his son's goddamn soccer game?"

Something tells me there's been a shift in aggressor when Dylan's arms slip from around me and I'm unceremoniously set aside. I watch as he stalks over to where Jeremy is now straightening up, no longer wearing the cocky smirk.

Shit. I set off after him. It's one thing for me to throw a punch at my ex, but for Dylan that could mean the end of his career. I catch up with him just as he comes to a stop no more than a few feet from Jeremy. "I'll need you to leave."

"I'm just watching my boy play soccer, not that it's any of your business."

Dylan takes another step forward, his body coiled with tension.

"Please don't," I plead, shoving my arm through his. Not that I have any hope of holding him back if he decides to put on a beating, but it makes me feel better.

"A little young for you, isn't he, Marya?"

I cling onto Dylan's arm a little tighter when I hear his low growl in response to Jeremy's taunt. "Your son is here," I quickly whisper under my breath, while casting a glance at the field where the game is still in full swing. Thank God for that. "Please...don't do anything I *know* you'll regret. It's exactly what he wants."

"Everything okay here? Barnes?" A guy I recognize as the father of one of the boys on the team comes walking up.

"Thanks, Rick. It's under control," Dylan says, easing his arm from my hold and reaching for his back pocket. He pulls out a wallet, flips it open, and shoves it at Jeremy. "FBI Special Agent Dylan Barnes. I believed I asked you to leave."

"I have a right to be here," Jeremy sputters, clearly a bit taken aback finding the man he was just taunting is law enforcement. "I'm his father."

"Don't even think about it, Marya," Dylan warns when I huff in protest, taking a step forward. He uses his free arm to move me behind him. To Jeremy he says, "I'm not going to ask again."

For a moment he looks like he's going to balk again, but then Rick casually walks up to him. "Look, buddy," he says, putting a nonchalant arm around his shoulders. "I'm not sure what's going on, but this is not the time or the place. Trust me, you don't want to get into a battle of wills with Barnes here, you'll lose. He won't just wipe the floor with you, he'll slap handcuffs on for the trouble." While he's talking, he slowly guides Jeremy away from the field and toward the parking lot.

"You need to file for a restraining order," Dylan

says as he turns to face me, a firm hand on my shoulder.

"I know."

"I don't know what his game is, but he's not just going to disappear again."

"I know, Dylan."

"You can't take any chances, Marya. Guys like that, they don't just give up," he pushes, and I lose my cool.

Pissed, I shrug off his hand and step out of his reach. "You're preaching to the fucking choir, Dylan. I know exactly what that man is capable of."

"Mom?"

Oh shit. My eyes dart to the parking lot where Jeremy is just getting into a shiny new Lexus, Rick holding the door open. I turn to Liam, who is leaning against the fence, concern on his face as his coach is yelling at him from the sideline.

"Buddy, get back in the game."

"Who was that?" he persists, his eyes trying to catch a glimpse, but Dylan's large form is blocking most of the view.

"Someone I used to know. Now get back on the field, Liam."

"Best do as your mother says," Dylan adds. "Looks like Coach is about to bench you."

Liam takes one last glance at the parking lot then gives me a hard stare, before turning and jogging back onto the field.

I let out a deep breath.

CHAPTER 10

Dylan

I ignore Marya's scowl as I steer her into the FBI offices, the boys following behind.

She's pissed because after the game I manipulated the situation and loaded both boys into the back of my Bronco, leaving her no choice but to follow me. Straight to Rock Point Drive.

Luna is sitting at her desk and looks up when we walk in.

"Hey." She sounds surprised and looks questioningly at me. I give her an almost imperceptible nod and her gaze shifts briefly to Marya before settling on the boys. "Hey, guys." The boys mumble their hellos.

"Is the conference room free?"

Her eyes shoot back to me and she immediately gets up out of her chair. "I think so, but let me make sure."

She disappears into the conference room and I can tell she's rolling the case boards we usually have up into the small interrogation room down the hall.

Luna Roosberg is sharp. She's not only a force to be reckoned with in the field, she's invaluable in outlining psychological profiles we use in our investigations. She's the one person in our office aside from maybe Damian, who is very familiar with the ins and outs of the judicial system. And last but not least, she's a woman, which may make it a little easier for Marya to share the kind of information I know a judge wants to see on a request for a protection order.

"Yup. All clear."

"Why don't you have a seat, Marya? I'll set the boys up next door."

I quickly get the kids sorted, logging into my Netflix account to stream a movie they both agree on to the flat-screen TV mounted on the wall. When I walk back into the office, I see Luna is already taking notes, and instead of interrupting, I sit down at my desk and check emails keeping half an ear to the conversation.

"…would he get physical?" I hear Luna ask, and I shift my full attention on the two women.

"He never really beat me senseless or anything," Marya answers with a denial that's ambivalent at best. "He'd get a little rough sometimes. Shove me, purposely squeeze my arm a little too hard in front of the kids, sometimes he'd bite, daring me to flinch or cry out. It was all a game to him. He knew I would do anything to shield the kids. It was nothing major. "

Luna catches the strangled sound I make—trying to hold back the growl working its way up my gullet—and shoots me a warning glare, before turning her attention back to Marya.

"I get that it's easier telling yourself it was nothing of real importance, but for the purpose of filing for a protective order, it's imperative not to minimize the reasons you feel he might be a threat. Both physically *and* psychologically."

By some divine power, I manage to stay quiet and in my seat for the next forty-five minutes while Luna helps Marya fill out the required forms. I do end up with a much better understanding of her, which is why, when Luna offers to take Marya to the courthouse Monday morning to see if they can expedite this in front of a judge, I don't object.

When we leave the office—at the urging of a couple of hungry kids—I suggest picking up some Mexican at Los Amigos.

"Are the other boys going to be home soon?" I ask Marya, as she gets behind the wheel of her Jeep while the boys climb in my truck.

"No. They won't be home until tomorrow."

"Okay, we'll pick up food and meet you at your place?"

It's slight, but the hesitation is still there in her eyes. "Okay, sure. You'll need the address, though."

I lean into the open door. "Sweetheart, I know where you live."

"You do?" She sounds surprised and I grin.

"Yup," I confirm. "Looked it up after the first time seeing you at the game."

"Oh."

Her lips purse into a perfect circle I want to penetrate with my tongue—or other parts of my anatomy—but the kids are watching. Instead I rap my knuckles on her roof before getting into my truck and turning to the boys.

"You guys have your orders ready?"

I grin at their emphatic. "Yes."

"Max? Juice or ice tea?"

"Joosh, pfeeze," he answers, nearly spraying Marya with a quarter burrito in his mouth.

"Manners, Max," I bark and his guilty eyes shoot my way.

"Sorry," he mumbles, after swallowing.

Marya grins, winking at Max before she turns to her son. "Liam?" The boy shoots his mother a scowl and doesn't answer, instead shoving another bite in his mouth. "Juice or tea?" she tries again, but he still doesn't answer. Max's eyes flit from one to the other. It's clear Marya is uncomfortable and doesn't want to draw attention to her son's rude behavior.

I know I may be overstepping but I can't help wade in. "Kid, you may wanna answer your mother."

"Juice," he bites off the single syllable at his mom, before turning his eyes to me, and adding in a normal tone, "Please."

I open my mouth to say something but catch Marya shake her head. Right. Maybe not my battle, but I plan to find out what it's all about.

I don't need to wait long.

"Wanna play *Fortnite*?" Max asks his friend, having just finished his second burrito.

Liam throws his mother a dirty look across the table before turning to Max. "Can't. I don't have my PlayStation."

"Liam," she cautions in a warning tone.

Suddenly the boy shoots up from his chair back, pointing an accusing finger at Marya. "It was him, wasn't it? At the game?"

She blanches and without using words the answer is plain on her face. "Liam…"

"I knew it," he hisses. "You sent him away, just like last time." His face red, close to tears, the boy kicks over the chair and storms up the stairs.

Marya claps a hand over her mouth and mumbles a barely audible apology, her eyes filling.

"Max, let me set you up in the living room, okay?" My son looks up at me with big eyes and nods. I get up, and give Marya's arm a squeeze in passing.

"Basement," she whispers.

"Sorry?"

"Set him up in the basement. He can use one of the boys' game systems there."

I'm surprised at the sweet setup her kids have in the basement, each with their own gaming cubicle.

Max clearly agrees, flinging himself into one of the massive beanbags. "This is awesome."

"No going online, okay, Kiddo?"

"I know, Dad."

By the time I leave him to it and head back upstairs, Max has all but forgotten the scene at the table. I haven't.

Marya's at the sink, hand-washing the dishes, her shoulders drawn up almost to her ears. The moment I put a hand on her back, she lets the plate in her hand slide in the soapy water, spins around, and does a faceplant in my chest.

"Hey…" I slip an arm around her waist, anchoring her to me, and slide my other hand up under her hair, curving my fingers around the back of her neck.

"I hate him so much." She sniffs in my shirt.

"Your ex," I clarify.

"Of course," she snaps, lifting her head back to throw me a glare. "Who else?"

I press her face back against my chest, deciding it's probably safer just to keep my mouth shut.

MARYA

"Hey, Bub."

The room is gloomy with the last of the day's light disappearing outside. Liam is facedown on his bed, his pillow pulled over his head, not moving. I'm wondering if he's asleep.

I spent the past half hour sitting next to a very quiet

Dylan on the couch, unloading everything from the demise of my marriage to the change in my middle child these past few months. It was Dylan who finally urged me to go up and talk to my son, while he checked on Max.

I sit down beside him on the bed, placing a hand on his back.

"I didn't send Dad away when he left us, Liam. He did that on his own. But I did send him away this morning." The fact it had been Dylan who said the words was beside the point, since I wanted the same thing. I can feel the muscles in his back tighten so I know he's awake, but he isn't talking. "Your father…" I'm not quite sure where to go from there without hurting my child. There isn't anything to say that would make the truth easier for him to hear, so I decide to give him the story straight. "He never contacted us, Liam. Not once. In fact, the few times I tried to get in touch with him in the first few months, he told me not to contact him again." I don't mention Jeremy telling me to leave him the fuck alone, since he had a new family now. There's no need to rub salt in the wound. "So I didn't. Instead I focused on building a good life for us without his help."

The pillow lifts away, and Liam's red-rimmed eyes peer up at me. "So if he didn't want us, why did he come to my game?"

My heart breaks at the dejection on his face, but I stop myself from making excuses for his father. No more. I've done that for years and probably would've continued if the asshole hadn't forced my hand by blindsiding us.

"I don't know why, Bub. He called out of the blue a few weeks ago, and said he wanted to see you boys. I told him no. He chose not to be involved in your lives at all for the past five years, he doesn't get to waltz back in and disrupt our lives. I don't even know how he found out about your game, but showing up there was totally out of line, which is why I wanted him to leave."

Liam seems to be thinking on that for a bit, before he pushes himself into a sitting position. "What if we want to see *him*?"

I try not to wince visibly, but it hurts. I busted my ass for years so my boys were looked after, and I'm the first in line to get shit on when they're in a mood, and all that bastard needs to do is show his face once.

I take in a deep breath and try to sound reasonable. "If that is the case, there are proper ways to go about seeing if we can make that happen."

For a minute, it looks like he might have something to say, but then he just nods and looks away, his face once again sullen. A thought occurs to me, sending chills down my spine.

"Liam? Has your dad tried to contact you before? Is that why you've been so angry the past months? Has he approached you at school? Talked to you?"

The puzzled look on my son's face fills me with relief. "Dad? No."

I reach out and brush the hair that's getting to be

too long again from his face. "Then what happened to make you so unhappy you're fighting with your brothers—angry with me? What's going on?"

It's like throwing a switch, how fast he shuts down. I can tell just by looking at him, whatever few moments of honesty he gave me are over. "Nothing."

In a last ditch effort to win back a little goodwill—I am not above bribing when it suits me—I tell him, "Max is downstairs playing on your brother's system. If you want, you can get yours from my closet and hook it back up. No more fighting, Liam."

He shoots up off the bed, and I hear him rummaging in my bedroom before his feet thunder on the stairs. I let out a deep sigh, get up off the bed, and close his bedroom door behind me on my way down.

Stubborn damn kid. Not even a thank you.

"Judging from the way he just tore down the stairs, clutching his game system, I'm guessing your talk went okay?"

Dylan is sitting in the corner of my couch, his eyes on me as I walk into the living room and lean on the armrest opposite him. "It did, until I pushed my luck, and then it didn't. Can I get you a drink? I may have a beer."

"Beer would be good."

I can feel him following my movements, as I unearth a beer from the bottom of the fridge and pour myself a healthy helping of pinot grigio. Both left from a barbecue with Kerry and Damian this summer. I only really drink when I have company.

Handing him the bottle, I sit down on the other side of the couch, pull my legs under me, and take a gulp of wine.

"So what happened?"

"I told him as much of the truth about his father as I feel he needs to know. Guess I'll have to do the same with Theo and Harry when they get home tomorrow. I don't want to run the chance he'll pull another stunt like today without them being prepared."

"They have no idea what happened?"

"Harry doesn't have a clue. He can barely remember Jeremy. Theo probably has a better sense of what went on, being the oldest. I suspect it's the reason he's always been protective of me. Liam's the one who's always missed him most, would ask about him regularly at first. I thought I was protecting them by skirting the truth when it came to answering questions. Why make life harder for them? Guess that didn't pan out so well. Anyway," I continue, after taking another healthy swig of my wine, "as it turns out, it wasn't his father that set off his sour attitude the past few months."

"What was?"

"Don't have a clue. He totally clammed up on me." I set my glass down and fall back in the couch pillows. "Total mom fail."

Dylan snorts and I watch from the corner of my eye as he scoots closer, settling beside me. He twists toward me, cocks his knee on the seat and proceeds to pull my feet from under me. He drops one on his lap and his thumbs rub firm circles on the sole of the other.

I almost groan out loud. *Bliss.*

A small satisfied grin on his lips tells me he's well aware of his effect on me. "Don't beat yourself up," he suggests softly. "I discovered that's something that seems to come natural to parents, when we all just try to do the best we can in the circumstances we've been dealt. I could blame myself 'til the cows come home for the ways I fucked up as a person, and a parent, in the past, but that's not gonna do my boy any good. So I try to do better—be better—and hope that's the lesson Max will walk away with."

My mind gets stuck on the ways he may have fucked up. Somehow it doesn't compute. I've tried hard to find fault with him, determined not to let my attraction run away with me, but I haven't been able to uncover a single thing.

"You mean you're not perfect?" I tease him, smiling.

The wine, confession, and foot massage have me feeling playful, and a giggle escapes me when he tugs on my feet, pulling me flat on my back. The next moment his weight pins me in place, his eyes almost black with heat.

"I'm not," he admits, "but you are."

Any thought of kids evaporates the moment his tongue spears between my lips, tasting me deep. I slide a hand into his hair, fingers tangling in the strands, as I wrap one leg around his, grinding my hips into the hard to ignore bulge behind his fly. Quickly losing control, I drop my other hand, shoving it down the back of his jeans, encountering sleek hard muscle.

From zero to sixty.

His kiss is relentless, nipping, tasting, and teasing as I writhe against him. I whimper my complaint in his mouth when he rolls us slightly—missing his weight and that solid steel pressing between my legs—but it quickly turns into a deep moan when his free hand dives under my shirt, zeroing in on my sensitive breast.

I could probably come just from the hunger of his kiss and the raspy rub of his thumb over my nipple, but I'll never find out.

If I wasn't teetering on the edge of what promises to be a deep and delicious orgasm, I probably would've been thrilled hearing my son's familiar footsteps clomping up the basement stairs as his voice calls out for me.

"Mom! We're starving, can we have some chips?"

CHAPTER 11

DYLAN

"Morning." Jasper walks into the office and tosses his jacket over the back of his chair. "You're early."

"Was hoping to catch you before the office gets busy," I confess.

"Oh?"

Since leaving Marya's place Saturday night, after almost getting caught with my hand up her shirt, I've been thinking. A lot actually. I don't like how vulnerable she is. That scene at the soccer field could've had a different outcome that might not have ended well for her.

But what really bugs me is how he found out about the game at all. The possibility he's been watching her scares me. She's often alone in the bookstore, and in addition works occasional nights cleaning offices. Wouldn't be that hard for her douchebag ex to catch her alone.

Hopefully she'll get a temporary protection order today, but that may just piss him off even more. We don't even know what his motivation is for barging back into her life. I spent all day yesterday digging online, but other than he married one Sylvia Keswick before the ink was dry on his divorce from Marya, and had a child with her just three months after that, I can't find a whole lot. The guy doesn't seem to keep a job very long; he's gone through seven in the past five years, as far as I can tell. All that tells me he's an asshole and a loser, but it doesn't give me a reason for his sudden resurfacing. Besides, I need to know where he is right now, so I can keep an eye on him.

That's one of the things I need to talk to Jasper about and I want to do it before Toni shows up.

"It's about Marya and her boys. I think she might be in some trouble."

"Marya, Kerry's friend?" He raises an eyebrow and scrutinizes me. "You've got something going on with her?"

I ignore the question and proceed to lay out the situation and the little I was able to discover about Jeremy Berger. I also voice my concern about the impact of a protective order and hand over my printouts and copies of the paperwork Luna prepared.

"So that's a yes?" Jasper grins as he pokes fun at me, but he immediately turns serious and turns to his computer screen. "Any reason she's kept her married name after the divorce?" he asks without looking at me, his fingers flying over the keyboard.

"Probably easier with the kids."

"Also easier for him to con his way into getting access to her information," he comments. "All he'd need is an old marriage certificate and a good story. You'd be surprised how many take one look at an official document and take it for granted." He digs through the papers I handed him and pulls out Luna's notes. "Let's see if we can find him."

Within five minutes he has Jeremy's phone records, his address in Montrose, and his credit card information up on the screen.

"That's the school," I point out, indicating a phone number I recognize.

"He's been in touch a few times. First call was in July."

"He wouldn't have gotten far, school would've been closed for the summer."

"When she spoke with him, it was on her cell phone, right?" Jasper asks and I confirm, but Jas taps the screen. "Then why is there a four and a half minute conversation to her home phone on July twelfth?"

Shit.

One of the kids. Marya mentioned Liam had given her trouble for a few months. She didn't think it had anything to do with the kids' father, but now I wonder.

I'm about to say something when Damian walks in, Toni right behind him. We exchange the perfunctory good mornings when Damian's eyes land on Jasper's screen.

"Why are you looking into Marya's ex?" He pins me with a look and I shoot a glance over at Toni, who is observing us closely.

"Happy to explain," I tell him before adding, "in private." No way I want to discuss Marya's personal business in front of Toni.

His jaw set, he leads the way into his office.

"How the fuck did he happen to show up at the soccer field?" Damian's anger is evident when I catch him up.

"That's what I'm trying to find out. According to the phone records Jasper pulled, he lives in Montrose. Seems like a long way to come for a soccer game, even if it was his kid playing."

"That man doesn't give a flying fuck about his kids. He wants something," Damian confirms my thoughts.

"My thoughts exactly."

"Right. Keep digging and from here on in, keep me in the loop," he says sternly.

"Will do."

I start to get up when he leans across his desk, eyeing me sharply. "Before you go...mind telling me in on what the fuck your issue is with Agent Linden?"

His hot glare follows me out of his office five minutes later. He's not happy with me. All I was willing to share with him is the fact she and I knew each other in Denver, had a brief thing, and it didn't end amicably. I then sat through a brief lecture about mixing work and pleasure—which is ironic, since I know how he and Kerry hooked up—before he warned me not to let whatever happened between Toni and I bleed into the job.

Easier said than done.

MARYA

"Guys, get on that homework, please. Grandma will be here in twenty minutes, and I want it done by then."

Loud giggling sounds from upstairs, where I'm pretty sure the boys are engaged in something other than homework. They're not fighting though, which I guess is a bonus. Still, I have three places to clean tonight, and I don't want to leave Mom to chasing after the boys.

What a crazy day. First waiting for forty-five minutes for my turn with the judge in an almost full courtroom, Luna sitting beside me showing more patience than I felt. Then the embarrassment of airing my dirty laundry in front of about fifteen strangers. I had to catch myself several times not to minimize the circumstances. After another twenty-minute wait, we walked out of the courthouse, a temporary protection order in hand.

Luna suggested I come back to the office with her to figure out how to find Jeremy to serve him with the judge's paperwork, which apparently is my responsibility. Since I had to hurry to relieve one of our part-timers at the store, who'd agreed to cover for me last minute, I told her I'd call her later. I barely had time to shoot off a quick message to give Dylan a heads-up, when another new shipment was delivered, taking almost all afternoon to unpack, price, and process.

I almost didn't make it home in time before the boys got off the bus at the corner, and I never had a chance to call Luna as promised.

Thank God Mom said she'd bring over a lasagna she'd made this morning, it means I don't have to figure out what to feed them before I go.

I quickly make myself a sandwich before I have to leave, when Mom comes in the front door.

"Why are you eating when I told you I'd bring food?" She walks in carrying a large aluminum tray covered in tinfoil and slides it onto the counter.

"I'll eat some when I get home tonight, Mom. I don't have time now."

"You work too hard," she says, wagging a finger in my face. "You won't last burning the candle at both ends, girlie. Take it from me."

She would know. After my father left when I was little, she worked several jobs at once to keep a roof over our heads. Never took the time to look after herself and still is more concerned about having the kids and me taken care of.

"I know, Mom." I give her arm a squeeze. "I promise I'll do better once this thing with Jeremy is behind us."

"I'm not saying it's not wrong to work hard for your family, honey. What I'm saying is not to spend so much of yourself, there's no room left for your own needs."

I hear her loud and clear. She met Dylan, she's not blind, but still it's uncanny sometimes how well she knows me.

"I gotta go, Mom." I pull her into a quick hug before yelling up the stairs. "Boys! I have to go. You'd better have that homework done before you show your face down here! Be good to Grandma!"

I smile when my oldest and my youngest call out, "Later, Mom," and "Love you," but it slides off my face when there's silence from Liam.

I'm about to back out of the driveway when I hear a text come in on my phone. A quick glance at the screen shows a message from Dylan.

Dylan: We need to talk

Me: Working late tonight

Dylan: Where are you?

I don't have time for this, if I don't get a move on, I won't be home before midnight. I tuck my phone back in my purse and head for my first address. Dylan will have to wait.

My first stop is an easy one, a large local real estate office. Darla, a woman I've only worked with a few times before, is waiting for me in the parking lot. With two of us, we can each take a floor and the job won't take more than an hour and a half, tops. Not much in-depth cleaning to be done here. Unlike the next two places, they require substantially larger amounts of elbow grease to keep clean.

I'm glad to see the clock in my dashboard shows just seven thirty when we pull in the parking lot of the Yooba Yoga Studio and The Edge Boxing Gym. Both these places are owned by Arrow's Edge, a local motorcycle club. I dread doing them, especially the gym, but the club pays well, leaving a generous tip for whatever cleaners draw the short end of the stick that week.

The yoga studio isn't that bad, but the blend of aromatic oils and body sweat can be a bit much, and the full wall of mirrors is a nightmare to clean.

We save the gym for last, knowing that the sooner we get it done, the faster we can get home. Being the mother of three boys, I can handle the acrid locker room stench permeating the place better than most, but it still hits me like a concrete wall every time I step through the doors.

The ringing of a phone pierces the dead silence of the gym. It's Darla's, and I leave her to take the call, while I get a start in the locker room.

As always, there's an assortment of stray towels, single socks, shirts, and underwear under and around the benches and showers to be collected and shoved in the stackable laundry combo in the small kitchen in the back. I don't sort the stuff, I just shove it all in on the same setting. If these guys don't care enough to pick up their shit, then I'm sure as hell not going to make an effort to keep the whites from the darks. Screw that.

Darla walks into the small kitchen, an apology already on her face. *Shit*.

"I hate to do this to you," she starts. "But my daughter is having an asthma attack and my boyfriend is in a panic—"

I hold up my hand to stop her. "Go. Don't even worry about it. I've got this."

"I don't live that far, I'll just go—"

"Seriously, just get home and stay with your girl. Kids come first." She still hesitates so I take her arm and walk her to the door, unlocking it for her. "Go."

"Thanks, Marya. Anytime you need me to cover for you…"

"I'm a mother of three boys, I'm sure it'll happen." I grin at her and she waves as she gets into her car.

Back inside the gym, I lock up and rest my back against the heavy glass door, sighing deeply. Things were going so well…

It's close to eleven thirty when I pull the stuff from the small dryer and add it to the lost and found bin in the corner of the gym. Flicking the lights off, I make my way to the front of the gym. As I'm unlocking the door, I notice a car on the far side of the dark parking lot that wasn't there earlier. I can't tell the make, but it's a dark color and a light from across the street shines off the exterior and reveals the shadow of someone in the driver's seat.

My eyes stay locked on the silhouette as my hand

is already digging the phone from my purse. I dial the first person that comes to mind, but as soon as I put the phone to my ear, the car's headlights come on, blinding me.

"Marya?" I hear Dylan's voice, but I'm focused on the car pulling out of the parking lot and taking off down the street. "Jesus, Marya? Everything okay?"

"I'm sorry, I...I shouldn't have called. It's probably nothing," I stammer, annoyed that I may have overreacted.

"What's nothing?" he asks sternly.

"I...uhm...was just getting ready to leave and got spooked when I spotted someone in a car in the parking lot. It's fine now, he's gone," I add quickly.

"Where are you?"

"Seriously, it's fine, he took off. Was probably just looking for a quiet spot to do...whatever."

"Marya, where are you?"

"There's a good chance I spooked him more than he did me," I try to brush it off, but Dylan won't have any of it.

"Babe, don't make me ask you again." Despite the endearment, there's an edge of steel to his voice I haven't heard before. I'm not sure if I like it, although the head to toe tingle it entices would suggest my body is on board.

"Fine, The Edge Gym. It's on—"

"I know where it is. You're inside?"

"Yeah, but—"

"Doors locked?"

"They are, but—"

"Do not move until I get there."

I take in a deep breath to tell him off, when I hear the line go dead, and I let the air go in a sharp hiss.

At least I'm no longer freaked out. Now I'm pissed.

CHAPTER 12

DYLAN

Good thing Max is already at my mother's tonight.

When Luna walked into the office with the paperwork from the judge, I'd wanted to head out and serve Marya's ex right away. Jasper told me to check in with Damian before doing anything. When I got hold of him, he suggested I not go without backup. He also pointed out that rather than trying to catch him during the day, and have him see us coming, it would make more sense to surprise him first thing in the morning.

We'd tracked his credit card charges to a small cabin he rented through Airbnb, just south of Hermosa. A full month. An indication he intends to hang around for a while.

The cabin is tucked away in the trees near Tripp Gulch and shouldn't be too hard to approach. Luna offered to meet me at the office at five thirty in the morning, so we could be in place before sunup.

That's why Max is at Ma's, and why I am speeding over to the boxing gym in the middle of the night. *Jesus*.

When I pull into the parking lot, the interior is dark and if not for the familiar Jeep still parked in the lot, I might've thought Marya took off, despite my instructions.

Still, relief floods me when I see a shadow move around inside. I get out of my truck and hear the click of a lock releasing before the door opens.

"I can't believe you hung up on me," are the first words out of her mouth.

I'll take her aggravated over scared or hurt any day. "Had some calls to make." In a few long strides I reach her, slamming my mouth over hers as I pull her tight into my body.

Really fucking relieved.

"Talk to me," I urge her when I reluctantly peel my lips from hers, but keep her circled in my arms.

"Who did you have to call?"

"The owners; Arrow's Edge. Had to make sure it wasn't one of their own guys."

She rolls her eyes, clearly annoyed when the rumble of motorcycles approaching can be heard. "Great," she huffs snidely. "Bad enough I got you out here for nothing, but you had to call in the troops."

The crunch of boots on the gravel has her lift her gaze over my shoulder, and I watch with amusement, as her eyes get big. "Your mouth is open," I whisper, giving her a wink before I turn to the two bikers sauntering up to us.

"Ouray, Paco." I shake the men's hands before introducing them to Marya, who mumbles cutely, but squints her eyes at me.

"Did you catch who was behind the wheel?" Ouray asks her.

"I couldn't really see more than a shape and then he suddenly turned his headlights on, and I couldn't see anything at all. Maybe he saw me on the phone."

"You say he," I point out. "Sure it was a man?"

"Pretty sure it was, unless it was a six foot something woman with short-cropped hair wearing shoulder pads I thought were outlawed after the eighties. They should've been anyway." There is clearly more bite in Marya's tone when she answers me.

Ouray checks his boots but the corner of his mouth twitches. "Anything about the car you remember?" he asks when he has his amusement in check.

"Not much. Dark, four-door sedan. I do remember it looked new, shiny."

"Think it could've been Jeremy?" I ask her.

Her eyes flit to the other two men before she answers, "Could be."

"That the ex?" Ouray wants to know and I hear Marya's sharp intake of breath.

"You told them?"

I open my mouth to answer but Ouray beats me to it. "He didn't, but I'll leave it to your man to explain."

Then he turns to me. "We'll check the feed, if there's anything I'll give it to my wife. Take her home, she looks about ready to drop." With that he lifts his chin and rounds us, Paco on his heels, and disappears into the gym.

"What the hell was that all about?" Marya swings on me, her hands balled into fists by her side.

"There are cameras." I point at the corner of the building where one is mounted next to the downspout. "They'll check if there's anything usable on the tape and Ouray will hand it over to Luna."

"Luna?"

"His wife. She's the one who told him about Jeremy. The club mentors young boys, mostly runaways they take in. Sometimes they keep an eye out for kids in the community. A few of them will be at the boys' soccer game this Saturday."

"Wow," she mouths, still looking a bit confused. "I'm not sure how to take that."

"For starters, let's take it home," I tell her, taking her by the arm and leading her to my truck. "You can barely stand straight."

"But my Jeep…"

"We'll pick it up tomorrow morning." I open the passenger door, but she's not getting in.

"Hey, where is Max?"

"He's at Ma's. Now, Marya…get in the truck, babe."

MARYA

It's after midnight by the time we get to my place, and Mom looks like she's dozing off on the couch. The moment she spots Dylan behind me, she sits up straight and checks her hair.

"Good, you've got company. I didn't know you planned on going out."

"I hadn't. I—"

"I'll just make another plate." She ignores me, gets up, and heads straight for the kitchen.

"Mom, hold—"

"Homemade lasagna," she informs Dylan, as if I hadn't spoken, already loading up a second plate. "There's still plenty here for leftovers tomorrow."

"Sounds good, Lydia. Not too much though, I had dinner earlier."

I throw up my hands when he walks into the kitchen, giving my arm a little rub in passing, and sits down on a stool. Mom's putting the plate in the microwave to heat.

From the moment I called him earlier, it's like I've lost any and all control.

"Just pop the other plate in at a minute and a half when this one is done," Mom instructs Dylan. "I'll just grab my purse and be on my way home."

"Mom." I try to stop her. "It's late. You should just stay the night. I don't think you should be driving."

"Hogwash. You kids don't need me around. Oh, and by the way, the boys were in bed by ten. Tomorrow's lunches are in the fridge."

"Thanks, Mom," I reply automatically. "You didn't

have to do that."

She's already by the door, shrugging in her jacket. "I don't mind. Okay, I'm off, give me a call tomorrow?"

When the microwave beeps she's already out the door, and I just catch Dylan slipping the second plate in. "Come eat."

I move to the kitchen, too stunned to even think about objecting. It's been a weird night, and apparently getting even weirder. I'm sitting at my counter—next to Dylan—in the middle of the night, eating my mother's lasagna. It feels like I've landed in an alternate universe.

"Did you have a chance to talk to the boys about their father?"

I wince. I was going to, yesterday, but we were having a good day and I didn't want to spoil it.

"Not yet," I confess.

"It's important they understand, Marya. Especially considering what happened Saturday and tonight. Until we get him served with the order, there's nothing stopping him from showing up at their school. You don't want them caught unaware."

"I'll do it tomorrow," I promise, knowing he's right. "I'll call the school first thing, and talk to the boys when they get home."

"I can be here tomorrow. Help you talk to the boys, give them some tips on how stay safe."

My head is heavy with the weight of all this stress, which is probably why I just nod. It's always been a lot to carry my family on my own, financially and otherwise, but with their father stirring up trouble, the responsibility seems almost impossible. The offer to shoulder even a small bit of that load with me, is welcome.

I barely hear Dylan telling me they've found out where Jeremy is staying and plan to serve him with the protection order tomorrow morning. All I manage is a nod. It's like I have my ears stuffed with cotton and concentrating on what he says takes what little energy I have left.

"Marya?"

I blink a few times and turn to him. "Yeah?"

"Babe, you're sleeping where you sit. Why don't you head up to bed, I'll lock up."

"I need a shower first. I smell like dirty socks."

Dylan chuckles. "Do what you need to do, but get your cute butt upstairs. I'll sort things down here." He drops a light kiss on my lips, to which I don't protest either. Apparently along with my energy, all common sense has left me.

I'm halfway up the stairs when I realize he just called my butt cute. Huh.

I'm hauling my ass into bed after the fastest shower in the history of running water, when it occurs to me the TV is still on downstairs. Dylan must've forgotten to turn it off.

I slip down the stairs on my bare feet and pad over to the TV to turn it off.

"Hey, I thought you were in bed."

I almost jump out of my skin at the sound of Dylan's voice and swing around. He's lying on my couch, the afghan my mother knitted years ago covering his legs, but his chest is bare.

"Jesus, you scared the crap out of me. What are you doing?"

"Trying to sleep." He slowly sits up, swinging his long legs on the floor. I never thought bare feet sexy. In fact, most of the time I try not to look at them because they repulse me a little, but somehow his mesmerize me. Naked feet on my couch make me wonder what else is bare under my mother's afghan. "Are you all right?"

My head snaps up at the question. "Uhh…yes, fine. I just don't get…I thought you were going home."

"It's almost one, I have to meet Luna at five thirty at the office, you just had a scare, so I thought I'd crash on your couch."

I have questions; I just can't seem to get them formulated in my head. Especially not with him looking at me like that. "What?"

"Cute nightie."

I look down at the favorite sleep shirt I haven't been able to throw out, even with holes from frequent washings. It's not cute. It's hideous and not fit for a cleaning rag, but it's the most comfortable nightie I own.

What it definitely isn't, is sexy, but you wouldn't get that from the look on Dylan's face.

"I should let you sleep," I rasp, suddenly very

aware of the tension in the semi-dark room.

Wrapping my arms around myself, I start moving to the stairs, trying to scoot by the half-naked body on my couch when suddenly his arm shoots out. Before I can react, I'm hauled off my feet, pulled over the armrest, and end up squarely straddling his lap. I scramble to get off but his arm locks me in place. With his other hand he brushes the still damp hair from my face.

"I don't think—"

"Then don't," he whispers, his lips already brushing mine.

This kiss is different: soft, gently exploring, and leisurely. The lazy stroke of his tongue has my body relax into him. Hands—his and mine—explore the heat of exposed skin as the world falls away around us.

My nightshirt is lifted and my arms go up automatically, without even a single thought to anything but this moment.

I'm melting, a puddle of goo carefully stroked and molded by skilled hands. His lips draw a hot trail down my neck and lower, over the swell of my breast, until I feel his warm, wet lips pull a nipple into his mouth. The sudden charge zipping through my body has me cry out in response.

"Shhh," he mumbles against my skin as he moves to my other breast, and again draws the hard bud in his mouth. This time I bite my lip and moan deep in my throat.

Underneath me his hard cock presses against me, evidence he's as primed as I am, despite his careful control. I test him with a roll of my hips.

"*Shit,*" he hisses, his fingers digging in my hips to keep me still as his eyes bore into me. I guess that control has a limit. I press my lips together to hide the small, satisfied smile, but he sees it anyway, narrowing his eyes. "Minx," he growls, but it sounds more like a caress than an accusation.

The next moment I'm up in his arms, my legs rounding his hips for purchase, as he uses the afghan to cover me up. Like that, he carries me up the stairs and into the open door of my bedroom, carefully closing it behind us.

"Bed," I order, rubbing myself shamelessly on his hard length between us.

"Fuck, yes."

He walks me two steps before dropping me on the mattress, but instead of covering me with his body, he pulls me to the edge and drops to his knees. Before my inner sexpot can pump her fist in celebration, he throws my legs over his shoulders, hooks a finger in the gusset of my panties, and yanks it aside. There is no tentative taste, no flick of the tongue, no hesitation at all when he covers me with his lips, kissing me as deeply there as he did my mouth.

The heat, the hunger, the sheer hedonistic pleasure of our combined moans is unlike anything I have ever experienced. He's as much into what he is doing as I am, his sounds of pleasure vibrating against my sensitive skin.

DYLAN

Fuck me.

I'm going to blow my load just watching her from between those plump thighs pressed against my head, as she comes undone right before my eyes. Her toes dig into my shoulders as she tilts her head back, long neck strained, and erupts in a rough groan of release.

I lick her gently, the occasional shiver running through her as her body relaxes in the aftermath of her orgasm.

With a last kiss on the sensitive skin on the inside of her thigh, I sit back carefully lowering her legs. My cock is distended with the need for release, precum leaking from the tip.

"Dylan…" My eyes lift to see her gazing down the bed at me.

She holds out a hand and opens her legs. It's all the invitation I need.

I climb up and sit on my knees between her legs, taking in her body on full display in front of me. Her softly lush and mature hourglass shape beautiful and welcoming for my much harder one. The white lines decorating her soft breasts and stomach a testament to the three boys she carried. With her expressive eyes observing me, I run the tips of my fingers from the dent between her collarbones to the crescent-shaped scar just above her pubic hair. I trail it with my index finger from one hip to the other.

"Theo ended up a C-section," she explains in a soft voice and I just nod, oddly moved by the trust she shows me.

There's no attempt to cover herself from my scrutiny, which is an invitation better than the spread of her legs. Maybe she's opening up as a result of her orgasm, maybe it's the fatigue still lining her face, but it doesn't matter; I'm finding my way inside and plan to stick around.

"I'll never get tired of looking at you," I confess, my eyes mapping every dip, mark, and freckle on her soft, white skin.

She sits up, hooks a hand around my neck, and draws me to her mouth. She doesn't seem to care I still have her taste on my lips as she kisses me deeply, pulling me down on top of her. My hips fit between her thighs, and she instinctively tips up to align my cock to her entrance.

"Condom," I grind between my teeth, clenched as I try to hold back against the urge to bury myself inside her warm body. "Tell me you have one."

"*Shit*." Despite my painful dick, I grin at her reaction, briefly dropping my forehead to hers.

"We'll plan better next time."

I reluctantly roll off her onto my back, covering my eyes with my forearm. Fucking hell, I might as well give up on any sleep tonight.

A slight rustle of sheets beside me, and a warm hand on my abs has me lift my arm, just in time to see Marya's pink lips slide over my cock. My mouth falls open and my hands grab onto the headboard, hips inadvertently surging off the bed.

Holy son of a...

CHAPTER 13

DYLAN

Daylight is just breaking when we leave the Bureau Expedition on the side of Tripp Creek Road and set off on foot.

I'd been a few minutes late, and Luna had already been waiting in the parking lot at the office, a knowing smirk on her face. I didn't even bother asking why, it was clear her husband had shared last night's events and Luna is all but stupid. Never mind I smelled like a fucking floral shop, finding only Marya's bodywash in the shower this morning.

I'd come so hard in her mouth; I ended up having no trouble falling asleep with her soft body curled into mine. Neither of us had been thinking straight, because we would've been fucked if one of her kids had come looking for her in the middle of the night. Can't take chances like that next time.

Luckily, all was still quiet when I dislodged myself from Marya's hold this morning. She didn't do much more than grumble, roll into the spot I just vacated, and bury her face in my pillow. The sound of her contented sigh was enough temptation to have me rush into her bathroom and rub one out in the shower—with the help of her rose-scented bodywash. The scent will forever be linked to sex and Marya in my brain.

"That's the car," Luna whispers beside me as a Lexus in the cabin's driveway becomes visible through the trees. "Rims are identical."

Apparently the camera feed had provided a little more detail than Marya was able to recall with the naked eye. The custom five-spoke bronze rims Luna mentioned visible on the video Ouray supplied her with, stand out clearly against the shiny black finish. Not exactly a car you'd expect parked outside of a rustic mountain retreat. It clarifies who was outside the gym last night, watching Marya, but that raises even more questions about why the hell he's here.

I haven't had a chance to try and contact his current wife, to see if she has some insight, but that might need to be done with the kind of finesse I doubt I can pull off. She could be in on whatever he is up to. May be something to ask Luna if she'd be willing to take it on.

"Why don't you keep an eye on the back, let me knock on the door?" Luna suggests, and I'm instantly defensive. I wanted the satisfaction of being the one to slap the order in his hand.

"Because I may be good, but your odds of bringing down a full-grown man charging out the back are still better."

She pulls up an eyebrow in challenge, but I easily capitulate to her reasoning. She's right. He's also more likely to open the door for a small, innocent-looking woman than he would be seeing my mug outside.

I nod my agreement, lift my hand up—all fingers extended—so Luna knows to give me five minutes before she knocks on the door. I slowly make my way around the cabin, staying within the tree line. There's no door at the back, just two windows and one is too small to fit a grown man. Probably the bathroom. That should make it even easier should he try to come out this way.

I sneak up under the window the moment I hear the sharp rap of Luna's fist on the door. I'm guessing this is his bedroom, judging from the sound of creaking bedsprings.

With only the birds for background noise, I easily make out Luna's loud and clear words, "You've been served," and jog around to the front, just in time to see the fucker take her down. Not for long—you'd have to be well-trained to beat her in hand-to-hand combat—but long enough for him to land a solid fist to her jaw. Before I can even get to them, Luna has him flipped over and sitting on his back, cutting off his airway in a chokehold.

"Easy, Roosberg. I've got better things to do than

filling out endless damn paperwork if you off the asshole."

The asshole's already bulging eyes open impossibly wider, giving me some satisfaction.

"Fine," she mumbles, letting the guy go.

He scrambles to his feet and points a shaking finger at Luna. "That's assault. You assaulted me. I'll sue."

"Nah." I shake my head. "Not gonna happen, my friend. I'd like you to meet FBI Agent Luna Roosberg; she's my partner. We'll take a few pictures of that nice bruise she's going to have on her face, thanks to your sucker punch. You're lucky I'd prefer you to disappear, or I might be tempted to arrest you for assaulting a law enforcement officer." I turn to Luna. "Got your phone ready? Be nice to have something to remember this moment by." I wink at her, before bending down to pick up the judge's order the idiot dropped on the front step. I throw a jovial arm around his shoulder. "You dropped something." Without thinking he reaches out his hand and takes the papers. "Smile," I tell him, already grinning at the phone Luna is holding up. "In case you missed it the first time, asshole…You've been served."

"Fuck you!" he spits out, pivoting away from me as he waves the paper around. "If that bitch thinks she can keep me away from my kids, she has another thing coming."

"Barnes…" Luna warns me.

She knows me well. I see red and have to stuff my clenched fists in my pocket to make sure I wouldn't let one fly. I take a deep breath in before setting him straight.

"Wrong again, friend. I would read that order very carefully before you get a wild hair. You come anywhere near Marya or her sons, I will personally make sure your ass lands in jail for a good long time. Think long and hard, Jeremy."

His face is almost purple, and I know he's trying hard not to lash out again. Finally, he turns on his heel, stalks into the cabin, and slams the door shut.

"Well," Luna says, a smirk on her face as she tucks the phone in her pocket and starts walking down the driveway. "That was fun."

I bark out a laugh and follow her.

"Not sure your husband will agree when he sees that bruise," I tease her, grunting when she swings her arm around, catching me in the gut. "Ouch."

"Then don't bust my bubble."

━━━

"Hey, Kiddo. Whatcha up to?"

"Homework," he grumbles and I smile. Max is not a fan of homework; it's like pulling teeth to get him to put the effort in. The kid is smart, so once he applies himself, he's done in no time, but getting him there is tough. Ma is much better at it than I am.

"Good for you. Get it out of the way."

"Dad? If I get it done, can we get pizza tonight?"

"I'm sorry, Max, I won't be able to get away in time for dinner, but I'll pick you up after, and maybe we can make peanut butter and chocolate sundaes for dessert instead?"

"Yeah! Sweet. Can I crush the peanuts?"

"Check and see if your grammy has any, kid. I think we're out."

I feel bad about skipping out of yet another dinner with my son, but I don't feel any guilt promising him a rare treat if that makes him feel better. Call it poor parenting, I don't give a damn. All I care about is making sure my child is happy, and he always is when I pull out his favorite dessert.

I'm parked in her driveway, beside Marya's Jeep Luna and I had dropped off this morning. I watch her house as I listen to Max talking to his grandma.

"She's got the peanuts."

"That's great. Don't forget them when I pick you up. Should be there before eight, okay?"

"Yeah. Later, Dad."

Marya must've seen me in her driveway because the door is already opening when I come up her walk, her face showing relief.

"I've been stalling," she explains when I step inside. I brush my hand against hers, needing to touch her. I'd prefer pinning her against the door and plunging my tongue in her mouth, but with the three boys sitting at the dining table, all looking this way, that's probably not a good idea.

I turn my back on the boys and address their mother. "Stalling?"

"Apparently Liam said something on the bus."

"Gotcha." Swinging around I find all three boys still looking. "Hey, kids."

"Hey, Mr. B," Harry chirps, but his middle brother jabs him with a sharp elbow.

As I walk to the table, Liam's eyes never leave me. "Why are you here?"

"William Berger," Marya snaps behind me. "Mind your manners."

MARYA

Shit. Already this is not going well.

I'm not sure what Liam said to them, but Theo and him rolled in the door fighting, throwing punches, and calling each other names. Liam appeared to have gotten the worst, his lip was bleeding, Harry seemed stunned and was on the verge of crying, and my firstborn just looked pissed.

When I asked what was going on, it was Harry who blurted out it was about their dad. For the past five minutes, I've been trying to get more out of them, but neither Liam nor Theo are talking—and each time Harry tries to say something—he's shut down by the older two.

"Can I get you a beer?" I ask Dylan, who ignores Liam's comment and takes a seat at the counter, his eyes on the boys.

"I'll hold off until after, thanks," he says, with an encouraging smile. He knows I'm delaying.

"All right," I start, sitting at the table with the kids.

"There's really no way to ease into this, so I'll lay it out. Your dad's been gone for five years. He made it clear at the time he didn't want to hear from me and we certainly didn't hear from him. I can understand walking out on me, but I've never been able to understand how he could walk away from you three, but he did." I take in a deep breath before I spill it all. "A few weeks ago, he called out of the blue, making demands. It wasn't pleasant. He called again, and that was even less pleasant. Then he suddenly showed up at Liam's game on Saturday."

"Why?" This from Theo, who looks at me sternly. My little protector.

"Honestly? I don't even know. I don't know what moved him to show up like that, Bub. What I do know is that it doesn't spell much good. He's made some threats, which is why I went to see a judge yesterday, who signed a protective order."

"What's that?" Harry pipes up, but before I can answer Theo does, his face hard.

"It means he's not allowed to come close to us, right, Mom?"

My boy, so smart and so much more mature than I'd like him to be at thirteen.

"That's bullshit," Liam interjects, angry.

"You don't know anything," Theo fires back.

"Boys," I draw their attention before another fight breaks out and quickly look at Dylan, who's been quiet so far. He just nods his encouragement. "Liam, I already explained to you, if your father wants to see

151

you there is a right way to go about that. Threatening me, showing up where I'm working, that's not okay. That's just plain scary."

"Why were you scared?" Harry wants to know, his eyes worried. My sensitive kid.

Time for more truth I would've preferred to keep from the kids, but I need them to understand how dangerous their father can be. "Because he's hurt me before, Bub."

"You mean, like hit you?"

"Yeah, baby."

"I don't believe you." I look at Liam, who is furiously blinking at tears and my heart breaks for him.

"You're so stupid. Our dad's an asshole." Before I can stop Theo, he jumps up, kicking his chair back from the table. "He was always a dick to Mom and I saw it. I saw him hit her, and I don't ever want to see him again. Never!"

Theo bails to the basement, Liam runs upstairs, and Harry sits across from me, big tears rolling down his face. I turn to Dylan, trying to keep my own emotions in check.

"Now what?"

He slips down the stool and closes the distance between us. I don't even complain when he bends down, hooks a hand behind my neck and presses a quick kiss to my trembling lips. "Now you take care of your youngest, and I'll tackle the other two." Another kiss to my forehead and he's off to the basement.

"Come here, baby," I tell Harry, who's trying to wipe the tears that seem to keep coming.

I don't have to tell him twice. He's up out of his chair and rounding the table. I barely have time to brace when he slams into my body.

"I'm sorry," he sobs into my shirt.

"You don't have anything to be sorry for, honey. None of this is your fault." I guide him to the couch where he cuddles right back into me.

"It is…my fault," he sniffs. "Liam said Dad left because of m—"

I quickly move my kid back a few inches so I can get in his face. "No. He. Did. Not. Your brother was wrong. Your father leaving had nothing to do with you."

I hope to God I got through to him when he ducks his head and shoves his face in my neck.

A few minutes later, I hear footsteps coming up the stairs. Theo sits down on the couch on my other side, pressing close. I tilt my head back to see Dylan watching us.

"Let me get Liam and we'll talk this through," he announces, and all I can do is nod, overcome with gratitude he's here.

It takes another ten before Liam shuffles into the room, his face blotchy from crying. I pull Harry onto my lap and pat the seat next to me.

"Come here, Bub. Sit by me."

I swear if ever I'm unlucky enough to see Jeremy's face again, I'll rip off his dick and shove it down his throat for putting my boys through this.

Dylan walks up behind Liam and gives him a little shove in my direction when he hesitates. When he sits down, leaving a gap between us, I lift my arm around his shoulders and tuck him closer.

"Right." Dylan takes a seat on the coffee table, right in front of us. "Here's the deal, and brace, because it sucks. Your dad wasn't a good dad, and so far he's shown he still isn't. What happened then and now is nobody's fault but his. Not your mom and not any of you. You guys are a family, and you need to start looking out for each other like your mom has done by herself these past years. You can start by not fighting." He directs a pointed look at each of the boys, and has them fidget against me. "But also by being smart, and being safe. You all need phones."

It takes the two youngest jumping up and cheering before it filters through what he just said. *Phones?*

"They're too young," I blurt out. "Theo just got one for his thirteenth."

"Mo-om," Harry complains, but I ignore him.

I'm focused on Dylan, who leans over and gives my knee a squeeze.

"Babe, you want them safe? You've gotta give them the tools."

I hate it when he makes sense. "It's not cheap," I point out.

"It's not that much either, if you get them flip phones on a plan without data. I have a plan for Max with straight phone and text. I'll hook you up."

"That's not fair, I want an iPhone like Theo," Liam complains, but I quickly pin him with a look, my mom reflexes thrown into high gear.

"When you're thirteen—like your brother; have a part-time job so you can pay for it—like your brother; and most important of all, work hard to improve your attitude. Until then you'll have to make do with a flip phone."

I know, even as I'm saying it, I just caved to giving my kids phones. Dylan tries to hide his smile, but Harry makes no such effort, he's grinning ear to ear. *Drat.*

"Now that's settled," Dylan continues, ignoring my glare. "Let's talk codes…"

The boys are riveted when he starts explaining how radio codes work, but when they start making references to what I assume are games, it all becomes noise to me. I retreat to the kitchen and dig through the fridge for quick meal ideas, since it's already nearing on six.

I'm just putting my sausage bake in the oven—sliced smoked sausage, potato, chunks of pepper and onion, some spices, an egg, and grated cheese—when I feel Dylan's hand on my hip. I close the oven door and turn to face him.

"The boys are putting together their own list of 10-codes," he informs me with a grin. "They just dubbed 10-99 *Mom alert.* As one responsible parent to another, I thought you should know."

"Appreciate it." I grin back at him. "What are they

gonna do with the codes?"

I dart a quick glance into the living room, where the boys are bent over the coffee table, scribbling on pieces of paper, when Dylan slips an arm around my waist, fitting me against him. "It'll be their custom designed alarm system. A way to communicate quickly if they ever find themselves in trouble. We'll add both our numbers at the top of their speed dial, and make sure we all have an explanation of the codes on our phones."

"You got them to work together," I note, checking on the kids, the one blond head between the two darker ones.

"Kills a few birds with one stone: it creates a common goal, adds to their sense of responsibility, makes them feel in control—and last but not least—has them focused on something other than their father being a certifiable cocksucker."

I throw my head back and laugh, a sound that I guess has become so rare, all three boys curiously look my way. I wink at them and wait until their attention is back on their list before I put a hand in the middle of Dylan's chest.

"You're a miracle worker."

CHAPTER 14

DYLAN

You're a miracle worker.

Her laugh had been nothing short of amazing, but hearing those words after had settled deep under my skin.

Her boys had come up with a list of codes. Some of them were cause for hilarity, but others had been sobering, showing the kinds of things kids—even at that young age—worry about.

We ate Marya's sausage bake—delicious—and after, she let me pull her outside on her front step so I could kiss her goodbye.

Work had kept both of us busy yesterday, but we connected via text last night, when I told her I'd drop off the phones for the boys today. That almost resulted in a stupid argument about who was going to pay for the phones, but it swung my way when I explained I wanted to get Jasper to install a tracker, the same one he installed on Max's, just in case. She liked the idea of added security, but insisted she'd pay me back, and took my silence as agreement. Her mistake.

"It'll run in the background," Jasper explains. "It's as simple to install as any other app, except you have to upload it from the computer since it's not on the market."

"And you say it'll work on Marya and her oldest's iPhones as well?"

"Yup. Installed it on Bella's. Takes all of two minutes. I'll send you a copy."

"Okay, I'll do that tonight."

"What's that?"

Jasper points at the list with emergency codes I'm entering into a reference file on the boys' phones. I don't think they'll need them, they were already quizzing each other over dinner on Tuesday, but the cheat sheet won't hurt. It's already on Marya's, Theo's, and my phone, and figured I might as well add it to Max's as well.

I turn the list around to show him.

10-1 Dad alert
10-2 stranger danger
10-3 SOS
10-4 Gotcha
10-5 Zombie attack
10-6 fire
10-7 hiding

10-8 kidnapper
10-9 lost
10-10 red alert
10-11 gun
10-12 urgent
10-13 starving
10-14 pizza tonight
10-15 need pick up
10-99 Mom alert

"These are not your standard 10-codes," Jasper snickers. "Zombie attack?"

"Boys put it together," I share by way of explanation.

"I can tell." He picks up his phone and takes a quick picture. "For reference," he explains.

"Whatever. You almost done?"

"Yeah. Oh, by the way." He shoves a sheet of paper my way.

"What's this? Copy of a police report?"

Jasper nods. "Talked to a guy I know in the Montrose PD, earlier in the week, to see if they have anything on Jeremy Berger. He called me back this morning. Sent me that."

I catch the complainant's name, Sylvia Berger, and quickly skim the content: a domestic abuse claim on none other than Marya's ex.

"The wife apparently kicked his ass to the curb a while ago, changed the locks on him and everything. Told him to leave her alone or she'd file a report on him. She says she doesn't know where he stayed, but he showed up last week, wanting to see his kid, and forced himself into the house. Smacked her around with their little girl looking on. Guess that motivated her to finally file that report."

"Jesus. Guy's a piece of work. Assume that's why he set up in that cabin in Hermosa."

"Yup, passed on the address and filled Jimmy in on what was going on here. Word of warning though, he's interested in talking to Marya. May want to give her a heads-up."

"*Fuck.* She needs that on top of everything else." I rub a hand over my face.

"He do the same thing to her? Put his hands on her?"

I can't bring myself to answer, so I growl in response.

I'd suspected it—Marya had never quite spelled it out—until Theo blurted a few nights ago what he'd witnessed.

A heavy silence stretches as I watch Jasper's jaw work. "*Shit,*" he finally barks, flaring his nostrils as he sucks in a deep breath. "Now I wish you'd have let Luna have a decent go at him on Monday."

When we'd walked into the office after serving that dirtbag with the protection order, the bruise forming on Luna's cheek had not gone unnoticed, and she hadn't hesitated giving the guys the blow-by-blow. Including me stepping in before she could do him more damage.

Heck, I'd thought the same thing Tuesday night after hearing those strangled words come from her oldest, as he described exactly what he'd witnessed when I was in the basement with him. If not for the state of those boys, I'd have hightailed it out of there, back up to Hermosa, to finish the job Luna started.

"Not as much as me," I grunt.

"I bet." Jasper hands me the second phone. "All set up. Get out of here. I'll shoot over that software."

I tuck both flip phones in my pocket and snatch up the copy of the police report. "Takin' this."

"About time that woman has a good man looking out for her."

The unfamiliar compliment startles me as warmth spreads into my limbs. There'd been too many years of not being a good man, a good son, a good father. Since joining the team as the junior agent, I'd tried hard to do better—be better—because of the caliber of the people I work with. I didn't grow up with siblings, or even many friends, but my teammates have become the brothers and sister I never had. Hearing a man I look up to say something like that means something.

It means a lot.

Still, all I manage is a mumbled, "Thanks," and a chin lift before walking out the door.

"I meant to ask you," Marya says, pulling apart the pork in her slow cooker.

I'd picked up Max from school and came right

here. Marya had made good on her promise of last night to cook Max and me dinner, in return for me taking care of the phones for her.

Apparently pulled pork, and it smells phenomenal.

Since tomorrow is a professional development day and homework can be done later, the boys disappeared down to the basement after the excitement of the new cell phones had worn off. I reminded them to stay offline.

"Is there any news on what happened to that Flora Vista boy?"

"Not really our case, but we're helping check out a few tips."

I can't tell her much more, in part because our office doesn't have lead on this case, but also because I don't want to get into details with her. Like the fact the coroner found semen on the boy, or that the investigation turned up a surprising number of registered sex offenders living within a fifty-mile radius from where the boy went missing. That's what we've been doing most of this week, knocking on doors of those registered in our county. It's a slow, tedious process that requires a lot of sorting through background information on these deviants to see if there's anything we could link to Seth's case.

Some of the shit is so disturbing, I mentioned to Luna this morning it's almost enough to lose your faith in the justice system we're here to uphold. How some of these guys—mostly—are even walking around free is beyond comprehension.

"You can't talk about it," she says with a grimace, noticing my hesitation. "I'm sorry, I shouldn't have asked."

I put a hand on her arm, stilling her movements. "You can ask me anything, just know it's not personal when I can't always answer. Especially if it's an ongoing investigation."

"Okay. It's just...that's the second time I hear you mention for the kids to stay offline, I was just wondering if there's something..." She lets her voice trail off.

Current circumstances have made her hyper-vigilant, so it shouldn't really surprise me she picked up on that. Should've had a talk with her about that sooner. This case, her dick ex, keeping up with my own kid, this new relationship—I feel like I focus on too many things at the same time and missing the mark on all of them.

Time to get my head out of my ass.

"I should've mentioned this before. Max came to me a little over a week ago and mentioned one of the players in his PS4 group made him uncomfortable. Jasper and I were going to look into it, but then Seth disappeared and we got wrapped up in that. Should've said something."

"Is that the same group Liam is part of?" The concern is evident on her face and that's on me too.

"I think so." I realize I should probably ask Liam if he's noticed anyone acting weird.

Marya drops the forks she'd been using on the pork

onto the counter and marches to the entertainment center in her living room. She pulls a router tucked back on one of the shelves, and yanks out the cord. With the appliance tucked under her arm, she heads to the top of the basement stairs.

"Guys, just a heads-up. There's something wrong with the router, I have to take it in to get it fixed!"

"Mo-om!"

"Deal with it, Harry," she calls back to her youngest. "You can just play with your brothers." She walks up to the fridge, stuffs the router into the small cupboard above, and picks up her forks again.

"You figure it out, let me know. Until then, no more online gaming."

Not pissed off—matter-of-fact—and without any hint of recrimination.

Fuck, she's perfect.

MARYA

I can tell he's beating himself up about it, something I've noticed he does easily—taking responsibility—but he won't get a hard time from me. He has enough on his mind.

He's already stepping in with Jeremy—which I'm grateful for, don't get me wrong—but with a kid of his own, a demanding job, and a devastating case on his plate, he shouldn't feel he also has to carry responsibility for my guys. That's my job.

His hands slip around my waist, pushing low on

my belly. I can feel his prominent erection pressing into me.

"Feel that?" His voice sounds right by my ear.

"Mmmm."

"That's how much I liked watching you getting things done without fucking around."

"The kids…" I mumble, even as I'm grinding my ass against him.

"Yeah." He slides one hand up my front and curves his fingers around my jaw, tilting my head back. His dark gaze pierces through me. "Need to carve out some time." The fire in those brown eyes and his deep raspy sound are hypnotizing. "Soon."

"Yes." My own voice sounds thready.

"So fucking beautiful."

The next moment his lips are bruising mine in a consuming kiss that has me wobble on my feet. Dylan's hand tightens on my stomach, keeping me steady as his mouth lifts away.

"Soon," he repeats on a whisper.

"I have to work tomorrow night, but I'm off Saturday night," I blurt out, blushing at my own boldness, when he turns me around and cups my face with his hands.

"Would love taking you up on that, Sweetheart. Problem is, I can't guarantee I won't get called away."

A bit embarrassed I pull back, putting a smile on my face. "Not to worry, it was a silly idea." I turn to the stove where my potatoes have probably mashed themselves by now. I reach out to take the pot off the burner, when he grabs my elbow and turns me around.

"Not silly at all, and you didn't let me finish." His eyes smile looking down on me. "What I was trying to get to is that I'm on call this weekend, so Max will be staying at my parents. I'll have to be at the office for some time during the day, but unless there's an emergency, I plan to be home around six. If your mother is on board coming here to look after the boys, so they don't have to be disrupted—however the night pans out—we could plan to meet at my place. I'll pick up dinner on the way." He smiles and brushes the pad of his thumb over my cheek. "That is, if you're willing to take the risk I may have to bail in case of an emergency."

"I can check with Mom," I tell him, trying hard not to give myself away by grinning like a loon.

"So we have a plan."

"Looks that way."

He lightly brushes my lips with his before carefully setting me aside. He takes the pan from the stove, and drains the water in the sink. "Do you have cream cheese?" he asks, as he pulls the potato masher from the stone utensil pot sitting next to the stove.

He takes me by surprise; apparently, he's making the mashed potatoes. I open the fridge, pull out the makings for a quick salad, and a brick of Philly I leave next to him on the counter.

I do all of this grinning like the Cheshire cat.

"See you Saturday morning?"

We're back on my front step. Max is already buckled up in the car and Dylan holds my hand in his.

Dinner had been a lively affair, with the exception of Liam, who kept mostly quiet. Between Max and Harry, though, conversation was never lacking.

My pulled pork was fabulous, if I say so myself, and Dylan's fluffy potatoes were the best I've ever tasted. But the absolute winner was the dessert he threw together with ingredients from my pantry and freezer, at the boys' urging. Peanut butter chocolate sundaes.

According to Max, they're even better with crushed salted peanuts—which I didn't have—but the plain vanilla ice cream, stirred with semi-sweet chocolate chips and drizzled with melted peanut butter, was to die for.

It was also a million calories, and on top of an already rich dinner, it feels like I've put on twenty pounds in the past hour and a half.

Just as Dylan starts bending toward me, I stifle a yawn, making him smile.

"Tired?"

"Food coma." I grin back and his eyes fix on my mouth, his intent obvious. "Max is watching," I caution him.

"Don't care. He'll have to get used to me kissing you," he counters, right before his lips touch mine, his tongue sliding inside.

The kiss is short, but so exquisite; I'm still blinking away my daze when he backs out of my driveway a few minutes later.

CHAPTER 15

DYLAN

"You getting ready for work?"

It's Friday afternoon and I'm sitting at the conference table in the office, looking for some privacy to call Marya.

We've been whittling down the list of registered sex offenders all day. With the lab working on the semen found on Seth during the autopsy to get a DNA profile—hopefully sooner than later—we're focusing on those for whom we don't have a viable DNA sample on file.

We'd been about to head out to get a start on the grunt work of collecting swabs, when I was digging around my pockets for my keys and my hand encountered a folded piece of paper. The Montrose police report.

With everything going on last night, I'd

completely forgotten about it, so I told Toni—who was unfortunately once again assigned to come with me—to hold on so I could make a call.

"Mom should be here soon, and uh…" Marya adds in a softer voice that shoots straight to my dick. "She can do tomorrow night as well."

I push the heel of my hand down on my crotch, discouraging my cock from rising to the occasion. I have no desire to go interview a sexual deviant, with Toni in tow, about to bust out of my fly. "That's good news, Sweetheart. There's something I should have told you last night, but didn't get around to."

"Oh?"

I hate the reserved caution I can hear in the single syllable and quickly give her the details. Ripping off the bandage so to speak.

"I'm not exactly a fan, but I'm sorry this happened to her. No one deserves that."

"You've got that right."

She's quiet for a moment, and then asks, "Why would they want to talk to me?"

"Jasper was looking to find something on Jeremy, talked to the Montrose PD and discovered they're looking for him. I assume they want to ask some questions about your recent run-ins, but fair warning, I think they'll also be asking you about your history with him."

"Okay," she mumbles, sounding reluctantly resigned. "Not exactly a proud time in my life, but I guess I can't change what happened."

"Look, I can't begin to understand what it must like be to relive that, but maybe the information you can add will strengthen this woman's case against him. A way for you to get some justice of your own for what he did to you."

Silence again.

"Babe?"

Her voice is low and full of emotion when she answers. "She's stronger than I am. I should've done what she's doing, but instead I—"

"Instead you focused all your energy on making sure three young boys had a good life. Christ, Marya, you denied yourself the opportunity for justice, so his crap wouldn't come near your kids. If that kind of sacrifice doesn't spell strength, I don't know what does."

I berate myself for not bringing this up last night. I could've held her so she could look me in the eye and see I mean every word.

"Thanks, but…oh, Mom's here."

I can hear muffled greetings in the background. "I'll let you go."

"Okay."

"I'm gonna try and be there at least for the first half of the game tomorrow. Clint and Ma will be there to take Max after."

"I could've dropped him off at theirs after the game."

"Appreciate that. I didn't ask because Ma already said they'd be there. Anyway, I should let you get to work and I'll catch you tomorrow."

"Yes, you will," she almost whispers. "Looking forward to it."

"Not as much as I am, Sweetheart."

With that I quickly end the call, adjust my fly, and walk out of the conference room, almost knocking into Toni who's leaning against the wall just outside the door.

"Ready?" she chirps, hiding a flash of shock behind a toothy smile, and I know in that moment she's been listening in.

I briefly consider calling her out on it, but decide on a sharp look before marching past her instead. Probably best not to validate whatever fucked-up shit is going on in her head by giving it more attention.

The one positive: my hard-on is instantly subdued.

"Are you with her?"

We're just leaving our first stop when she hits me with that.

I whip my head around. "Are you for fucking real?" At least she has the sense to look almost embarrassed.

"I'm just curious—" She immediately silences when I snap my hand up from the steering wheel, taking a deep breath in.

"I see you still haven't gotten the message," I bite off. "There is absolutely nothing—not a single fucking thing—appropriate about your question. Whatever makes you think you get to ask me something like that, get it out of your fucking head. You're a grunt I have to put up with at the boss's orders, because there's no other way I'd be willing to even share the same air. You tossed the last of your rights in the trash last time I saw you, coming out of that clinic in Denver."

I have to slam on the brakes when the lights turn red, the Expedition skidding a few feet into the intersection. Better keep my head, or I'm gonna get us both killed.

"Please don't fucking talk," I snap when I hear her suck in a breath. "Don't say a word or, so help me God, I won't be responsible for the consequences."

There is no way I can work with this woman. The rage still blazes like it was yesterday when she's around me. I'm going to have to talk to Damian first chance I get.

Rather than heading to the next address on our list, I turn us around and head straight back to the office. Damian's truck is still in the parking lot. Ignoring her, I slam the SUV in park, get out, and head inside to have a talk with my boss. No time like the present.

I can hear her heels clicking behind me when I take the stairs two at a time.

"Dylan, please wait."

I don't listen and barge into the office. Damian and Jasper are bent over a map, both their heads snapping up at my noisy entrance. Two sets of eyes regard me curiously.

"Got a minute?" I direct at Damian, indicating his

office.

He nods and starts heading there when the door flies open behind me, stopping him in his tracks. I force myself not to look behind me, but keep my eyes focused on my boss, who shoots glances from me to her and back. Then he starts moving again and I follow him into his office, closing the door behind me.

"It's bleeding into the job, Barnes," he starts before his ass is in his chair.

"It is, but it's not me probing the wound," I fire back immediately.

"You sure about that? The woman looks like she's suffering."

I'm surprised at the statement, but I also know she's a hell of an actress.

"Wouldn't be the first time and have it be a lie."

Damian's turn to look surprised. Although, whether it's because of what I'm implying, or my unusually callous delivery, I don't know.

"Maybe you'd like to clarify."

"Honestly? No. She hasn't left me another option, though, so you're getting the whole sordid story." I lift my ankle on my knee, mostly to stop my leg from bopping up and down as I poke around in memories I've tried to bury. "I met Toni early on, while I was working that assignment for Aiken in Denver a few years ago. We hooked up; it was fun. We hung out for a couple of months; both knowing it had an expiration date. Or so I thought. Took me a while to discover she was angling for more, but the moment I did, I explained things weren't like that for me and bowed out."

"I don't see what—"

"That's because I'm not done," I interrupt Damian rudely. In my defense, this shit is costing me and I was having a pretty good fucking day before. "Three weeks later, she shows up at my apartment, telling me she's pregnant, and the baby is mine." I'm looking at my fingers, picking at the seam of my jeans, but I still feel the air change in the room around me.

"Go on."

I need another deep breath in to keep my voice level as I spill the rest. "She was eight weeks pregnant. I demanded to go with her for an ultrasound. Fucking heartbeat on the screen and everything. Wasn't planned, but from that moment it was fucking wanted. I thought about Max, and this new baby brother or sister, and I knew I was gonna give this thing a go with Toni. We started planning, even brought her home to Durango one weekend to meet Max and my folks. Two weeks after that, I'm at a coffee shop near my place, when I get a call from a friend of hers. She tells me I need to get my ass over to a clinic in Englewood." I bark out a painful laugh. "Fucking place is called Healthy Futures, believe it or not. I'm arguing with a fucking guard to let me in, even wave my FBI badge, but it's already too late. The friend who called me walks out, an apology on her face and an arm around Toni."

"*Jesus.*"

My eyes burn with the memory of hot pain hitting my gut, realizing what she'd done, and puking right there on the sidewalk, the knowledge almost bringing me to my knees. "She never wanted a kid. She just wanted me and had since the beginning. She orchestrated the pregnancy, gauging the kind of guy I am, knowing I was gonna do the right thing. She had me hooked, got rid of the baby she never wanted, and was gonna claim a miscarriage, using that instead to keep me around."

"That's all kinds of fucked up."

"Ya think?"

"What the hell is she doing here?" he wants to know.

"Fuck if I know. The fact she's FBI now doesn't necessarily mean anything, but it's the fact she's FBI, and she's assigned to my field office. This afternoon I caught her listening in on my call with Marya, and to top it off, she had the balls to ask me about my relationship with her." I finally look up to find Damian observing me, a muscle ticking in his jaw. "I can't do it, man. I'm still so fucking angry, I'm afraid I'll do something I regret. I can't work with her."

"Fuck!" I flinch when Damian's hand slams down on the desk, sending papers scattering on the floor. "Shoulda told me, kid. Right away. The moment you heard her name, you shoulda laid it out. I never would've put you in that position had I known."

"I'm…shit piled up quick."

Damian shakes his head sharply. "I get it. I'm

pissed at the situation. I'm fucking furious with that manipulative bitch out there, and I have to figure out a way to explain to Aiken his first candidate is already not working out, when I should be concerned with a sexual predator and child killer on the loose."

"Tell him the truth," I suggest. My shit is out there now. No way to put the genie back in the bottle, and whatever blows back my way I'll deal with.

"Get out of here, Dylan. Walk out that door, go straight to your truck, and get yourself home. Regardless of how this pans out, you won't need to deal with her. Leave it to me."

"Thanks."

I push out of the chair, when he suddenly gets up too and rounds the desk. He claps a hand on my shoulder and curves the other around my neck, giving it a squeeze.

"So fucking sorry, kid."

I barely manage to nod when he lets me go and I hurry out the door, not seeing anything but the exit.

My eyes are too blurry.

MARYA

I haven't stopped smiling since I left my house this morning.

Darla was teasing me earlier before she took off to do a medical clinic on the south side, while I headed over to a spa downtown.

It's a small, one-story building that'll take me

another ten minutes or so to finish and then I can head home to bed.

My phone vibrates in my back pocket and I fish it out.

Dylan: Where are you?

Me: Still working

Dylan: Where?

Me: The Pampered Princess on 3rd, why?

Dylan: Geezus. How long?

Me: Maybe another 10 or so, why?

I wait a few seconds, but when there's no response I tuck the phone back in my pocket, and finish cleaning out the footbaths.

Not sure what that was all about. I don't want to assume anything, so I tamp down the butterflies in my belly getting all excited. No need to set myself up for disappointment.

Damn, what I wouldn't give for a pedicure every so often. It's one of those luxuries I afford myself once a year, at the start of summer, but the rest of the year I make do. Being on my feet a ton lately, they are in a dire state. I could probably sand my kitchen cabinets with my bare heels.

Fifteen minutes later, I tuck the cleaning supplies back in the closet, turn off the lights, and let myself out, locking the door behind me.

I see him right away, leaning against my Jeep in the parking lot.

He doesn't move as I walk up to him.

"Hey," I barely manage to get the single word out when his arm sneaks out, hooks me around the waist, and turns me so my back is pressed up against the fender—his body plastered against my front—and his mouth showing me he's happy to see me with a desperation that's new to me.

It's only when he finally lets me up for air I see the deep creases around his mouth and on his forehead. Lifting both hands to his face I pull him closer.

"You all right, honey?"

Something twists inside me when I see him grimace as if in pain, before his face evens out again. "I'm good now," he whispers, his forehead resting against mine.

"Wanna talk about it?"

"I've got a neighbor sitting with Max for a few, I should get back. I just…needed to see you."

I pull him down as I lift my face, meeting his lips in what I hope is a soothing kiss. He seems torn up and I'm afraid something else bad happened he can't talk to me about. "Whatever you need, honey."

His arms wrap around and crush me to his chest, his face pressed in my hair.

Something is definitely wrong.

"This exactly what I need," he mumbles. "Some bad memories resurfaced today. I'll tell you, I promise, but not tonight."

"Whenever you're ready, Dylan," I whisper, my hand stroking his head.

His mouth finds mine in a hard kiss before stepping back.

"Fuck, you're perfect."

CHAPTER 16

MARYA

"There they are," Liam says, pointing ahead.

I recognize the team jerseys on the field farthest from the golf course.

This is the first time they're playing at the Sports Complex in Farmington, and I had no flipping idea the place was this massive.

We missed the first turnoff, but caught the second one, parked the Jeep, and started walking. We passed a huge pond, tons of baseball fields—already busy on a Saturday morning—but didn't see the soccer fields. We discovered those after traipsing through a golf course—to the chagrin of a foursome of late season golfers—to find there was parking right along the fields on the other side. Should've taken that first entrance.

I spot restrooms, and seeing as I downed my second

coffee of the morning earlier, I need to make a stop.

"Boys, go ahead and follow Liam, I'll just be a minute."

Bathrooms at sports fields are a hit and miss I've discovered, but I'm pleased to find this one was recently cleaned. The pungent smell of bleach greets me when I pull open the door.

Maybe it's a good thing I'm not that familiar around Farmington and didn't stop for another fix of caffeine. It would've made us even later. The boys and I were already slow getting up, last night's movie night had gone a little long.

It's nippy this morning. Even with my warm hoodie and down vest I can feel the chill seeping in. I see some parents sitting on the sidelines who were smarter than me and brought blankets. I didn't even bring a hot drink to keep me warm. Maybe next year, I'll have this soccer mom thing down.

It's clear Dylan has more experience, since he's sitting with a huge thermos beside him, talking to my boys. Clint and Beth sit one higher, and clearly also came better prepared since Beth's knees are covered with a throw.

"Morning." Dylan grins at me, looking a whole lot better than when I saw him last night. Just a shadow of whatever was haunting him is visible in his eyes.

"Hey. Hi, guys," I toss at Beth and Clint as I sit down beside Dylan, who uses my distraction to lean in for a surprising touch of his lips to mine.

I feel my face flush and my eyes immediately dart

to my boys, sitting on the other side of him. Harry is oblivious but Theo noticed. I'm not sure what I expected, but the sardonic lift of his eyebrow and barely contained grin wasn't it. I bulge my eyes at him and the grin breaks free. A quick peek over my shoulder gleans me a similar smirk on Beth's face and a rumbly chuckle from Clint. Guess I'm the only one a little freaked by the public display of affection.

"Mom, can we get something to drink?" Harry pipes up; his best 'please' face in place.

"Boy, we just walked a half-marathon to get here and now you tell me?"

"It's cold," he complains, like that explains it all.

Before I have a chance to shut him down—because there's no way I'm going to leave the warmth of Dylan's thigh pressed against mine—Beth comes to the rescue.

"Anyone for hot chocolate? Hand me the thermos, Dylan." The boys make it known they'd love some, and I send her a grateful smile. She pulls some foam cups from the tote between her legs. "You hold these and I'll pour," she instructs me. When everyone is taken care of, she dives back in the tote and pulls out a large Tupperware container, handing it to Clint. "Pass these around, would you, honey?"

"Take two," Clint rumbles when he offers the boys what look to be giant oatmeal cookies.

"They're practically a breakfast food," Beth says behind me, and I throw a smile over my shoulder.

"Let me guess," I say softly, leaning into Dylan.

"You played soccer when you were a kid?"

He grins in response. "Six years. Ma never missed a game."

"Figures," I mumble, sipping my hot chocolate, thinking Beth knows her shit.

When the coaches call the teams to the sidelines for their final instructions before kick-off, I hear the low rumble of a motorcycle. I spot it rolling down the path on the far side of the soccer fields, carrying two people.

It's not until the pair is walking this way I recognize Ouray, and the smaller figure is Luna.

"Morning," she says easily as she plants her butt on my other side, her silver-fox hubby simply lifting his chin before sitting down beside her.

"What are you doing here?" my curiosity has me blurting out, instead of the friendly *hey* or *good morning* they received from everyone else.

"Just out for a Saturday morning ride before winter settles in," Luna answers with a grin.

Ouray leans in front of her, "Got a guy keepin' an eye out in the parking lot."

Dylan bumps my shoulder and whispers in my ear, "Told you they'd show up."

Now that he mentions it, I recall him saying something about that.

It had slipped my mind.

DYLAN

I listen with half an ear to Marya chatting with Ma and Luna beside me, when the halftime whistle sounds.

I'd like to hang around, but I've got to get to the office, so I tap Marya on the shoulder.

"I've gotta head out, babe. Call you this afternoon?"

Her face lifts to me and I don't hesitate in covering the slight pout on her lips with a quick kiss. Wedged between her kids, my folks, and my partner, I can't do much more than that, which sucks.

"Okay, honey," she mumbles, the cute blush back on her face.

"Mom, I've gotta go to the bathroom."

I look at Harry. "I'm heading out anyway, kid, I'll take you." I'm surprised when he easily slips his hand in mine. It's been a few years since Max held my hand, and it occurs to me I miss it.

"I'll come too," Marya's oldest boy announces, jumping up as well.

"Straight back, you guys," she calls after us.

I drop the boys at the bathrooms on my way to the parking lot, where I spot Paco having a smoke leaning on his bike.

"This is why I ain't never havin' kids," he grumbles when I walk over. "The little shits keep you up at night or get you up at the butt crack a' dawn. Either way, they mess up your sleep. I fuckin' need my sleep, man."

"It's near eleven, Paco," I tell him, biting my lip to keep from grinning. "Hardly the butt crack of dawn."

"Was fuckin' nine when we rode out, smart-ass,"

he retorts, and this time I don't bother holding back on the grin.

"Sun rose a few hours before that, my friend."

"The fact you know that just proves my point, brother." He tosses his cigarette on the ground and crushes it under the heel of his boot. "Kids. Sheeet..."

I'm still chuckling when I drive off the parking lot.

The good mood sticks with me until I'm in Aztec, waiting to turn north on Highway 550 and my phone—tossed in the cupholder when I got behind the wheel—buzzes with a message. I glance over at the screen.

Marya: Harry still with you?

It's been twenty minutes at most since I left the sports fields. I turn the truck around first chance I get and pull off to the side, my fingers already dialing.

Marya's phone bumps me right into voicemail.

MARYA

I watch as the kids head back out on the field, before my eyes return to the buildings on the far side, where I know the bathrooms to be.

Ouray gets up and walks over to the fence behind the bench, appearing casual, but I note his eyes aren't on the field either.

Time crawls along as the slightest twist in my stomach coils itself into a tight knot, until finally I see the familiar lanky form of Theo jogging this way. There's no sign of his younger brother, though. Something Ouray apparently has noticed, because he swings around and looks straight at me, a frown between his eyes, before stalking away to intercept Theo.

I immediately pull out my phone and dial Harry's new number, noticing Luna standing up beside me, as the phone keeps ringing until a generic voice invites me to leave a message. My fingers whip over the screen, shooting off a text to Dylan and then I try Harry's number again.

Same result.

"What's going on?" Beth leans down over my shoulder.

"I'm not sure." My voice is already shaking as I watch Luna join the huddle with Ouray and Theo. He's gesturing wildly, pointing toward the bathrooms.

I try Harry's number again, my body shaking now. Same automated message. I don't seem to be able to do anything other than sit frozen in my spot, while hitting the redial button over and over, my eyes locked on the huddle. Ouray breaks off and starts jogging to the bathrooms.

"Marya, Theo says you didn't park in the main parking lot?"

I look up at Luna who walks up, an arm slung around Theo's hunched shoulders. I can't take my eyes off my boy, who won't look straight at me.

"Marya," she repeats a little more sharply.

"Uhh…we missed the main entrance and ended up parking by the baseball diamonds, on the other side of the golf course." I point at the tree line. "Back there."

"Shit," she hisses, letting go of Theo to pull out her phone.

The bench moves when Clint climbs down and stalks off along the fence line on this side.

"Yeah, there's a second entrance down the road," Luna informs whoever is on the phone. "A parking lot by the baseball diamonds—Right, I'll call him now—Yes, I'll tell her. "

I'm listening as I reach out for my son, grabbing his hand, and pulling him down on the bench beside me. He still won't show me his eyes.

"What's happening?" I ask Luna, not even sure what exactly I'm asking myself. I feel disconnected, like I'm watching a movie, except I'm in the middle of it. It's almost like an out-of-body experience and I hold on tightly to Theo's hand.

"He's sending a guy to your car, in case he went there. Ouray is checking the skate park and the putting green. He says to let you know they'll find him. I've gotta call Dylan."

She walks off and puts the phone back to her ear.

The game on the field continues uninterrupted.

"I thought he was still in there." Theo buries his face in my neck. "I waited, Mom. I promise. I even went back in to see what the hold up was. He wasn't there."

I twist in my seat so I can wrap my arms around

him. "I know, baby. They'll find him."

My mouth spouts out the words in response, like the automated message on Harry's phone. I feel paralyzed. Terrified if I move, if I get up, I acknowledge this is happening and I can't deal with that. So I'll just sit here, with my arms around the only thing that feels real.

"You think Dad has him?"

He lifts his head and finally meets my eyes, his red-rimmed and frightened, begging for reassurance. His question cuts right through the paralysis and finds hot anger.

"He does, it won't be for long. I can promise you that," I tell my son, fire in my voice.

"Atta girl," I hear Beth mumble behind me.

"Go sit with Max's grandma, Bub, I'll be right back."

He does as I ask and I walk over to Luna, who's just ending her call.

"Stay put, Dylan's just pulling into the parking lot."

"Like hell, my kid is out there."

"Marya…" Luna puts a restrictive hand on my arm when I try to pass by her. "Best you can do is sit tight."

The anger erupts; I twist my arm loose and get in Luna's face. "Don't touch me," I hiss, and take off running toward the bathrooms.

"Marya!" I look up to find Dylan approaching the building from the other side. He doesn't stop moving until I'm in his arms. Just for a second, I let his strength soak in before I try to wiggle free.

"I've gotta find him." I shove against his chest and he takes a step back but grabs onto my wrists.

"And we will, but we can't go running off half—"

"Harry!" Dylan swings around when I rip my arms from his hold and start running to where I just caught sight of my baby coming out of the trees edging the golf course. Beside him is the dark-haired biker I saw with Ouray the other day, holding fast to his hand.

I drop down on my knees in front of my baby and pull him down on my lap, wrapping my arms around him. I vaguely hear the crunch of footsteps stop behind me, and the deep rumble of men's voices over my head, but I'm focused on my boy in my arms.

"I'm sorry," he whispers.

DYLAN

I look at Marya sitting in the passenger seat beside me, her face pale.

She didn't object much when I told her I would drive her and the boys home. I wasn't going to let her get behind the wheel, not in her state. Luna offered to drive her Jeep back to Durango. Max went with Ma and Clint for the rest of the weekend.

The boys are unusually quiet in the back seat.

Paco had found Harry by Marya's Jeep. He'd crawled underneath to hide, he said. Apparently he'd come out of the bathroom, didn't see his brother, and wanted to go have a look at the pond, where he'd seen people fishing earlier. He walked around the water's edge, to where the small dock juts into the water, near where his mother's Jeep was parked.

That's when he says he saw his father park a silver car just a few spots away from his mom's Jeep, get out, and head for the path through the golf course toward the soccer fields. Harry got scared, wanted to let his mom know, but had accidentally left his new phone on the back seat of the Jeep. Of course the doors were locked, and afraid his father might come back and see him, he figured he'd be safe hiding under his mom's vehicle.

The kid had been gone for forty-five minutes. A fuckofalot can happen in forty-five minutes.

By the time I helped both Marya and Harry on their feet, the teams were already coming off the field. I left them in the care of my folks, with Paco standing guard, while Ouray, Luna, and I went to check out the supposed silver car.

There were seven of them in that damn parking lot, but none parked near his mother's Jeep. If it had been there before, it was gone now.

"Weren't you supposed to be at the office?" Marya asks and I take her hand, pressing to my thigh.

"Luna's already let Damian know I'll be a little later. I'll get you settled in at home first."

I'm also curious how Harry would've recognized his father, but any questions will have to wait until I get them home. I don't want to grill the kid when I can still hear him sniffle every so often in the back seat.

CHAPTER 17

MARYA

"Answer the question, Bub."

Harry's eyes drift from me to his brother. He's hiding something and Liam's in on it, judging by the tight press of his lips.

We arrived home ten minutes ago, got some sandwiches for lunch ready, and just sat down with the boys at my dining table. Dylan caught me in the kitchen earlier, wanting to know if I was okay with him trying to get some more information from Harry over lunch. I agreed, I was actually curious about a few things myself.

Dylan was casual and relaxed when he asked Harry how he'd been able to tell it was Jeremy in the parking lot. I immediately saw the change in my youngest though; he froze up with his sandwich halfway to his mouth and then quickly took a massive bite. Boy knows he's not to talk with his mouth full. I guess he thought we'd forget.

I'm a mom. I don't forget.

"Harrison Berger, I'm not going to tell you again."

He throws another furtive glance at his brother before turning to Dylan. "I saw pictures of him."

"Bub," I call him out. "I'm not buying it. The last pictures of your father we have left; his hair came down to his shoulders and he was wearing glasses. I saw him last weekend, I was married to him for ten years, and it took me a bit before I recognized it was him. Try again."

"Don't." The low voice is Liam's. He's glaring at his brother.

"Don't what, Liam?" I demand to know, standing up and bracing myself with my hands on the table.

He's engaged in a staredown with Harry, who looks near tears and doesn't answer me.

"Leave him alone, Liam," Theo jumps to his little brother's defense.

"I saw him, okay?" Harry sobs, his big teary eyes now on me. "He was outside the school."

"When?" Dylan's been quiet for most of the exchange. So focused on the boys, I almost forgot he was there.

"Liam?"

Defiance on his face as he reluctantly turns to me; but it's Theo who answers.

"Harry saw him talking to Liam on Tuesday by the bus stop outside the school. I was late because Mr.

Robbins asked me to stay after class, so I didn't see him, but I walked in on them fighting." He cocks a thumb at his brothers.

"Is that why you guys were fighting when you got home that day?" I ask, remembering them walking in, Liam with a bleeding lip.

"Liam was pushing Harry around," Theo volunteers with a shrug.

"Why didn't you tell me?" I throw up my hands, exasperated. "I asked you what was going on, and you guys went mum on me. I don't get why you wouldn't tell me that." I direct the last at my oldest child specifically. He looks duly scolded, two spots of red appearing on his cheeks.

"I thought it was under control," he explains, but it doesn't help me. I still don't understand.

"Under control? I'm your mother, your father shows up out of the blue after *years*, and you don't think that's something you might wanna share with me?"

I know my voice is going shrill, but I can't help myself, if my kids don't share with me, how the fuck am I supposed to keep them safe?

"Marya," Dylan's deep cautioning rumble from behind me is paired with a firm hand on my shoulder. "My guess is Theo was trying to protect you. Take care of it without involving you."

"He's thirteen, it's not his job to protect me," I snap, and watch as the red spreads over my oldest boy's face.

"Sweetheart, he saw you get hurt by the man when he was too young to do anything about it. Now he could, by shielding you. I'm a guy, I get it."

Theo throws a look of gratitude over my head at Dylan, indicating he was right on the money.

Christ, I love my kids with all I am, but there are days when I'd like to pack them up and ship them off to boarding school. Of course that would require a budget I don't possess.

I miss the times when the biggest hurdle I would face any given day was getting them to brush their teeth and eat their vegetables. Looking at their faces, I feel powerless; Harry's is worried and guilty, Theo's stubborn and defiant, and Liam…Jesus, Liam…he's just so angry.

"Liam? Wanna tell me what your father said to you?" His answer is to push his chair back and stalk from the room. I look at his brothers. "Either of you know anything?"

Harry shakes his head and looks down, but Theo's eyes stay on me, his expression gentling. "He doesn't look like us," he says, baffling me.

"What do you mean?"

"Liam. Harry and me, we look alike, we look like you: dark hair, dark eyes. Liam doesn't. He looks like Dad. When he got mad, he started yelling that he doesn't even belong. That's when I punched him."

I sit down, shove my plate with the half-eaten sandwich aside, and drop my head on my arms on the table.

Sweet Jesus...my boy.

Tears burn my eyes. Why would he think that? More importantly, how did I miss that?

Dylan's hand curves around the back of my neck as I hear him address the kids.

"Right. It's important you get that what your father did, talk to one of you at school, is against the law. He's not allowed near the school, or near your house, or anywhere near you guys or your mom. Ever. You get me? The protection order the judge signed is there to do exactly that—*protect you*—but it's not gonna work if you don't tell your mom, or me, or your teachers when your dad breaks the rules."

"But we didn't know about that until after," Theo counters, which doesn't surprise me.

"Maybe not," Dylan comes right back. "But don't tell me you didn't know keeping that from your mom wasn't the right play to make, no matter how good your intentions." I can't see his face, but I hear my boy's grunt in response. "Now, why don't you guys give me a minute with your mom, okay?"

Chairs scrape over the floor and I keep my face hidden, not wanting the kids to see their mom come apart at the seams.

Then I feel arms awkwardly hugging me from behind. "Sorry, Mom," Harry says, his voice thick, before letting me go.

"Me too." This time it's Theo as he presses his head against mine. "Please don't cry," he whispers, before he too moves away.

As soon as I hear their feet hit the stairs, a sob rips from my throat and the next second my face is pressed against Dylan's shirt. His large hand rubs circles on my back as the events of the past day—fuck, of the past years—come pouring out of me.

"Knowledge is power, Sweetheart," he mumbles when my crying bout subsides.

"What do you mean?" I sniffle, leaving my face buried. I'm not a pretty crier with big crocodile tears rolling down; I blubber, and it gets messy.

"I bet that was hard to hear, but you won't be blindsided by it again. Always better to see what's coming."

I try to resist when he lifts my head away from his shoulder. He persists, leaving his hands to cup my sloppy cheeks, and I blindly grab for a napkin from the table to mop the worst off my face.

"I just don't know how to fix this."

"Been brewing for a while. Can't expect it to be a quick fix, Sweetheart."

I know that, of course, but the thought my kid feels he doesn't belong is gut-wrenching.

His thumb strokes my jaw as he presses a soft kiss on my lips.

"Weren't you supposed to be at the office?" I suddenly realize out loud, jerking my head away.

"Gotta look after my girl first."

Okay, that's sweet, even though I left my years as a girl behind me a long time ago.

"I'll be fine, Dylan. You should go."

He drops his chin and scrutinizes me closely. "Have you got an extra key?"

"Why?"

"I'm thinking you'll wanna stay here tonight—stick close to your boys. I'm gonna need a key to get in if I'm late."

I open my mouth to protest, only to close it again. Truth is, it feels good he wants to check in on me.

So instead of making a fuss, I get up, walk over to the kitchen, and pull the extra key from the magnet behind the fridge.

"Be safe," I tell him, pressing the key in his hand.

He tucks it in his pocket, hooks his other hand around my neck, and pulls me to his mouth. The moment my lips open his tongue slides in.

The kiss is like a shot of Valium straight to the bloodstream. Slow, thorough, and completely addictive.

I'm still swaying on my feet when he walks out a few moments later.

DYLAN

"Marya and the kids okay?"

Damian sticks his head out of his office when I walk in.

"Relatively," I answer honestly, tossing my jacket over the back of my chair before sitting down. "Discovering the asshole ex showed up at her sons' school didn't go over too well."

"You're shitting me." He leans against Jasper's desk, crossing his arms.

"Nope. Same afternoon we served him with the protective order. Walked right up to Liam."

"What did he want?"

"The boy's not sharing."

I relay what little I know.

"He's renting a place in Hermosa, right?" Damian scratches his fingers through his goatee. "I'm thinking maybe I should drop by on my way home. Sounds like he's not clear on the ramifications should he defy that order, I should make sure he understands."

"Couldn't hurt." I turn to the files on my desk.

"Barnes." My eyes meet his serious ones. "I briefly spoke with Agent Linden last night and have a call scheduled with Aiken first thing Monday. Giving you a heads-up, because she insists whatever happened between you is a thing of the past and won't impact work, and I have a gnawing suspicion that's what Aiken's line will be too—suck it up."

"Fuck."

A call comes in on the office line and Damian leans over to hit the speaker.

"La Plata County FBI, Gomez here."

"Gomez, it's Yeager." The voice on the other end sounds glum.

I shoot up straight in my seat. Yeager is the special agent in charge of the Farmington field office.

"We've got another one."

Damian rounds the desk, grabs a notepad and a

pen. "I've got you on speaker. Talk to me."

"I've got the distraught parents of one Thomas McKinley in my office. They were brought in by Farmington PD after their son disappeared after a soccer game."

"This is Dylan Barnes, by chance was this at the Sports Complex?" I ask, a nasty feeling in my gut.

"It was. After their son's game, the McKinleys were talking to some of the other parents. Thomas said he wanted to catch up with a buddy in the parking lot, and they told him to go ahead and wait by the car. By the time they got to there, the kid was gone. They tried finding him for an hour before they called it in."

"Jesus, I was just there for my son's game."

"Soccer?"

"Yup."

"Fuck, don't tell me his team is the Stingers."

"No, but they were playing them. My boy knew Seth Mayer from soccer as well. They play in the same league."

"Fuck," Yeager repeats. "Didn't want to think the two were connected. Hoping the kid was stupid and took off without telling his parents, but—"

"What do you need?" Damian cuts in.

"An Amber Alert is going out in the next five minutes, that's what I called to give you a heads-up on. I've got my guys and local PD out scouring the fields and the adjoining golf course. The McKinleys are local to you. Work it from that end, I'll work it from here and we'll be in touch."

Twenty minutes later, the entire team is in the conference room, including Agent Linden. Damian shot me an apologetic look when she walked in. I'll suck it up. Fuck, I'll do anything to find that boy.

I hand out printouts of everything Yeager sent us, a picture of Thomas on top.

I vaguely recognized the kid: blue-eyed and blond. Just like Seth.

Just like Liam.

"I need to make a quick call," I mutter, already on my way out to the hallway.

"Dylan?" Marya's voice is breathless when she answers. "The Amber Alert, it's one of the kids—"

"I know, Sweetheart. Listen, I don't have much time. Do me a favor; keep the boys home. If you need to go out for anything, ask your mom to sit with them. Please. I'll be in touch as soon as I can."

"Okay." I can hear her strangle a sob and it kills me I can't do anything about it right now. I know I'm probably freaking her out on a day she's been freaked out enough—and I fucking hate that too—but I need to focus on finding Thomas.

"Gotta let you go, babe."

"Go. Find him," she whispers back.

"No one is saying it, so I will." Luna looks around the table. "Anyone else thinking we should have a closer look at Jeremy Berger?"

"Absolutely, I'm on that. Heading up to Hermosa

shortly," Damian answers. "Linden, you're coming with me," he says to Toni, who's been quiet and only nods. "Jas, I want you to dig into the Four Corners League. Pull an address list for every kid on his team; call the parents. Any information that looks interesting, toss it to Luna and Dylan to follow up on. Next look at board, administration, coaches. Anyone even remotely connected to the league; I want it scrutinized front to back. You'll be in contact with Yeager." He turns to me. "Dylan, get in touch with Joe Benedetti and get him in the loop. Then you and Luna head over to the McKinley house. The parents are still in Farmington, but the boy's uncle is coming down from Dolores with a key. Everything and anything we find gets relayed into the office right away. Every fucking minute counts, people."

After I talk with Benedetti, our local chief of police who promises any and all support, Luna and I meet up with a very distraught Michael McKinley—Thomas' uncle—outside a nice house in a middle-class neighborhood near the college.

The McKinleys aren't hurting for money. Parked in the driveway is a fairly new Subaru Ascent, and I know from the reports the vehicle the family is currently driving is a Porsche Cayenne. I'm guessing the Subaru is mom's ride.

Thomas is the only child and it's easy to see which bedroom is his. Looks like a boy's dream; posters of superheroes and famous soccer players on the wall, a nice computer on his desk, a forty-inch flat-screen mounted across from one of those gaming chairs, and a PlayStation on the floor beside it.

"Big gamer? Your nephew?" I ask Michael, who follows us around.

"Yeah. Aside from the soccer, it's all he does these days."

"These days?" Luna, always perceptive, picks up on it as well.

"Well…" The man darts assessing glances between Luna and me before he appears to come to a decision. "My brother and his wife are going through a tough time," he says reluctantly. That explains why not only the master, but also the spare bedroom, look to be occupied. "The atmosphere in the house hasn't exactly been healthy, so I guess these past few months he mostly sticks to his room."

"I see." I send Luna a meaningful look. "Would you excuse me for a minute?" I announce, already pulling my phone from my pocket as I walk out of the room and down the stairs.

"Talk to me," Jasper answers.

"Get on the horn with Yeager. If he doesn't know it yet, the McKinleys are having marital issues. The kind that has them sleep in separate bedrooms and is bad enough the boy hides out in his room all the time."

"Gotcha."

"And, Jas? There's one other thing; Thomas has a PS4 sitting on the floor next to a state-of-the-art gaming chair, complete with headset and mic."

"Is that right?"

"Age, looks, soccer, and now PlayStation. If it was just the gaming, I wouldn't even consider it significant, but add it to the other similarities, it could well be. Want me to bring in the system?"

"You bet. I'll get hold of the Farmington office, see what they found on Seth's."

"Right." All this is hitting way too close to home. "What about that group that Max—"

"Already thinking of that, brother. Not taking any chances, but just to say; Max is not blond and blue-eyed."

Max may not be, but I know another boy who hits those marks perfectly.

CHAPTER 18

MARYA

I wake up at a gentle touch to my face.

"Why aren't you in bed?"

I blink my eyes open to find Dylan leaning over the back of the couch. From the TV the late-night sounds of *Saturday Night Live* filter through. It's been years since I watched it and decided to while waiting for word from Dylan.

"I'm watching *SNL*."

"With your eyes closed?"

I decide the best way to handle this is to ignore it.

I scoot my legs over the side of the couch, sit up, grab the remote, and mute the sound. "How are you? Do you need something to eat? A beer?" I turn around to face him and see the sign of fatigue mar his features. I badly want to ask if there's any news on the missing boy, but I'm pretty sure if he'd been found he would've told me.

"I had something at the office earlier, but I wouldn't mind a kiss."

I put my knee in the couch and reach my arms around his neck, lifting my face. "I can do that."

I'm surprised when his mouth is infinitely gentle on mine. Not sure what I was expecting—hunger, or frustration, or maybe both—but not the tenderness he is showing me. His eyes are haunted when he lifts his head and kisses the tip of my nose.

"Come sit down," I invite him, but he shakes his head.

"I don't want to sit down. What I want to do is take you to bed and make love to you," he says, his eyes filled with regret. "But with just a few hours to get some sleep before getting back to the search, I wouldn't be doing our first time together justice. I'll need time for that and I'm dead on my feet." He winces at his own choice of words. "I should go."

The thought of him driving home to an empty house doesn't sit well. "Stay here," I offer, getting up off the couch. "Head on upstairs, I'm just going to lock up and take care of the lights." I don't wait for an answer and head for the kitchen to put the last few things in the dishwasher before turning it on. By the time I turn around, he's no longer there.

I can't even imagine dealing with the most depraved aspects of society every day then coming home to try and instill morals and values in a child you're raising on your own. So many things I've come to learn about

Dylan, in the past few months, have not only made the eight-year gap disappear, but have slowly eroded any misgivings I've had about letting another man in.

My judgment hasn't exactly been the greatest, but I don't think I'm making a mistake letting Dylan in.

Throwing the deadbolt on the front door and turning off the hall light, I head upstairs.

He's already in bed, just the light on the nightstand left on. His clothes are tossed on the ladder-back chair, in front of the antique dressing table I bought at a garage sale and fixed up; the only nice piece of furniture in my bedroom. The rest is functional at best; an old dresser with half the handles missing off the drawers, a box spring and mattress on the floor serve as my bed, and a cheap metal Walmart side table is my nightstand.

I pull one of my nightshirts from the dresser and slip into the bathroom where I quickly change, brush my teeth, and wash my face, before walking out.

Dylan hasn't moved, he looks asleep, but when I turn off the lamp and slip under the covers, he immediately turns toward me. A strong arm snakes around my middle and pulls me snug with my back to his front. He tangles his legs with mine and pins my body to the mattress. His face burrows in my hair and I hear him let out a deep sigh. "Thank you," he mumbles, and within seconds his breathing deepens.

The hard body pressed against me is causing a hot ache between my legs, so it takes me a little longer to drift off.

I wake up when Dylan leaves the bed.

A quick glance at the alarm clock tells me it's just after four. A little over three and a half hours of sleep. *Ugh.*

I hear the toilet flush and then the shower turn on.

Dylan, naked in my shower.

My thighs rub together restlessly before I finally throw back the covers and swing my legs over the side. I should probably get some coffee going, toast him a bagel, so he doesn't have to start what's probably going to be another tough day on an empty stomach.

I get up, aiming for the door when I sneak a glance at the bathroom. The door is left open a crack, and I can see his vague outline behind the condensed glass shower doors.

So fucking tempting.

Making a split-second decision, I head downstairs. I get a pot of coffee going, pull a couple of bagels from the freezer—leaving them to defrost—before rushing back up.

"Oomph…"

I'm lifted off my feet the moment I enter the bedroom and tossed unceremoniously on the bed. Dylan's still wet body lands on mine.

"Where'd you go?" he rumbles, running his nose along mine.

"Jesus, you scared me." I'm still catching my breath, but my hands are already exploring the damp skin of his back. "I have coffee started, was going to toast some bagels."

He brushes impatiently at the wet hair dropping over his eyes. "You didn't have to do that." The hand that was at his hair now cups my face, his eyes on my mouth, thumb stroking along my bottom lip.

"Can't let you go on an empty stomach," I share, voice hoarse with arousal at that simple touch.

His hand travels down, over my throat brushing down between my breasts. My heart is racing against his palm.

"I was going for a different kind of breakfast." His eyes follow his hand trailing down to the hem of my nightshirt.

"Dylan…"

"Off, Sweetheart."

He tugs the material from under my hips and works it up over my breasts. I've barely lifted my arms when the shirt is whipped off and tossed blindly next to the bed. His mouth latches onto my nipple as his hands go to work on my panties.

"I was going to wait for a perfect time," he mumbles, his lips brushing my skin. "With our lives, perfect times don't exist, only opportunities. I'm taking it."

My panties go the route of my shirt and he uses his knees to spread my legs, dropping his pelvis in the V they create. His rigid cock is hot against me, and I instinctively pull a knee up to his hip, hooking my heel around the back of his leg. My hands slide down over the taut muscle of his ass, holding him in place as I tilt my hips.

"Condom." Again it's Dylan who has to remind me.

"Please don't stop…"

"Two seconds."

Before I know what's happening, he's off the bed and digging through his jeans pockets. His backside is phenomenal, when he turns the front only gets better. He stops at the foot of the bed, looking down at me as he rips at the foil with his teeth. The walls of my pussy contract at the sight and my legs spread wider in invitation.

"*Fuck*, so beautiful," he growls, nostrils flaring as he manages to roll on the condom blindly and puts a knee on the mattress. There's not a doubt in my mind he means that. No way a man could look at me the way he is and not mean it. I welcome the weight of his body and instinctively wrap my limbs around him. "Look at me, Sweetheart."

My eyes drift up to his, blowing out shallow breaths as I feel him line up his cock to my entrance.

"Please…ahhh…" The groan escapes me when the broad crown pushes inside.

"Eyes open, baby," he urges when they flutter shut. "I need you to know it's me inside you."

I force them open and look into eyes that are almost black with heat. Burning, like the stretch of my body to accommodate his girth as he slides deep.

As his hips set a rhythm, I feel full to the brim: with him, with emotions that should scare me, but don't. I can see every one of them reflected in his eyes. Time is endless there.

There's almost no room to breathe as the force of

his hips drives his cock impossibly deeper. It doesn't take long for me to stop breathing altogether when the world splinters apart, and Dylan swallows my cry with his mouth.

A few moments later, I do the same with the deep guttural groan as he jerks in my arms.

DYLAN

"Cream cheese?"

"Sure."

I watch as Marya putters around her kitchen in the same nightshirt I stripped off her, just half an hour ago. I'd rather she be naked, but I guess with a houseful of boys, that's not a viable option. Too bad.

More regrettable is I have a few things I want to talk to her about before I head back to the office. A talk I'm afraid will wipe that little satisfied smile from her lips.

"Sweetheart…"

"Yeah?" She turns around and slides a plate in front of me with a bagel and a bunch of grapes. I have to bite down a grin. She's in mom-mode.

"Grab your coffee and come sit with me, okay? Few things we need to discuss before I head out."

There goes the little smile. Shit.

"What?"

She takes the stool beside mine, wrapping her arms around herself. Bracing. I turn her to face me, and bracket her knees with mine, resting my hands on her thighs.

"A lot happened yesterday," I start, looking her in the eye. "Some of it I want you to be aware of, because it impacts you and the boys." I can feel her body jerk in response and add some pressure to keep her in her seat. "For a few reasons. One being that we're looking into Jeremy Berger's whereabouts. We only have Harry's word he was there, but the coincidence is enough we need to dig into it. It means at some point today, Damian will be here to ask a few questions of the boys about any contact with their father."

"Will you be there too?" Her voice sounds small.

"I can't make that promise, but I'll do my best," I reassure her as best I can. "There are a lot of moving pieces in this investigation, though. We're all on our toes." She nods her understanding.

"That's one lead we're looking into. Another is that we discovered both Seth and Thomas were...are..." I shake my head, reminding myself that Thomas could still be alive. "They're part of the same *Fortnite* group Max and Liam are. Now that doesn't have to mean anything," I quickly add, noting Marya's sharp inhale. "But it's something we need to look into."

"I'm confiscating all their game systems," she blurts out, two red spots high on her cheeks, and fire in her eyes.

"Sweetheart, I get your reaction, but you've already unplugged your router, so they won't be able to go online. Which reminds me, I should take that router with me, and if you don't mind, Liam's PS4. I picked up Max's yesterday. There may be useful information Jasper can pull from those."

Without saying anything, she pushes my hands aside and slides off her stool, heading straight for the cupboard over the kitchen to retrieve the router she stored there. "That's one," she bites off, setting it on the counter in front of me before turning toward the basement. A minute later she's back, carrying a game system and setting it next to the router. "And that's two. I wish you'd take them all."

I pull her between my legs and wrap my arms around the small of her back. "Seeing as it would be best if you guys stay here—indoors—for now, those systems may come in handy to keep them occupied."

"Liam will be pissed his is gone."

"I'm sure if you explain that it may help find Thomas, he won't be so upset." The reminder there's a boy out there missing deepens the shadows on her face.

"We're supposed to go to Mom's for dinner."

"Ask your mother to come here instead."

"I can do that," she agrees without a fuss.

"Good." I drop my mouth to hers for a soft kiss. "You should also know that at this time we can't get a bead on Jeremy's whereabouts, which is partly why I'd feel better if you stayed here."

"Do you think my boys are in danger?"

I tighten my hold on her. "I think every parent should be on alert right now," I respond without really answering her question, but Marya is smart enough to know the answer already.

It eats at my gut that I have to leave her with this—I'd rather she take the memory of the best fucking half hour of my life into her day—but she should be aware. I don't want anything else blindsiding her.

"I've gotta go."

"I know." She grabs my shirt and drops her head to my chest.

"I don't wanna go."

"I know that too," she mumbles there.

"Okay if I keep your key?" I stroke a hand over her tangled hair as she lifts her face, a small smile tugging at her lips.

"Yeah."

I bend down for a kiss. "I'll be in touch."

"Okay."

She reluctantly lets go of my shirt and I grab the electronics off the counter, tucking them under my arm. "Walk me to the door, Sweetheart." I turn to her in the small hallway. "Lock the door behind me, okay?" She nods. "And try to get some more sleep." She rolls her eyes at that, making me grin. "Now kiss me."

Her hands wrap around my neck as she lifts up on her toes, and her lips find mine. Soft, sweet, and not nearly enough to last me through the day.

"Be careful out there," she whispers, before letting me go.

I wink, pull the door open, and step outside.

"Marya?" I partially turn my body to her. "It wasn't nearly enough time—that would've required an entire weekend of exploring you. Still, I've never had better."

CHAPTER 19

MARYA

Perhaps a little late—given that Dylan's hands were all over me this morning—but it feels good to get rid of the stubble I've been cultivating for a few weeks.

Life gets busy and with three kids, grooming is definitely not a priority.

Not that Dylan seemed to care one way or another. It didn't put a damper in the way his body responded to mine.

I run my hand over the now smooth skin of my leg and lift the other one on the edge of the bathtub.

Of course I hadn't been able to go back to sleep after he left and instead decided to take the few hours before the kids inevitably roll out of bed looking for sustenance, to treat myself to a bath.

My body still primed from this morning's activities and Dylan's parting words, I distracted myself with my razor.

"Mom?"

Shit.

I toss the razor on the ledge and grab my washcloth to press over the fresh cut on my leg. Figures.

"Yeah, Bub?"

"I had a bad dream."

Poor Harry, sensitive little boy that he is, he often processes things in his sleep, resulting in occasional nightmares. I should've expected this.

"Give me a minute, okay, baby?" I hesitate briefly before adding, "Go ahead and get in my bed. I'm just getting out of the tub."

That's often all he needs: crawl in bed with me, tell me about the dream so he could let it go, and then he'd often fall right back to sleep. For a moment, I considered telling him to get back to his own bed, given what took place in mine this morning, but that's not what we'd normally do. Whatever happens between Dylan and me will have to find its place in my routine with the boys.

This is real—this is life with kids—you just deal with the next thing that comes along.

I quickly dry off, slap a Band-Aid on my shin, and put on my ratty robe. Harry is curled up under my covers, his eyes on the bathroom door, when I open it.

"Two secs, Bub." I grab clean undies, a T-shirt, some yoga pants, and dart back into the bathroom. I used to have no problem changing in front of the kids when they were much smaller, but these days I'm a little more careful.

"Wanna tell me?" I ask as my boy snuggles up against me.

"It's stupid," he mumbles.

"Not stupid if it freaked you out, Harry."

I wait him out, letting him come to his own decision. "It was weird," he finally speaks. "One minute I was under our Jeep, and then suddenly I was in a box. I was yelling 'til my throat hurt and I kept banging against the top, but no one could hear me so I stopped. Then suddenly you were there, pulling me out of the box. That's when I woke up."

"That sounds pretty scary to me. I hate dreams like that, where you're helpless."

"You get dreams too?"

I bark out a laugh, I've had more than my share, although not as much as when I was a kid.

"Not as many as I used to, but yes, baby, I get dreams too."

"Next time you have a dream, you can come tell me," my baby says, and a lump forms in my throat.

"Thanks, Bub," I whisper, kissing his mop of hair.

"I'll go get the kids."

Damian had arrived twenty minutes ago, with a female agent in tow. Damian introduced her as Agent Linden, on temporary assignment with the La Plata office. Her smile was wide, but it made me feel uncomfortable.

Dylan had sent me a message to expect them. He was apparently on his way to Montrose, and even though he didn't specify why, I'm not an idiot. I know they're looking into Jeremy.

I'd offered the agents coffee, and we settled in the kitchen, where Damian proceeded to ask me questions about Jeremy. Much of it I'm sure he already knew from either Luna or Dylan.

"Do you mind if I go downstairs?" Damian asks carefully. "It's possible they'll open up easier without you around. May hold back if they think it'll upset you."

I don't like it but I nod my understanding. It's not like he's not been here plenty of times before. After all, he's my best friend's husband. I know I can trust him. "Sure," I quickly agree, but the moment he disappears, I notice the chill in the kitchen.

I slowly turn to Agent Linden. The smile is back on her face but it doesn't reach her eyes.

"Would you like some more coffee?" I offer just to break the tension.

"Please." She slides her mug toward me.

"Would you care for something to eat? It's almost lunchtime, I have some cinnamon rolls left I made this morning." I know I'm babbling as I pour her coffee, but I feel her eyes follow my every move.

She doesn't say anything until I turn and hand her the full mug back. "No thanks. I'm careful what I put in my body," she says in a saccharine sweet tone, but the up and down look she affords me betrays her true intent.

I'm not one to put a lot of stock into what other women think of me, but for some reason from this woman it burrows under my skin, which is why the next words out of my mouth are sharp.

"I bet you do."

Her head tilts to the side and her eyes narrow. "You know…it's funny, when Dylan first mentioned you, I wasn't expecting someone…" She gives me another head to toe once-over, and I find myself straightening my back. "…quite as mature."

I try not to let the sting show and leave a blank mask on my face. "Maturity is unavoidable with three sons," I share, layering on the fake friendliness thick.

I have no fucking idea why this woman is trying to push my buttons, which I have no doubt she means to do. I just wish I knew why.

"I'm sure it is. All I meant to say is I've known Dylan for quite some time, and it just surprises me he'd elect to be with someone with baggage. Three of them, no less." The chuckle that follows is as malicious as the words.

"My children are *not* baggage," I hiss at her. "And if you know Dylan at all, you'd know he has a son of his own he dotes on."

Too late I notice the satisfied smirk on her face. "Oh, surely I didn't mean to imply they are, and I adore little Max." Another sharp knife to the gut with the familiarity. I'm starting to see a picture form and it has me off-balance. "All I meant to say is, I know from first-hand experience, he likes to keep life uncomplicated and more kids don't play into that."

She's been in his bed. I suspected it when I got a taste of her attitude, now I know it for a fact. Not a pleasant sensation, to be blindsided like that.

I suspect this is a case of a disgruntled ex-lover, but I'm surprised Dylan didn't think to give me a heads-up about her when he was laying everything else on me this morning. I'm not about to indulge the woman in her obvious game though and turn my attention to the dishwasher that needs emptying.

"Of course," she starts, and I know right off the bat this is her knockout punch, so I brace. "I would know, since he demanded I abort his child."

The two glasses slip from my hand, shattering on the floor.

DYLAN

"Wanna tell me what crawled up your ass?"

I throw an angry glare at Luna beside me.

"Nothing," I bite off.

"Bullshit. You've been giving off wounded bear vibes since we got on the road. What gives?"

I know Luna; she's like a goddamn bulldog once she gets hold of something. I know she's not going to let go unless I give her something.

"I'm involved with Marya."

"Tell me something new," she quips, but I'm not amused.

"Should've been me heading over there with Gomez."

I can feel her eyes on me but keep mine firmly on the road ahead. "I would think that's a pretty good reason for you not to be there."

"Yeah? You think it's better he brings Linden?"

"Look," she says in a softer tone. "I gather you have a history with her." She quickly raises her hand to silence me. "And no, no one told me. It was pretty obvious from the way she looks at you, and the way you freeze over when the two of you are in one room. I gather it didn't end well?"

I snort at the understatement. "Fucking right it didn't. She shouldn't be anywhere near Marya."

"You know we don't have the luxury to pick and choose right now, Dylan," she scolds me. "There's a kid missing and we're scrambling to grab hold of a good lead, so we can get that boy back to his family." I know she's right, which is the only reason I didn't risk my job for insubordination when I discovered she'd be heading out with Damian. Doesn't mean I have to like it. "Besides," Luna continues, "Damian will make sure she stays professional."

"I hope so, I haven't had a chance to share all of my history with Marya yet," I confess.

It's myself I'm most angry with. I should've fucking made the time, but there's already so much crap flying around, I thought I'd spare her the shit between Toni and me for now.

"Why the hell not?" I can hear the disapproval in

her voice and it doesn't sit well.

"Maybe because ever since this thing between us started, there hasn't been a moment's peace to even take her out on a proper date, let alone do a full dissection of my accumulated fuck-ups over the years."

Her hand lands on my arm for a squeeze. "I'm sure it'll be fine," she says, but she doesn't seem too sure.

The morning started out in the best possible way. How the hell did it get so fucked up?

—————

"Please call me Sylvia."

The blonde leads us from an opulent foyer with marble floors, a crystal chandelier, and an oak stairway curving to a second floor, to an equally swank sitting room. I can't call it a living room; the place looks more like a museum. Must've been a hard transition for Jeremy to go from this to a cabin in the woods.

Even more surprising is the presence of an older gentleman, already seated in the room. A familiar older gentleman. Connor Keswick. I just read something the other day about Contechs, his electronics manufacturing company, opening a third plant near Austin, Texas. I saw the name in the background check on Jeremy's wife, but I didn't make the connection to Contechs until just now. His picture's been in the news.

"This is my daddy, Connor Keswick. These are Agents Barnes and...I'm sorry," she turns to Luna,

"I'm afraid your name escapes me."

"Agent Roosberg," I answer for her, noting Keswick doesn't bother getting up.

"Of course. Please have a seat." She points at the ugly Louis XV-style bench on carved legs.

The seat is much lower than the other chairs in the room, and designed for discomfort. I'm well aware it's supposed to make us feel off-balance and inferior. At my height, though, I'm still able to look Keswick straight in the eye, something that appears to irritate the man. Good.

I let Luna handle the questioning of the daughter, while I am engaged in a silent standoff with the father. He's so bent on proving me inferior; he forgets to pay attention to the questions Luna fires off, until she asks about the assault Sylvia reported.

"You can read all of that in the police report," he suddenly interrupts. "My little girl's been through enough."

"Not a problem," I butt in, with what I hope is a friendly smile. "In that case, perhaps you could help us with just a few more questions."

The man didn't get where he is if he was stupid. He hears the challenge. "Of course. Pumpkin, why don't you go check on Amelia? I will see the agents out."

"Daddy?" The woman looks surprised. "But Alba is upstairs with—"

"Sylvia." Keswick's voice snaps like a whip and has the woman on her feet in an instant.

"Of course. Pleasure to meet you." She nods

awkwardly in our direction before leaving the room.

"You had questions?"

"Just a few," Luna takes over. "Your daughter mentions Jeremy works for your company? Strange, because we weren't able to find a record of that anywhere. In fact, from what we can tell, he hasn't reported employment income to the IRS in the past five years."

The man's face looks like he just ate something unpleasant. "It was my daughter's idea. The man was a useless waste of space from the start, but my little girl had her eyes set on him. I gave him a job, just so he'd have something to do, but he failed at that too. The only thing he ever did right is that little girl upstairs. She's a treasure."

"Is that her?" I ask, getting up when I spot a picture on the fireplace mantel. I walk over and pick up the frame. A beautiful little girl with blonde ringlets, looking more like a doll than a living, breathing child. The frame is pulled from my hands and placed back in its original spot on the mantel.

"That's Amelia. Now, if there is nothing else…" He stays on his feet, a clear indication he considers this interview over.

I look at Luna, who shrugs and gets up as well. "Is there a good number to call you, Mr. Keswick? Should we have some more questions?"

He glares at her, but pulls a golden business card holder from the inside pocket of his jacket. Instead of handing it to her, he drops it on the coffee table for her to pick up. The prick.

"Daddy is an asswipe," Luna comments when we get back in the SUV.

"Won't get an argument from me. Worth a pretty penny, though," I bring up, starting the Expedition.

"No kidding," Luna agrees. "From what I gather, Jeremy Berger was a kept man. Very generous of Keswick."

"I get the impression that's more about keeping his little girl happy. According to the records, the woman is thirty-four years old. She looks ten years younger, and I bet there's a plastic surgeon somewhere who made a mint on it."

"There's no record of that," Luna points out and I raise an eyebrow at her.

"Doesn't need to be if you have enough money."

"True enough. Are we hitting up the police station next?"

"That's the plan."

Luna's phone rings in her pocket.

"You've got Luna—Okay. Yes, okay—Right away."

"Who was that?" I ask when she tucks the phone away. A muscle ticks in her jaw. Something is up.

"Damian. Can you pull over for a minute?"

I'm puzzled at the request, but do as she asks. The moment I put the SUV in park, she gets out and rounds the hood opening the driver's side door.

"Scoot over."

"Why?"

"Just move over, okay? I'm driving."

"What did Damian want?"

"I'll tell you if you move your ass into the passenger

seat."

I have a very uneasy feeling, so I move over. "Luna? What the hell is going on?"

"Buckle up," she orders, waiting for me to finish the task before she pulls away from the shoulder making a sudden U-turn that throws me into the door.

"Are you nuts?"

"We're heading back to Durango. There's a situation."

"A situation," I repeat, my eyes on her, and I catch a quick worried glance in my direction.

"Keep your shit together."

That doesn't make me feel much better, but I nod in agreement.

"Damian called from Mercy Hospital."

CHAPTER 20

DYLAN

"I'll drop you off at the door."

I'm relieved to see Mercy Hospital. *Finally*. That was the longest fucking two and a half hours of my life.

Luna had moved at a fair clip, but there's only so much you can do when you get stuck behind a big Mack truck on a mountain road.

I was able to get some information from Damian while we were on the road. There'd apparently been an accident that left a large shard of glass embedded in Marya's knee. Details were still a little vague with the connection cutting in and out; the mountains are notorious for pockets of dead air. I finally connected with the office, but Jasper wasn't able to provide much more other than she was being looked after and the boys were in good hands.

I fucking hope that doesn't mean they were left with Toni.

Luna pulls into the hospital drive and stops in front of the main doors.

"Go, I'll park and catch up with you."

"Thanks," I manage to mumble as I exit the car.

I aim for the gray-haired lady behind the information desk and give her Marya's name, when I hear my own called. Turning to the sound, I see Theo running toward me.

"We were waiting for you," he says a little breathlessly when he gets close. I'm startled when he walks right into me, giving me an awkward little man hug. It takes me a second to clue in, but the moment he lets go of me, I hook my arm around his neck and pull him close.

"Thanks, kiddo."

Over his head I see Kerry approaching, Dante perched on her hip. My arm still hooked around Theo's neck, I start moving us toward her.

"Where's Marya?" I ask when we get close.

"There was some damage to her knee. The glass cut clear through the patellar tendon. They took her into surgery for repairs twenty minutes ago."

I take a deep breath in before looking behind her. "Where are the other kids?"

"I picked up Lydia on my way in. They're all in the surgical waiting room. We were waiting for you."

I follow her down a corridor and into a small room, Theo still pressed to my side. The moment I step inside, Harry—who's sitting cuddled up to his grandma—shoots up and barrels toward me, planting his face in my stomach. I wrap my free arm around him and look up to find Lydia taking in the scene, a faint smile on her face, Liam quiet beside her.

"Mom got cut," Harry volunteers, his head tilted back so he can look at me.

"I heard."

"There was blood *everywhere*," he adds, a shiver running through his little body.

I almost shiver myself at the thought of Marya bleeding, but I force a smile on my face. "We have a lot of blood in our body, did you know that?" He shakes his head, eyes big. "We do, and we can afford to lose a little."

"Come on, boys. Give Dylan a chance to sit down," Lydia suggests.

Harry darts back to his grandmother, but Theo stays beside me when I walk up to Liam, who hasn't moved yet. I hunch down so I'm face-to-face and put a hand on his knee. His worried eyes come up. "Your mom will be fine, Liam."

"She was crying," he says softly.

"I bet she was. That probably hurt really bad."

"Yeah." The single syllable sounds heavy with the weight of the world.

"Your mom is one of the toughest women I know, kid. She'll be back to bossing you guys around before you know it." I take in the slightest twitch of his mouth and get to my feet. "Where's Damian?" I ask Kerry.

"He had some stuff to tend to in the office."

Of course, an eleven-year-old boy is still missing.

MARYA

"I'm fine, Bub."

I stroke my hand over Harry's head. He crawled into bed beside me, right after the other two boys went with Kerry and Mom to the cafeteria to grab something to eat—apparently it's already past seven. Harry wouldn't leave my side.

Neither would Dylan.

I sneak a peek at him. He's still leaning with his shoulder against the doorpost. The same position he took up after I turned away from his kiss. The question is still in his eyes, but this is not a discussion I'm willing to get into with my child in the room.

I'm torn, I'm tired, and I'm sore, and even though I realize that woman was playing me, the whole scene left me confused.

I was so thrown by her claim, I wasn't thinking straight. The glasses broke and I immediately reacted, dropping down to clean it up only to drive a shard up my knee. The pain had been instant.

So stupid. One of those moments when you want to go back, even just a fraction of a second, so you can change the outcome. What was worse, I burst into tears right in front of that bitch. That was the ultimate humiliation.

All I could think about on the way to the hospital,

and while we were waiting for a doctor, had been Damian's reaction when he came storming up the stairs. "What the fuck did you do?" he'd fired off at Agent Linden the moment he saw me on the floor. It had struck me as odd he'd immediately assumed she had anything to do with it. Unless...he knew something. That would imply there could be at least some truth to the things she said.

This morning I trusted him enough to give him all of me, and within hours that trust was shaken to the core. Whether there was cause or not, what does that say about me?

"Sweetheart, I met her in—"

I stop him with a raised hand. I can hear regret in his voice and I believe it, but right now I can't get into this. Not when I'm trying to figure out how in hell I'm going to look after three boys, let alone myself for the next six weeks at least. I'm supposed to keep my leg elevated for a week, then my knee immobilized in a brace for at least another until I see the orthopedic surgeon for my follow-up. No driving for a minimum of six and three months anticipated until I return to normal activities.

It's impossible. I could probably return to the bookstore in a few weeks, if I was careful, but my cleaning days are over for the foreseeable future.

I'm fucked.

Dylan pushes off the wall when a hot tear rolls from the corner of my eye, soaking into my pillow, just as the door opens and the surgeon walks in followed by one of the nurses.

"Mrs. Berger, how are you feeling?"

"*Miz* Berger," I hear Dylan rumble behind the doctor before I have a chance to correct him.

"Of course," the man says with an apologetic grin.

"Sore, but I guess that's expected," I tell him honestly, as Harry lifts his head from my shoulder.

"Can we take Mom home?"

"We'd like to keep her overnight, but you should be able to have your mom home tomorrow. Is that a plan?"

"I guess," Harry grumbles, but the kind doctor just smiles.

"You'll have to promise to look after her, though, can you do that?"

"I'm almost nine," my youngest claims, as if that should answer the question. Never mind his birthday isn't until next January.

"Well, then, I guess that settles it." Still smiling he turns to me. "Don't hesitate taking your medication, you'll want to keep the pain in check. A physical therapist will be by in the morning to help you on your feet. I'll pop in during rounds at about eleven, check in on you, and barring any issues, we'll have you out of here around lunchtime."

With the doctor gone, the nurse approaches the bed with a small plastic cup.

"Your meds," she explains, handing me the pills and the cup of water from the night table. "I'll give you ten more minutes to say goodbye to your visitors, and then I suggest you get some sleep."

Not long after she leaves, Mom and Kerry are back with the boys. My eyes are already drooping when we're working out logistics. Dylan will drive the boys and Mom to pick up their stuff for school tomorrow and drop them at Mom's place.

I hear Kerry's offer to pick me up from the hospital and Dylan jumping in.

"I've got her, you'll have your hands full with the bookstore."

I can't bring up the energy to protest, and the last thing I'm aware of is Dylan's voice close to my ear.

"Rest up, Sweetheart, we have a lot to talk about tomorrow."

DYLAN

The boys are subdued in the back seat.

Unfortunately, there'd been no way to avoid the blood still on the kitchen floor and cupboards. I'll have to come back and clean that up later. I hustled the kids to grab what they need for tonight and tomorrow, and got them, their overnight bags, and backpacks in the Bronco as quickly as possible.

Luna had followed me into the hospital to get an update and a chance to give Damian a report, but then she left soon after discovering he'd gone back to the office. At some point during the afternoon, while we were still waiting for Marya to come out of surgery, Keith Blackfoot, a detective with the Durango PD and a friend, walked in. The keys to my truck I'd left on my desk earlier, dangling from his fingers.

He hadn't stayed long and asked me to walk him outside.

"That woman has had enough bad luck to last her a couple of lifetimes," he remarked, and my hair immediately stood on end, expecting another lecture like the one Damian treated me with, but then he surprised me. "Can't tell you how happy I am to see her luck has finally turned. About time she has a good man at her back." With that he clapped me on the shoulder and got into the patrol unit waiting for him out front.

The good feeling I was left with lasted until I saw the look in Marya's eyes when she caught sight of me walking into her hospital room. She wasn't feeling lucky at all.

"I'll help you get your stuff inside," I announce, pulling up to Lydia's place.

I grab a few of the boys' bags from the back and follow Lydia into the small bungalow. "The kids have bunks and their own little setup in the spare bedroom," she explains when she catches me taking in the small space. It's like she read my thoughts, because I had been wondering where she'd stick the three boys. "It's not the first time the boys stay over here, I just thought it might distract them from the fact their mother is in the hospital."

And, judging by Lydia's wet eyes, her as well. The boys all in one room and a senior's community wouldn't necessarily be the obvious place Jeremy might look for them.

I would've offered keep them for the night, but there's not a lot of time to take care of things before Marya comes home. Not the least of which is finding Thomas.

I leave Lydia with my number and give her a hug. Harry gives me a quick squeeze with his arms around my waist and Theo—a little more composed now that he knows his mom will be fine—opts for a fist bump. I hold my fist up for Liam as well, who seems to hesitate for a minute, before he bumps it too.

"Catch you guys tomorrow," I tell them before pulling the door shut behind me.

"What did you say to her?"

I stop in front of her desk, ignoring the other eyes I'm sure are on me.

"I don't...I didn't—"

"Cut the bull, Toni."

"Barnes..." The warning comes from Jasper. "Damian was there," he reminds me.

"Actually," I hear from behind me, and I turn to find my boss leaning against the doorpost of the conference room, not looking at me, but at Toni. "I was in the basement with the kids."

"You left her alone with Marya?"

Now his eyes are on me, dark and angry. "Yes, I did. My main concern is to find an eleven-year-old kid, who is out there being subjected to God knows what kind of atrocities. If he's even still alive!" I can count the times I've heard him raise his voice before on one hand, so I know he's good and pissed. So the fuck am I, but he makes a good point. I open my mouth, but I don't get the chance to tell him that. "Even with half the Durango PD helping us out, we've got nothing. It's like fucking looking for a needle in a haystack," he continues before turning to Toni. "The last thing I should be worrying about is some fucking trainee agent, with her own goddamn agenda, making it even harder. Do you hear me, Agent Linden?"

Her eyes dart back and forth between Damian and me. "Yes, sir, but I was only—"

"No buts. No excuses. I don't have time to dig through all the crap you're about to feed me. I have a young boy to find, and right now you are a distraction to this investigation and a disruption to my team. You're dismissed until further notice. The rest of you, get in here." He turns on his heel and disappears into the conference room.

Toni looks like she's had the wind knocked from her, but I can't find it in me to care.

"Go ahead," Jasper suggests, getting up. "I'll take care of things here."

I still want to know what it is she said to Marya that had her do a one-eighty from this morning, but Luna grabs my arm.

"Let's go, big guy, the boss is waiting."

It's almost midnight when Damian sends us home to get some rest. I get in my Bronco and am tempted to stop by my folks to check in on Max—I haven't seen him since yesterday morning—but I know he's in good hands, and I don't want to wake the whole household.

Instead I head home, going over the case in my mind.

We still don't know where the boy is, or who has him. Damian never had a chance to get Liam to talk, and Luna and I didn't bring back a solid lead from Montrose, but Jasper spent his day pulling files and IP addresses, sorting through chats and comparing groups and nicknames, and came up with something useful after talking to the tech specialist at the Farmington office.

Whoever has the handle, *SoccerLord,* was in touch through a peer-to-peer connection with both abducted boys, not long before they disappeared. The only problem is this guy's signal appears to move around a lot. Pings from at least twenty-seven different IP addresses, originating from the library in Farmington to a Starbucks in Hermosa.

A lot of fucking places for us to hit up tomorrow.

Luna pointed out he may have played on some common vulnerabilities in those two boys. Both kids had troubles at home. Seth's mother had a new boyfriend he wasn't too happy about, and as we found out from the uncle, the McKinleys are on the verge of a divorce.

It's not nearly enough, but at least it's something we can put our teeth into. We know whoever *SoccerLord* is has a type.

Unfortunately Liam ticks all those criteria as well.

CHAPTER 21

MARYA

"Put me down."

Dylan ignores me as he lifts me from the wheelchair and deposits me in the passenger seat of his truck, before tossing the crutches on the back seat. The nurse who accompanied us to the door titters as she turns back inside with the empty chair. I, however, am not amused.

I'm also cranky. They keep you overnight so you can supposedly 'rest' and then poke you awake all night long to make sure you're comfortable. Clearly, I never got much sleep.

My leg is sore as hell too. The whole damn leg, not just my knee.

I'm not in a good mood. At all.

To make it worse I had to wait half an hour for Dylan to get here after the nurse handed me my discharge papers. Which is another thing to be pissed at Dylan for. I have quite a list going.

"I need some decent coffee," I announce snippily when he pulls the Bronco out in traffic. "And a Danish," I add. "Maybe two. Breakfast was a piece of toasted cardboard with a boiled egg that oozed out the moment I cracked the damn shell. How they figure a person can heal without proper food, I have no idea." Yes, I'm also hangry.

Dylan stays silent through my annoyed rant; his eyes focused on the road ahead, his mouth a straight line. It's like he doesn't hear me at all.

With a huff, I cross my arms over my chest and turn my head to look out the side window, mentally scanning the contents of my fridge at home which— if memory serves—holds no more than some wilted lettuce, a few stray string cheese, and a half full jar of salsa. I never had a chance to get groceries this weekend.

He makes a sudden left turn into the drive-thru for Durango Joe's and stops at the window.

"One large latte with one sugar, one large black, two Danish, six cinnamon rolls, and a bran muffin," I hear him order.

It's the first time he's said anything since his, "Hey," when he walked into the hospital room.

Truth be told, I may have complained he was late. A little. In my defense, it really sucks to be cooped up in a hospital room, unable to sleep, with a head full of questions and no one to talk to. Add to that a throbbing leg, lukewarm tea, cardboard toast, and liquid egg for breakfast; you can see why I might not have been overly gracious.

"You eat bran muffins?" I'm struggling with my attempt to be civil, and that's all I can come up with.

"That's for you."

"I don't eat those."

He throws me a look and for the first time I see his mouth twitch. "You will. Trust me. After surgery, lack of physical activity for the foreseeable future, and eating shit like Danish, you'll be glad for that bran muffin."

My mouth falls open in disbelief when I clue in. "Are we seriously discussing my bowel movements?"

"I was in the hospital for a week a while back, and I can tell you that getting backed up is worse than getting shot."

I clap my hands over my ears. "Good Lord Almighty, that's too much information." When he catches me glaring at him, a grin breaks through. "I thought boys grew out of their poop fascination somewhere around fourteen. At least that's what I've been promising myself."

The glass slides back and a tray with the coffee is passed through the window. I snatch it from Dylan's hands, identify my cup and take a swig, scalding my mouth.

"Can you hold on to these?" Dylan holds up two paper bags.

I quickly set the coffees in the cupholders and take

them from him, taking a peek inside. When he merges back onto the road, I grab a Danish, ignoring the bran muffin the girl stuffed in the same bag. It's almost sacrilegious.

"What's with the cinnamon rolls?" I ask while masticating a hunk of my pastry.

"The boys. After school."

Okay, that's sweet. In fact, despite the fact Dylan's investment in the regularity of my bowel movements is slightly weird, the muffin is a sweet touch too. I could almost forget I'm pissed at him.

I feel a ton better by the time we pull up in my driveway.

"Stay put," Dylan orders as he slides from the truck. I watch him jog to the front door, unlock and open it wide, before heading back this way.

I don't even protest this time when he lifts me out of my seat and carries me straight inside, setting me down on the couch, my leg elevated on a pillow. I notice a strong smell of bleach. When he returns with the coffees and the bags, I ask him about it.

"Was someone here? I smell bleach."

He hands me my coffee and sits down on the coffee table across from me. "Cleaned the kitchen."

"You cleaned my kitchen?"

He shrugs it off. "Got busy this morning, so I didn't get to it until right before I had to pick you up. Took a bit of scrubbing by then."

So the reason he'd been a little late was because he was on *my* kitchen floor, scrubbing off *my* blood with bleach, so *I* could come home to a clean house.

"I'm sorry I was a bitch this morning," I apologize immediately, but he shrugs that off too.

"Been a trying twenty-four hours."

I snort. "No shit, Sherlock."

"We need to talk," he says seriously, and my mellower mood evaporates as I grab a toss pillow and clutch it to my front like a shield. He doesn't hesitate and wades right in. "I want to know what she said to you."

Immediately my snark is back. The best defense against getting hurt is to land the first blow. I don't hesitate.

"Who? Your ex? The woman you work with? The same one who was in *my* kitchen yesterday, making sure I knew she'd been in your bed? At least I fucking hope it's past tense."

I was wrong to think seeing him wince would give me some satisfaction. It doesn't.

"Yes, it fucking is," he hisses, before taking a deep breath in as he runs his hand through his hair. I only now notice the strain on his face. The dark shadows under his eyes and the scruff that's almost grown into a beard over the past days on his chin. "I met her in Denver, a few years ago, when I was there working a case. It was casual. That's all it was supposed to be. She had other ideas. A few weeks ago she showed up here, no longer a cop, but an FBI agent assigned to our office for three months. I don't know how she finagled that, but it was clear early on she has an agenda."

"You didn't tell me." My tone is accusatory. Jealousy is a ridiculous emotion and yet my stomach is churning with it.

"It's not like I've had much opportunity to," he snaps back, before once again taking a deep breath. "Look, I know I should've, but aside from the abductions, dealing with one crisis after another with your douchebag ex, and rarely having any time to ourselves without kids around, there hasn't really been a good moment to bring it up."

This time it's me wincing. "She warned me you didn't like kids to complicate your life. She—"

I don't get to finish my sentence. Dylan is on his feet, and his coffee splatters the wall by the stairs where he pelted it. *"Fucking bitch!"*

I clutch my pillow a little tighter as I watch him stalk back and forth in front of the fireplace, his hands in white-knuckled fists by his side. Suddenly, he stops in front of me; his eyes squinting and a thick vein throbbing on his forehead.

"What. Did. She. Say?"

He enunciates each word with careful control, and although he makes a threatening figure, I instinctively know his anger is not aimed at me.

Still, I keep the pillow in front of me when I answer. "She said when she got pregnant, you made it clear you had no interest in more kids and insisted she get an abortion."

Instead of the explosion I expect, Dylan sinks

down on the coffee table, head bent and his fingers clutching his hair.

When he lifts his eyes, the pain I see reflected there knocks the breath right out of me.

DYLAN

"How could she?"

Marya's voice wobbles as her eyes fill with tears and her fingers curl into the pillow she's been clutching in her lap.

"Fuck if I know. People do fucked-up shit all the time. A lot of the stuff I see in my job is incomprehensible, and I've given up trying to understand their motivation."

She lets go of the pillow and reaches for my hand. "I'm so sorry."

"Not your fault, Sweetheart." I smile at her but she shakes her head.

"I can't believe I allowed her to get under my skin, let her push all the right buttons, when I should've known better. That's what I'm sorry for, that she managed to shake my confidence in the good man I know you are."

Jesus, but that feels good. I lean over and kiss her lightly on the lips. This time she doesn't turn away and that feels fucking great too.

"She played me too, babe. She's good at figuring out weak spots and aims straight for them. She's also a great actress, but she overplayed her hand last night."

"How so?"

I outline the confrontation with Toni in the office last night, resulting in Damian sending her home. It had meant some reshuffling this morning so we'd still have two teams chasing down leads. Luna was hitting all the geographic locations Jasper had been able to connect *SoccerLord* to, with Keith Blackfoot as her backup. They'll be showing Berger's picture we downloaded from the DMV site. Damian and I are visiting as many of the kids in the under-twelve soccer league as we can after school is out. At least those whose names we were able to link up with the online *Fortnite* group. First one on Damian's list is Liam.

"Talked to your mom first thing this morning," I mention and watch her eyebrows lift. "Wanted to warn her about the DPD patrol car parked in front of her house. It's just a precaution," I quickly add when I see alarm on Marya's face. "They'll be at the school and following the boys on the bus home. Until we get a bead on Jeremy anyway."

"Okay."

I'm about to launch into the next thing I need to discuss with her when I hear a key being turned in the door lock and Lydia walks in, her arms full of groceries.

"Hey, Mom, what are you doing here?"

"Coming to look after my daughter, what do you think I'm doing here? Didn't your man tell you?"

I can feel Marya giving me the evil eye.

"Was about to get around to that, Lydia," I tell her mother, who shrugs and makes her way into the kitchen, dumping the bags on the counter.

"Well, never mind me then, I'm just gonna put some things away. Pretend I'm not here."

I bite off a grin, because that would be an impossible feat, but then I turn to Marya and the grin melts from my face.

"Again, precautionary," I explain. "Until you get back on your feet. I'll be here at night; your Mom will be around during the day. And a contact of Jasper's is coming by in a bit to install a security system."

"I can't afford that," she huffs at the suggestion. "I don't even know how I'm gonna keep my kids fed with me being out of commission."

"You don't have to worry about it. It's taken care of."

"What does that mean?"

"It means it's taken care of. Suck it up, buttercup," Lydia, who's clearly been paying close attention, suggests.

"It's important, Marya—as a precaution," I remind her when I see her lips press together. "None of this may be ideal, but we're all trying to do the best we can under the circumstances." The subtle reference there's a lot going on is enough to have her features soften.

"What about Max?"

That quiet question is enough to make me want to declare my undying love for this woman—concerned about my boy—but since I don't have the time to follow through on any such declaration, plus I can feel her mother's eyes burning a hole in my shirt, I curb the urge.

"He'll be okay at my folks' place."

"Or he can stay here too," she suggests. "There's plenty of room."

Oh yeah, I'm not just falling for her; I'm plummeting. "Why don't we see how things go tonight? Damian and I will need to chat with the boys when they get home from school, since Damian didn't get far yesterday. Might be best not to have Max in the mix today."

That seems to settle her and I lean in for a quick kiss before getting up. More chaste than I'd like it to be, but with Lydia looking on, it'll have to do.

I'll welcome the day when I don't have to hold back. When I don't feel the pressure of this case eating at me, or the guilt that inevitably follows a brief moment of happiness.

"I should head back to the office. Take a nap while you can, and I'll see you in a couple of hours."

I bend down and kiss the tip of her nose. I'm about to head out the door when her arm reaches around my neck and pulls me farther down instead. Her eyes lock on mine, but her words are for her mother.

"Mom? Close your eyes."

"Do you know Thomas?"

Liam's head drops even lower at Damian's question.

Damian suggested separating him from his brothers, in hopes he might have an easier time talking—we're in his bedroom—but he's wrapped up tight. Without discussing it beforehand, we've assumed abbreviated 'good cop-bad cop' positions. Damian is standing with his back against the door, and I'm sitting on the small desk chair, pulled up close to Liam who's perched on the edge of the bed.

"Liam," I call him to attention, "We just need some help finding him. You're not in any trouble, but Thomas is. He's been gone for forty-eight hours now."

"But I don't know anything about that. I didn't see anything," he says, lifting his head and looking at me pleadingly.

"I realize that, kiddo, but you know Thomas, am I right?" That earns me a nod.

"Did you know Thomas' handle is *Ace2McTank*?"

Liam's head swings around to Damian, his surprise evident. He didn't know that.

"And that Seth used the tag *MadGoalz*?" I add, hating to see the color drain from the boy's face, but he may have information that could help us find Thomas.

"For real?" His wide eyes come back to me and I see the wheels start turning.

"Yeah, kid. It shocked me too. Not only did you all play in the same soccer league, you've been gaming with those same guys and didn't even know it."

"Do you know who *SoccerLord* is?"

I can see it happen. The moment Damian asks the question, Liam's small body jerks as if hit and he shuts down. *Fuck.*

"Max came to me a few weeks ago." I hope to reach him by sharing maybe more than I should. "Told me someone in the group had made him feel uncomfortable. I was going to look into it when Seth went missing, but I didn't follow through because we were focused on finding him. If I had, we might've been able to stop Thomas from being taken. Maybe." I take in a deep breath, resisting the urge to do a victorious fist-pump when Liam's eyes focus on me. "We need to know all we can about *SoccerLord*, kiddo. And we need your help."

It takes everything out of me not to shake the boy as he wages some internal battle that is visible on his face. Finally he speaks.

"He was nice at first." His voice is barely above a whisper. "I thought he was my age, talking about stuff, you know; soccer, school, fun things to do. Then he started asking about my family, about my brothers and my dad. That's when I started thinking maybe he wasn't my age. Just some of the stuff he'd talk about got weird."

"Can you give us an example?" Damian asks in a surprisingly gentle voice, and I notice he's no longer towering over the boy, but is sitting on the floor with his back against the wall. Putting himself in a position where the kid might feel less threatened.

Liam looks embarrassed but forges on. "Like if I'd ever had naughty dreams...you know..."

"A wet dream?" I offer, vaguely remembering those early stirrings of hormones and curiosity.

"Yeah. I wasn't...I mean...I hadn't. Anyway, he said it was too bad I didn't have my dad to talk to. That he could try and find him. That we could set something up. Meet somewhere. Then the next day he called my house."

"Who did?"

"He said he was my dad. He wanted to see me. It was weird though, he didn't even know I played soccer when I told him my team name, so I hung up."

"You're a smart kid, Liam," I encourage him, trying hard to ignore the fire boiling in my gut.

"Not really," he says, dropping his eyes to his hands fidgeting in his lap. "When I asked *SoccerLord* later if that was him on the phone, he got mad. Said if he found out I'd told anyone about him, he'd hurt *GrootRules*."

"What's *GrootRules*?" Damian asks.

I don't need the confirmation, I already know who he's been protecting.

"That's my brother—Harry."

CHAPTER 22

DYLAN

"That was Ouray."

The way Luna says his name has all eyes turn to her as she walks back into the office.

Despite going balls to the wall these past days, talking to almost every kid we were able to link with both the Four Corners League and the *Fortnite* group. Still none of them had much to add to what Liam had contributed.

Jasper's been using my, Max's, and finally Liam's handle to try and lure *SoccerLord* out, with no result. He looks to have gone silent.

We're all beyond frustrated, feeling incompetent and helpless with Thomas still unaccounted for. Farmington doesn't have much more, although they have a lead they're chasing down. One of Thomas' teammates has come forward. He saw a boy he thinks might have been Thomas getting into a dark van with a sliding side door.

It's something, but we need more.

"What's he got?" Damian instinctively asks, like the rest of us knowing she wouldn't announce a call from her husband unless he had information to share.

"Berger."

Chairs scrape on the floor, as we all seem to move at once at the news.

"Thomas?"

Luna turns to me and shakes her head. "He can't confirm that. Hasn't seen the boy, just Jeremy."

"Where?" This from Damian, who's already shrugging into his FBI slicker.

"The RV park along the highway, south of town."

"You mean the Old Homestead?" Jasper's already pulling up a satellite view on his screen.

"No, not the trailer park, RVs, farther south. The club's been searching. The guys have been checking trailer parks, short-term private rentals like the place Berger had up in Hermosa. Figuring we'd be looking into hotels, motels, and the like, where registration would be required, they've focused on places where cash transactions aren't questioned and someone looking for privacy would be left alone."

"Durango RV," Jasper apparently has found it. "West side of the highway. Do we know which one?"

"Ouray says it's an older fifth-wheel with a single pop-out on the south side of the property. A trail that leads back out the highway right behind it. He's got eyes on it, but is getting itchy."

"There it is." Jasper points at the screen. "Coming in from the southwest gives us best coverage."

"Luna, call your man and tell him to fucking wait until we get there, and give Joe at DPD a heads-up. You've got the office. Okay, folks. Let's saddle up."

I ride with Damian, and Jasper follows in the Expedition outfitted for prisoner transportation.

It's a twenty-minute drive. We pass the RV park to get to the dirt road on the south side. I spot a silver four-door sedan parked next to a trailer that matches the description.

"Still here," I tell Damian.

"I see that."

We turn right the first chance we get. After about two hundred feet the dirt road takes a sharp right turn, but straight ahead we see two bikes parked side by side in a clearing. Damian pulls in behind them.

"Haven't seen movement for the past hour," Ouray shares, walking toward us from the shelter of the trees. "Paco's up there keeping an eye out."

"Decent cover?" Damian asks.

"Back end of the trailer, yeah. Twenty or so open feet to a ridge of rock at the edge of the tree line. No cover in front."

Ouray leads the way through the trees, until we have a visual on Paco crouched behind an outcropping up ahead and the trailer beyond. Damian stops us with a hand gesture.

"Door faces the road. I'd like to have a look at

those windows before we knock on the door though," he says, pointing at the three windows at the back of the trailer. "Jas, you're with me. Dylan, stay back in case he bolts and avoid fire."

"I wanna go in." I've never questioned an order in the field—never—but I want this guy. I want in on the action.

"Not gonna happen, Barnes. Don't need you losing your head."

"Like hell," I hiss back at Damian.

"Think, goddammit," he growls, leaning close as he pokes a finger in my chest. "You've already had an altercation with the guy. You're involved with his ex-wife. He takes one look at you, and right off the bat we've got a situation on our hands. You are not the right guy to go in, and you know it."

Fuck. I know he's right, even just standing here I can feel the adrenaline rage through my body. I know Damian sees the whole picture, when all I can think about is crushing that miserable bastard like the parasite he is.

I reluctantly nod my understanding and have to watch as my teammates join Paco behind the rock and from there, ducking low, approach the back of the trailer.

A large hand claps on my shoulder.

"You think this is bad," Ouray mumbles behind me. "Imagine being married to a woman half your size who can outfight you, outshoot you, and outsmart you."

"Fuck."

The hand gives my shoulder a squeeze. "Exactly," he says dryly.

I can see Jasper sneaking a look in one of the windows, before moving to the next. I try to catch the signals I know they're using to communicate, but their hands are shielded by their bodies.

As they round opposite sides of the trailer, I go on alert. I hear knocking, then, "FBI, open the door," and the next instant a window on the backside slides open and Berger hoists himself through. He hits the ground hard but scrambles to his feet and takes off almost straight for us.

"Mine," I growl at Ouray, but just as Berger darts past the outcropping, Paco bolts out and tackles him by the legs, bringing him down instantly.

I'm already moving and launch myself on top of him, shoving his face in the dirt.

"I dare you to move," I hiss in his ear. "All I need is an excuse."

I'm not sure if he knows who is pinning him to the ground, but he freezes instantly. Too bad.

"Cuffs," I hear Ouray behind me, and holding Berger down with one hand I pull them off my belt, holding them out.

There's no resistance from the man as Ouray snaps the cuffs in place and reluctantly I let him go, just as Damian comes jogging around the trailer.

He takes one look at the scene and gives me a nod. Barely distinguishable but praise nonetheless.

Normally I'd feel that in my bones, but not this time.

"Thomas?" I ask instead, my eyes on Damian.

"Not here."

MARYA

"I thought you said Max would be here tonight?"

Harry's barely cleared the front door when he calls out.

"Don't leave your bags there," I automatically respond. Every day when the kids come home I have to repeat the same thing over again. You'd think they'd clue in eventually. "He's going to do homework at his grandparents until Dylan picks him up after work, Bub. I suggest you guys do the same so you're free to play when he gets here."

Each of the boys—even Liam, who almost made me emotional—stops by the couch to kiss me hello, haul their backpacks upstairs, and return for the snack Mom set out for them on the kitchen counter.

"So he'll be here for dinner?"

"That's the plan."

Initially Max was supposed to stay here last night as well, but when Mom spilled the beans to Dylan I'd had a tough recovery day, he insisted we wait. He didn't get here until after dinner these past two nights and spent them on my couch. I would've preferred him in my bed, but seeing as I'm still recovering and not feeling at all sexy—with an immobilized leg and having not had a proper shower in days—I didn't object when he took a pillow and sheets and bunked downstairs.

He'd been up with the kids, getting them off to school in the mornings. He'd wait for Mom to get here, bring me up a coffee, and kiss me goodbye before heading to work.

I felt better today. Able to move around with my crutches a little easier, and Mom helped me take a shower. A little clumsy trying to keep my leg wrapped in plastic from getting wet, but we managed to get my hair washed, which made me feel ten times better. Thank God for the handheld, so I could give the rest of me a good scrub before Mom had to come back in and help me get dressed.

It's a little weird, at forty-one, getting bathed by your aging mother, but I was grateful for the help. Sure made my day a lot more enjoyable.

Kerry called this morning, checking in on me and to tell me she'd hired extra help for the store. She also reminded me I have eight sick days I haven't touched yet for the year, and my employee benefits will cover me for eight weeks of short-term disability at eighty percent after that. The alternative, if I felt up to it by then, would be to take over some of her duties I could do from home.

Finances are still a worry without my cleaning pay, but I can handle tight, I just can't do without.

Which makes me feel a whole lot better about the monster grocery run I know my mother is on. She's off to Farmington to hit up Sam's Club with a friend this afternoon. Since she spent most of the morning making room in my pantry, and asked to take my Jeep instead of her Ford Focus, I'm prepared for the worst. Knowing I have money coming in, I can transfer some to her to cover what she's been paying for.

She should be back shortly. The chili she left simmering in the Crock-Pot is starting to smell mouthwatering, and I know she's planning to throw together some cornbread, which won't take long. I'm considering sneaking a taste when my phone buzzes with a message.

Dylan: Held up at office. Don't wait with dinner.

I feel a pang of selfish disappointment but quickly squash it. He has more important things to do right now. I shoot off a message back.

Me: We'll save you some chili.

Dylan: You're killing me. ♡

An emoticon.

He sent me an emoticon. A heart.

Dylan is an attentive man, but a pretty straightforward one; not exactly the type I would expect hearts and flowers from. Certainly not someone who randomly drops emoticons in his messages, but there it is—a heart.

Is he telling me something? Should I send him one

back?

Geezus, I'm fawning like a twelve-year-old who just caught a glimpse of her crush by the locker rooms. Ridiculous.

The decision is taken out of my hands when the front door opens and Mom walks in, balancing enough toilet paper in her arms to last a year.

"Mom, alarm," I warn her when she leaves the door wide open and marches straight through to the pantry. As I've tried to explain to her about fifteen times since the alarm was installed Monday afternoon, you have all of thirty seconds to punch in the code before it goes off.

Sure enough, the incessant beep fires up and the boys come barreling down the stairs. I try to get my crutches under me when Mom comes stomping out of the pantry, cursing under her breath about that "blasted noise-maker."

"What's the number again?" she yells over the din, having beaten me to the small panel in the hall.

"I'll do it," Harry volunteers, but he gets shoved aside by Theo.

"I've got it," he says and punches in the numbers. Now the alarm double beeps.

"It's two-nine-*four*-three. You punched in a five," Harry helpfully announces at full volume to the world at large.

"No it's not."

"It so is, right, Mom?"

I give up and sink back down on the couch.

Three minutes later, after Mom was able to silence the noise by entering the correct number, there's a knock at the door I was expecting. Just like the other two times a patrol car stopped by to check after we accidentally set off the alarm.

Mom opens the door and apologizes to whoever knocked, when I hear Keith's chuckle.

"How are you doing?" he asks, walking into the living room.

"I'd be better if my family stopped setting off the goddamn alarm." I throw a glare at Mom, who shrugs and heads outside to grab more groceries, I presume.

"Don't worry about it. It takes a little time to get used to."

"Right," I snort. "By the time that happens, the alarm center, as well as Durango PD, will have learned to ignore any alerts coming from this address."

"The security company is used to it, and in your case, because a lot of stuff is happening, we don't wait for confirmation, we just send out the closest unit."

"I'm sorry."

He grins at me. "Don't be. Besides, I just heard there's a development that makes me hopeful you won't have to worry about alarms anymore soon."

"Really? Dylan just sent me a message saying he was held up. So something's happened? Did they find Thomas?"

Mom hears my last comment, just as she comes walking in, dumps the bags in the hallway, and walks over to listen in.

"They found your ex."

It was ten when I sent Mom home.

That took some doing—she initially insisted on staying until Dylan showed—but I reminded her that with Jeremy no longer a threat out there, we'd be fine. She finally conceded and left, but not until she left a covered plate out for Dylan with a little note.

I just closed the door behind her, armed the alarm, and turned off lights. The kids are in bed, or so I thought. Harry stumbles out of his room when I hoist myself up the stairs on my ass, pulling my crutches along with me.

"Max here?" He's rubbing his sleepy eyes.

"Don't think he's coming tonight, baby. His dad is working late, so I think Max crashed at his grandparents. Why don't you go back to bed?"

"Can I sleep with you?"

I wince at the thought. Harry is high energy, even in sleep. It's like trying to cuddle with kicking horse, and I don't want those size sevens of his pounding my poor knee.

"When I'm better, Bub. I'll come tuck you in."

He's almost back under by the time I have him tucked in and press a kiss on his floppy hair.

I do my thing in the bathroom, change into my nightshirt, and settle myself in bed; with my leg elevated and my book within reach. I don't even manage to read a single page before my eyes get too heavy.

I'm not sure what time it is when I feel a hand slip under my shirt and over my stomach.

"Dylan?"

"Go back to sleep, Sweetheart," he mumbles, settling in on my good side, his head on the pillow next to me, hand still under my shirt.

"You got Jeremy." In the dark room I feel more than see his head come up.

"How'd you know?"

"Mom set off the alarm again and Keith showed up. He mentioned it."

"Right." He lies back down, his head closer so he can reach to kiss my shoulder. "We got a tip and found him in a rented RV south of town."

"Any sign of Thomas?" All Keith had told us was they'd brought in my ex, but he couldn't elaborate further and I've been dying to know.

"No, and Jeremy clammed up. Asked for a lawyer."

I hate hearing defeat in his voice. "You'll find him."

"Fuck, I hope so, Sweetheart."

CHAPTER 23

MARYA

Like the last night when Dylan slept in my bed, he leaves it before the sun comes up. The toilet flushes and I wait for the shower to be turned on, but instead there's a splash of water in the sink before I can hear him come back in the room. The mattress moves under his weight as he gets in, and his body curves again mine.

"Do you need to leave early again?" My voice sounds rough with sleep, even though my body is fast coming alive.

I feel his lips brush my neck and then my shoulder. "Yes," he mumbles, "Need to start my day with a fill of you first, though."

A charge skips over my skin when his large hand slides over my stomach, and up between my breasts, coming to rest at the base of my throat. There's something deeply possessive about the weight of his forearm pressing between my breasts as his fingers brush the pulse in my neck.

"You're so warm. So soft. So fucking sexy, all rumpled with sleep."

"My leg," I remind him when his touch travels south, playing with the trimmed curls at the apex of my thighs before dipping a finger through the wet. I hiss at the almost casual brush against my clit.

"We'll be careful, and creative."

"Yes…" I moan, pulling up my good leg to give his nimble digits room. With my foot planted in the mattress I try to lift my hips into his touch.

"Stay still, Sweetheart. I don't want you to hurt yourself. Trust me to do the work."

He works me all right, with lips and tongue, hands and fingers, until tears of need squeeze from my eyes.

"Please…"

"I've got you."

He does. In every aspect, he has me: my body, my needs, my back, my trust, and yes, my heart too. In the care he takes when he positions me under him, rolling me partly on my side, hooking his arm under my good knee to spread me wide. Straddling my immobile leg, he plants a hand in the mattress in front of me and braces as his cock brushes along my slit, gently probing.

"Honey…" I whisper on an exhale when he slides in, filling me up.

The muscles in his arm bulge when he shifts all

his weight there, keeping it off me, as his hips pump deep.

"Work your clit, babe," he grunts, the strain showing in the tendons of his neck and the lines of his face. "Hurry."

My hand slides down, two fingers rolling over the slick tight bundle as he grinds his cock deep. I feel my body tensing, reaching for release as my touch becomes frantic. The moment his strong rhythm starts to falter, I slide my fingers wide over our connection and feel the pulse of his release, triggering my own.

All too soon he slides out and rolls off on his side, facing me, as we both catch our breath. His eyes are deep warm pools, just inches from mine, as he wipes the hair from my face and leans in for a lazy kiss.

"There isn't a day I can't handle if I can start every morning like that," he mumbles, his lips still on mine.

My heart full, I slide a hand along his jaw and let the words spill over.

"I'm falling in love with you," I find myself whispering, drowning in his eyes.

"I know," he whispers back. "I promise it'll be a soft landing; I'm already there, ready to catch you."

I'm not sure how long we lie there, breaths mingling and our souls in our eyes. Cocooned in a safe, early-morning vacuum keeping the world at bay. Nothing in the moment but the two of us, hearing each other in silence.

"Mom?" Harry's soft voice sounds as the bedroom door is pushed open.

Dylan barely manages to yank the covers up over us when my youngest pads in, rubbing his fists in his eyes.

"Yeah, Bub," I manage, pushing myself up a little, thankful I'm still wearing my nightshirt, even if the bottom is wrapped around my waist under the sheets.

"I threw up." He stops at the foot of the bed; the front of his pj's a mess as he blinks at us. He seems to take finding Dylan in my bed in stride, not even reacting.

"You feeling sick?" I ask, struggling to get my nightie to cover my ass before I try to slide out of bed. I belatedly remember the state of my leg and hiss in pain.

"Stay put," Dylan rumbles beside me, as he swings his legs over the other side, keeping himself covered with a corner of the sheet while grabbing for his jeans.

"My stomach hurts," Harry announces, his tearful eyes still focused on me. Thank God. From the corner of my eye, I spot Dylan pull the jeans up over the tight globes of his ass.

"I'll get him cleaned up and take him downstairs," Dylan says, putting a hand in Harry's neck. "Come on, sport, let's get the puke washed off you. You reek."

Even through his misery, Harry manages to grin. Must be a guy thing.

I gingerly get out of bed—this time—the moment they disappear down the hall. My leg is throbbing, but I know it'll get better once I start moving around some. Grabbing my crutches, I snag some clean clothes and head for the bathroom to clean up.

I skip the shower; it takes too long, but give myself a sponge bath by the sink. Since my hair looks like a gale-force storm is blowing in from the left, I feel the need to stick my head under the hand-held shower over the side of the tub. It's a pain in the ass but I feel better after.

I'm about to head down on my ass when Dylan comes up, two steps at a time, and swings me up in his arms.

"I can walk, you know."

"Yup," he says with an easy grin.

Despite my words, I wrap my arms around his neck, holding on tight as he carries me downstairs. Harry is curled up on the couch covered in a quilt, a bucket beside him.

"He feels feverish, you may want to check." He sets me on my feet and I make my way over to the couch. "I'm just gonna strip his bed and hop in the shower, okay? Coffee is brewing."

I'm about to tell him not to bother, that I'll take care of the mess later, but he's already disappeared upstairs.

Harry turns out to have a bit of a fever, but I hold off on giving him anything until he can keep down the piece of toast I'm trying to feed him. He's just dozing off when Dylan comes back down, his arms full with Harry's dirty sheets and pj's.

"Drop it on the floor of the laundry room, I'll pop it in the washer later."

Of course he doesn't listen and is rummaging around in there, probably looking for detergent. A moment later, I hear water flooding the washer as he walks into the kitchen, straight for where I'm waiting with a travel mug for him.

"Thank you."

"I believe that's my line," I correct him. "Thank you for cleaning up my kid's puke first thing in the morning."

He hooks his free arm around my waist. "First thing this morning I was buried to the hilt inside you."

"Mmmm," I mumble at the memory, a smile on my lips he bends down to kiss. "Still," I persist. "You didn't have to clean up, I could've done that later."

He shrugs. "I love you," he declares, as if that explains it all.

One more brief press of his lips and he's out the door.

I swallow hard at the emotions his words evoke and let that safe and treasured feeling settle deep in my soul, realizing he's right.

It does explain it all.

DYLAN

"Yeager is driving up."

I look up to find Damian standing in the doorway.

"Berger?" I ask.

"Yup, he should be at the police station in about forty minutes. I talked to Joe, the public defense attorney just walked in to meet with his client." Since it was obvious last night Berger wasn't going to talk without a lawyer there, he was held overnight at the police station. "I'd like you to sit in. See if maybe your presence will get him worked up enough to start talking."

"Sure," I respond immediately. Yesterday I was relegated to watch Luna and Damian have a go at him from behind the one-sided mirror in our single interrogation room here in the office, which was frustrating to say the least. I wouldn't mind having a go at him.

"Just remember we want *him* worked up, not you," Damian cautions, a stern look on his face.

"Gotcha." Seeing as I was the one with my dick in Marya this morning—her sweet declaration in my ears—I'm pretty confident little the man says can get me rattled. "Does Yeager have anything more to report?" I ask.

"They still have a few search parties going out during the day, but it's been five days, Thomas could be anywhere in the world by now." The strain on Damian's face is the same I imagine we all wear. We all want Thomas found, which is what makes Berger's silence so infuriating. "So far no luck with the IP addresses in Farmington or Aztec. No one seems to recognize Berger from his DMV picture." He turns to Luna. "You're heading back out to the Starbucks in Hermosa?"

"Yes. The one barista who was on vacation should

be back on shift today. I'm leaving in twenty minutes."

"Fucking hope she has better eyes than the rest," Jasper mumbles from behind his screen.

As pumped as we all were to find and bring in Berger sixteen hours ago, the shine came off immediately when he didn't give us an inch. He'd blanched when we brought up Thomas' disappearance. Was adamant in his claim of no involvement with the boy's disappearance and clammed up altogether when Seth's name was brought up. We went over that trailer with a fine-tooth comb. The Colorado Bureau of Investigation had their forensics team there last night, going over every inch of the place to find any evidence Thomas had been there. Nothing had jumped out and sadly analysis of anything they collected would take some time.

Time Thomas likely didn't have. If he had any left at all.

"How old were you when you realized you had a fascination with little boys."

Yeager's first question is a doozy. Designed to have the suspect off-balance right from the get go, and the wet-behind-the-ears public defender plays right into Yeager's hands with his standard response.

"I advise my client not to answer that question," he says, placing a hand on Berger's arm, who seems unsure what to do.

"I've never…I mean I don't…I'm not like that!"

"Mr. Berger, please don't say another word," the lawyer, Brendan Addison, hisses at his client, but Berger has a wild look in his eyes, looking from one to the other.

"I don't like boys," he blurts out.

"You prefer little girls?" Yeager persists.

"Yes! I mean no. I—"

"I think this interview is—" his lawyer tries to cut the questioning short, but I'm not about to let him and jump in.

"Why are you hanging around the soccer fields?" I ask, trying to keep Jeremy in defensive mode and talking.

"I just wanna see my son."

"Don't you mean sons? You have three." That seems to throw him, and his lawyer once again puts a restraining hand on Berger's arm, but this time he bats the hand away impatiently. I feel for the younger man in the ill-fitting Brooks Brothers suit.

"Yes, of course," he mutters, but it's clear I hit on something there, even if I don't have a fucking clue what it is.

"Why are you so focused on Liam?" I probe a little deeper.

"I'm not at all. Liam's just…he's always been…"

"Your favorite?" I jump in, making use of his hesitation. "The one kid who favors you in looks?"

"Amelia does too." The defensive tone when he corrects me is interesting. He hasn't mentioned the other two boys by name, only Liam and now his daughter.

"Yes. She's a pretty girl, isn't she? Like a little angel, all that blonde hair, those blue eyes...pretty pink lips."

My taunt has the desired effect, as Berger shoots up from his chair and lunges over the table at me.

"No one touches my daughter!" he yells, as Brendan tries to pull his client back in his seat.

Interesting.

"Of course not," I use a soothing tone to settle him down before I slam my fist on the table, startling him. "Where is Thomas, Jeremy?" I bark.

"I don't know," he whines, clearly flustered as he looks to help from his attorney.

"Where's the Lexus?" I drop right away, keeping him on his toes.

"What?"

"The new shiny Lexus, Jeremy, where is it?"

"It's gone."

"I know it's gone, I've seen the piece of junk parked outside the trailer, but where is the pretty Lexus? Did you dump it?" He shakes his head. "Afraid we might find Seth's blood in the car?"

"What? No! There's no blood. I needed the money."

"Mr. Berger," Brooks Brothers cautions his client, even though he knows he's already lost control.

"So you beat him to death after you got him out of the car?" Yeager jumps in.

"I never touched him!"

"Before or after you raped him?" Yeager fires off.

"I didn't—"

"Mr. Berger! Jeremy, that's enough!" his lawyer yells to be heard, but he's still ignored.

"What did you need the money for, Jeremy?" the Farmington SAC asks in a much softer voice.

I sit back and glance over at Damian, who gives me a barely-there nod of approval, while Yeager continues to draw information bit by bit from the unwilling Jeremy Berger.

After two hours of the cat and mouse game, the public defender has had enough as he stands up from the table.

"I'm afraid we'll have to end this here. I'm due in court in fifteen minutes. I ask that my client be released immediately."

Joe, who's been quietly observing while leaning against the wall, steps forward.

"I'm afraid that won't be possible," he announces. "We've reason to believe Mr. Berger has breached an order of protection against him on more than one occasion. We'll need some time to question him with regard to those incidents."

"Are you serious?" Brendan snaps incredulously.

"Dead," Joe responds expressionless.

The young guy rolls his eyes heavenward before turning to his client. "Right, Jeremy? Looks like you'll be the guest of the Durango PD a little longer. I'll be back this afternoon." He scoops up his file, grabs his briefcase, and marches out the door.

Berger seems stunned as two of Joe's officers—

who were standing outside the door—walk in, take him by the arms, and lead him back to the holding cell.

I can just hear his muttered protest, "But…"

CHAPTER 24

MARYA

"I'm bored."

Mom lifts her head from the massive pan of lasagna she's been assembling at the kitchen counter.

"Last time I heard those words out of your mouth, you had pigtails and were home for weeks with mono."

"Yeah, well, I'm not used to having nothing to do."

She rolls her eyes at me. "Most people would be thankful if they were waited on and could watch Netflix all day. Guilt free."

"I'm not most people."

"I'm your mother, I think I know that."

I'm being a whiner and I know it, but there's a big difference between choosing to laze about and being forced to take it easy. I like feeling productive, having something to show for my time, but watching three seasons of *Sherlock* in four days just leaves me with a moderate crush on Benedict Cumberbatch.

Call me a bad mother, but I'd hoped to keep Harry home after the early morning wake-up call with him throwing up. I'd have sat through another Marvel marathon with him just to hear him chatter. Instead, he insisted he was fine after a brief nap on the couch, and since they had a local wildlife presentation in class, he wanted to go school. Live snakes are apparently a big draw for an eight-year-old. *Yuck.*

"Why don't you give Kerry a call? Didn't you say she could set you up with some work to do at home? You'll have enough distraction over the weekend with those boys, but you can tell her Monday you're ready."

She washes her hands at the sink and covers the pan with tinfoil. The lasagna was at Theo's request; it's his favorite. That's part of why she's making an ungodly amount. The other part being that Max is supposed to come here after school, and Dylan was going to try to make it in time for dinner. We'll have a full table, and I'm oddly excited at the prospect.

Max has been with his grandparents all week, but apparently they're leaving on a cruise tomorrow. According to Dylan, this had long been in the plans. At least on Clint's part. Beth always dreamed of traveling but never had the opportunity. So for their anniversary Clint is taking her on a Caribbean cruise, although from what I gather, he's not too keen on finding his sea legs.

With this investigation taking up a lot of Dylan's time, his mother made noises earlier this week about cancelling, but both men had put their foot down. Therefore, Max would hang out here for the week, and I have to admit, it feels a little like playing house. I like it.

"Shit," Mom mumbles, her head stuck in the fridge. "How come you don't have anchovy paste in your fridge?"

I twist around on the couch. "Why on earth would I want anchovy paste in my fridge?"

Her head pops up over the door and she looks at me in disbelief. "Don't you ever make Caesar dressing?"

"Mom, they sell that stuff in bottles. I've got three boys and two jobs, what am I gonna make dressing for if I can get it ready-made?"

"Well, I'm not serving Caesar salad with bottled dressing, which means I need anchovy paste." She grabs her purse from the counter and heads for the small front hall to shrug on her coat. "Need anything from the store?"

"Do we have enough eggs? Chocolate chips?" I ask her. "I want to make waffles tomorrow for breakfast."

"I'll pick some up. See you in a bit, I shouldn't be too long."

I grab the phone and dial Kerry the moment the door closes behind her.

"How's the knee?" is the first thing she says when she answers.

"Healing, but I can feel myself dumbing down. I

need something to do. How are things at the store?"

Her warm chuckle puts a smile on my face. "Things are fine here. Samantha is working out really well. She worked at Barnes & Noble in Flagstaff before moving here, and she's got some great ideas."

"Good," I mumble, feeling a touch of jealousy for the faceless Samantha. At least she's productive.

"So what's this about needing something to do?"

"My follow-up appointment with the surgeon isn't until next Wednesday, and I know you said to wait until after, but I'm going nuts here. Surely there's better ways to occupy my brain than staring mindlessly at Benedict's lips moving."

"Ah, you're finally watching *Sherlock*?"

"Kerry, I haven't been home a week and I'm starting season four. I need help."

"Right," she snickers. "How about I pop in Sunday? I'll bring Dante over for a visit, and I'll get you set up managing the web store for me. That'll take a load off me."

Even though my computer skills are passable at best, the prospect of having something to contribute already makes me feel better.

I realize after I hang up with Kerry, I'll need Wi-Fi for that. As far as I know my router is still at the FBI office. A quick look at the clock tells me I have another half hour before the boys get here, so I quickly call Dylan.

"Hey."

"I'm sorry to bug you at work," I start apologizing

the moment I hear his voice.

"Not bugging me, babe. In fact, I can safely say your call is the highlight of my day."

"Ouch. That doesn't imply good things," I sympathize, hearing the frustration in his voice. "I'm sorry, I wish there was something I could do."

"You're doing it," he says, and this time I hear a smile. "Did you just call to hear my voice?"

I find myself grinning at the tease. "Let's call that a perk, but I called with a question. You guys still have my router, right?"

"Jasper does, yes. Why?"

"Kerry's popping in on Sunday to get me set up with her web store, but I just realized I can't get online."

"Right. Let me talk to Jas, okay? We'll get it sorted."

"Thanks, honey."

"I like that." His voice sounds sexy but muffled, and I envision him covering his mouth with his hand for privacy.

"What?"

"You calling me honey. Makes this whole fucked-up day a lot better."

"That bad?"

"Worse. We may have to let our only lead walk out the door."

"Jeremy?" I can hear rustling and then a door close.

"Had to step out of the office," he shares, the sound of his voice echoing. "Big guns showed up today. A pair of lawyers on daddy-in-law's payroll. Somehow the domestic violence charges against him were dropped in the past twenty-four hours, and they are fighting the violation of the temporary protective order. And, Sweetheart? Brace. It looks like they're digging in."

"Shit."

"Good news is, we know the judge who signed the protective order, and they'll find the man doesn't respond well to pressure, but that doesn't mean it can't get unpleasant."

"Nothing about dealing with Jeremy is pleasant, Dylan," I remind him.

"I realize that, but these don't sound like guys who'd lose any sleep ripping you apart if they thought it would help their client, Marya."

I swallow hard. The whole ripping apart thing doesn't sound appealing, and though I work hard at being a good mother—a good provider—Lord knows I'm far from perfect. I've made not so sound choices in my life. Ones that might draw my judgment into question.

"Oh."

"Yeah. So brace, baby, but know you have all of Durango law enforcement at your back."

Well, fuck.

I'm about to respond when the doorbell rings.

DYLAN

"I've gotta go. Someone's at the door and I need both hands to walk."

I'm about to ask where her mother is but she's already ended the call.

"Marya?" Jasper asks when I reenter the office.

"Yeah. You done with her router? She needs it back to do some work."

"You don't want her to have that old thing back, it only uses WEP encryption. Any primate with opposable thumbs can get through that. I'll get her set up with one that has WPA3 capability. I'll probably double it."

I don't understand most of what he said, but I trust he knows what he's talking about. "That'd be good."

"Did you warn her about Berger?"

"I did."

The two attorneys interrupted our third attempt to get some information from the asshole this afternoon. Barged right in, demanding some time with their client. Of course, the public defender took exception to that, which resulted in a small legal standoff that predictably ended with Brendan Addison handing over his client. It didn't take long to realize these guys were willing to do whatever it'll take to get their client out of the charges against him. I'd been about to call Marya when she beat me to it.

"Judge Fanshaw won't easily back down on that protection order," Jasper assures me. "But I have a feeling those two sharks won't hesitate to throw your girl under the bus, if they find a way to do that."

"I know. I told her as much."

Marya's name pops up on my phone with a message.

Marya: CPS is here.

"Son of a bitch," I bark out, already grabbing for my keys.

"What's up?"

"Those bastards are in a hurry. They've got Child Protective Services on her fucking doorstep." I'm already on my way out the door and don't hang around for a reaction.

It's a long fucking ten-minute drive to her house. I'm worried when I don't see Lydia's car in the driveway and realize she's alone.

There are two of them facing a very upset Marya across the dining room table. Her eyes dart over the moment I walk in the door.

"Dylan, these are—" she starts, but I don't let her finish.

"You need to keep your leg elevated," I remind her, ignoring the two women assessing me as I approach. I don't give a fuck.

I bend down, slide an arm under Marya's legs and another around her waist and lift her straight out of her chair, carrying her to the couch. When she's installed with her leg elevated, I finally turn to the two women.

"Excuse me, Mister…" the older of the two drags the word out, clearly hoping I'll fill in the blank.

"It's Special Agent Barnes, and you are?"

"Agent Barnes we were informed there were—"

"I didn't catch your names," I interrupt and the woman is clearly irritated. Again, I don't give a fuck.

"This is Brenda Davids and my name is Kelly White, Child and Family Services," she concedes. "We have reason to believe three minors by the names of…" she looks at the file in front of her.

"Theo, Liam, and Harry Berger," I fill in for her. "Let me guess, you received a call within the last hour?" I catch the furtive glances between the two. "Slow day, was it?"

"Dylan!" Marya admonishes from the couch but I keep my eyes on the old shark.

"Mr. Barnes, there's no need—"

"Agent. It's Agent Barnes."

"Whenever we receive a call on our emergency hotline, we're compelled to investigate," the younger woman shares almost apologetically.

"What was the complaint?"

"Excuse me?"

"The hotline call, what was the claim?" I clarify.

"Neglect and child endangerment," the older one—White—snaps.

"Ironic, since I presume the call was made by the boys' father?" That seems to surprise them, but the younger one nods. "The same man who walked out on these kids five years ago and never looked back? The man who never paid a single penny for their support? Same guy who's being investigated in the abduction, rape, and murder of one, perhaps two young boys? Is that who we're talking about?"

Shock is evident on their faces, but Ms. White does not give up easily. "We're simply following protocol."

"I'm sure you are, but I would suggest next time, before you waste your time investigating a mother who busted her ass for five years, working two jobs to provide for her three young children without any help from their deadbeat father, you take a closer look at the source of the complaint."

"Let's go, Kelly," the younger woman gets up from the table.

"We haven't seen the children yet," she snarks at her colleague.

"And we're not going to traumatize three young boys if there's any chance this call was a sham. Now let's go." She turns to me, holding out her hand. "I'm so sorry for the inconvenience."

I ignore her hand. "You're apologizing to the wrong person."

I'm just seeing the two out when Lydia comes walking up the driveway, her arms full of bags.

"You took my spot," she says, clearly put out. Then she looks at the two women.

"Jehovah's Witnesses? On a Friday? Since when are you guys diversifying to other days of the week?"

"Ladies are here to investigate whether Marya is a fit mother," I explain.

"They're what?"

Ms. Davids seems to be the smarter one, raising

her hands defensively when she feels the full force of Lydia's scorching glare. "We'll just be on our way."

We don't have much of a chance to discuss anything because the boys come barging in—all four of them—by the time we have the groceries Lydia bought squared away.

I disappear out the back door to give Damian a call and quickly update him. When I walk back inside, Lydia is behind the stove, the boys have disappeared downstairs, but Marya's eyes are on me.

"Do you need to go back to the office?" she asks, worry on her face.

I sit down beside her and wrap an arm around her, tugging her close. "No, I'm staying. We're gonna have a nice dinner with the kids, then we're going to watch movies and binge on all the snack food your mom picked up. What we're not gonna do is let that asshole take up any of that precious time."

"Hear, hear," Lydia—who evidently still has perfect hearing—contributes from the kitchen.

Ignoring her, I slide my free hand in Marya's hair, tug her head back, and take her mouth.

"You good?" I ask when I lift away and note to my satisfaction the worry lines are gone.

"Yeah," she says almost drowsily.

"Good. We all need a little normalcy. Tomorrow morning I'll feed the boys and take Max and Liam to soccer. The other two can hang back with you."

Her smile is sweet, but I can see concern creeping back as her eyes drift off. "I was gonna make chocolate chip waffles for breakfast."

"Hey." Her gaze comes back to me. "I've never had chocolate chip waffles. Sounds good to me."

"Okay."

Still a little too glum for my liking, but I can't blame her. Her life's been in a spin cycle, and every time she thinks she's gaining a foothold something else happens to keep her off-balance.

"Are you still on those painkillers?"

She shakes her head. "Not since Tuesday. They made me loopy."

"How about a drink then?"

"I bought some wine. You were all out," Lydia announces and Marya rolls her eyes to the ceiling. I snicker.

"Fine, I'll have a glass," she surrenders.

I lean in for another kiss, wishing we didn't have an audience, and get up. When I move toward the kitchen, I spot Liam standing at the top of the basement stairs. His lips are pressed in a tight line, but before I can even react, he storms straight through upstairs, slamming the door to his bedroom.

Fuck.

CHAPTER 25

MARYA

"Have a good game, Bub."

Liam—who's barely talked to me since last night—stalks out the door after Max.

I tried, labored my way up to his room and sat on the edge of his bed, asking why seeing me with Dylan had him upset. No reaction. I asked him if it was Dylan, or just the idea of me dating anyone, and he threw me a dirty glare. Then I wanted to know if it was the age-difference between us that made him uncomfortable. To that I received a puzzled look and a mumbled, "Whatever."

He did come down for Mom's lasagna, and watched movies with us. He also ate his chocolate chip waffles this morning, which is a hopeful sign. At least whatever is up with him is not affecting his appetite. As a mom, I have to take comfort somewhere.

"I'll talk to him," Dylan says, leaning over me for a kiss. "You and the boys gonna be okay? Your mom said she'd come if—"

"We'll be fine. I'm not completely useless," I snap, a tad acerbic.

"I wouldn't dare to imply such a thing," Dylan says in an amused tone, brushing my lips once again before he too heads for the door. I'm already feeling guilty.

"Thank you," I call after him, and he turns a wide grin my way just before he pulls the door closed.

I'm irritable. My mind is restless, my skin is crawling with anxiety, and I'm taking it out on Dylan. The guy who, once again, dropped everything so he could come to my rescue when fucking Jeremy played his dirty hand. I was full-on scared when those women showed up. I wanted to be angry, indignant—as I'd otherwise be—but instead I was overwhelmed and frankly, terrified.

There comes a point when the blows keep knocking you down, you just can't get up anymore. Not under your own steam anyway. That point was yesterday afternoon for me.

I had the presence of mind to shoot Dylan a quick text, and he came—like the proverbial knight in shining armor—and did what I no longer had in me to do. Fight.

This morning I'm snapping at the guy, when he's being nice.

Fuck, I want this mess to be over.

"I like him, Mom."

I turn and watch Theo come out of the kitchen. "Bub?"

"Dylan. He's cool. He's totally into you."

I press my lips together, forcing back tears that suddenly burn my eyes. My little protector is not so little anymore. "I'm glad," I manage to utter in a steady voice. "For the record, I'm into him too."

Theo rolls his eyes. "Duh, Mom. You'd have to be blind not to catch that. Your face goes all goofy when you look at him," he says with a shrug and a grin.

I pelt a throw pillow at him. "Goofy, huh?" He catches it easily.

"Totally."

"Get your skinny butt over here and give your mom a hug, smart-ass."

He makes his way over to the couch, a suffering look on his face—which is all for show—judging by the strength of his arms wrapping around me.

"Love you, Theo."

"Love you too, Mom," he mumbles, squeezing me extra hard before he lets go.

"How long since you've had a shower, Bub?" I ask, scrunching my nose when I get a whiff of eau de adolescence.

"Dunno." He sniffs his pits and shrugs. "It's not that bad."

"You're ripe. Get on it." I smile when his lanky frame heads for the stairs without argument. "And when you're done, get your brother to take one too."

A house full of boys requires constant monitoring of personal hygiene, or before you know it, the place smells like a locker room.

I slide sideways until my head hits the armrest and close my eyes. A catnap sounds like a good idea after Dylan's early morning wakeup call between my legs, and forty-five minutes on my feet in the kitchen making enough waffles to feed a battalion.

Five guys under my roof. I must be out of my mind.

Still, I doze off with a smile on my face, the mess my life is in momentarily forgotten.

DYLAN

I look in my rearview mirror, catching Liam glowering at the back of my head.

"Liam." He visibly jerks at my voice and catches my eyes in the reflection. "I care about your mom. A lot." He turns his head to stare out the side window. "She cares about me too," I continue undeterred. "I get it might be a bit weird seeing us together—it's something we all have to get used to, I guess—but I need you to understand it will happen. I don't plan to stop touching or kissing her."

"I don't think it's weird," Max pipes up beside me. "Grammy and Grandpa touch all the time, and they're like...*old.*"

I toss a grin at my son. "Just don't tell 'em that, Kiddo. Not sure Grammy will appreciate being called *old.*"

In the mirror I spot Liam's focus on Max, then his eyes meet mine before he turns his attention back out the window, but he does it with a smile playing on his lips.

"I want your mom to be happy, kid. Things haven't always been easy for her, but I'd like a chance at changing that. I don't think that's a bad thing, do you?"

The snort from the back seat is loud, and I decide to give it a rest. Max is watching me, a little confused, so I shoot him a reassuring wink.

"Until she ends up in the hospital," I hear Liam mumble under his breath.

I get where he's coming from. She ended in the hospital, battered at the hands of the last man his mom was involved with. He also just found out his own father had taken his hands to her. He has no reason to trust I wouldn't end up doing the same.

This week the boys play in town, at the soccer fields by Fort Lewis College, so I hold off responding until I can pull into a parking spot, shut off the engine, and turn in my seat.

"Liam, I'm not gonna hurt your mom. That's not going to happen. *Ever*," I emphasize, observing his tepid reaction to my words. "I also never make promises I can't keep."

"He doesn't," Max confirms in my support as he twists around in his seat. "He like…*really* likes your mom. I can tell." I bite off a grin at my son's vote of confidence. He isn't done yet. "And think about it, we could end up living in the same house, how cool would that be?"

Before my kid totally freaks Liam out, I intervene. "We should get a move on. Coach is waiting."

The boys get out and dart ahead. By the time I collect my coffee from the Bronco and take a seat on the bleachers, they're already running around the field for their warm-up.

Rick plops down on the bench beside me.

"Where's the hot babe today?"

"Watch what you call my woman," I grunt, taking a much-needed sip of coffee.

These early mornings are beginning to wear on me, even though sliding into Marya's warm, sleepy body first thing is the best way to start my day.

Rick's chuckle sounds beside me. "Well, excuse me for noticing," he quips. "I'm guessing things are good?"

"What is this? We're having a girl-talk now?" I look at him with an eyebrow raised, but his smirk only gets bigger.

"Living vicariously through you, my man. You're walking up here with that I-just-got-me-some swagger, making the rest of us poor single saps green with envy."

"Whatever," I mumble, but with a grin of my own.

"Guess a boys' trip into the mountains is out?"

Rick Henderson's son, Jamie, has been playing soccer with Max since the boys were six. The boys have had occasional playdates, and last year Rick and

I took them on a weekend campout up in San Juan National Park.

"Not necessarily," I consider out loud, thinking I wouldn't mind taking Marya's three along. "I may just have a couple more kids in tow."

"You're a lucky bastard, you know that?"

"Yup."

We watch the first half of the game in companionable silence, except when the Chargers score a goal toward the end, and we're on our feet cheering.

It's not until partway through the second half my phone rings. Damian calling.

"Boss."

"Our boy walked."

"Berger?"

"Yup. Benedetti called. He tried to stall, but there was little he could do."

"Tell me he's got a tail."

"Ramirez is on it. Just talked to him, looks like he's holed up with his lawyers at the DoubleTree. Where are you?"

"Up at the sports fields by the college. There's about ten minutes left in the game. Anything changes—he moves—let me know right away."

"Will do. Marya with you?"

"Nope. Home with the other boys."

"Want me to send Luna?"

"I'd rather tell her face-to-face." After yesterday, the last thing she needs is another surprise visit with bad news. "I shouldn't be too much longer here."

"Everything okay?" Rick asks beside me when I end the call.

"Fuck no."

He takes his cue and stays quiet the rest of the game while I seethe in silence.

Of course, in the last two minutes the opposing team scores the equalizer and both boys come off the field disappointed. Even my, "Tough break, guys, but you played a good game," does nothing to change the mood.

The drive home is silent other than the Eagles playing on the radio. I'm just turning onto Marya's street when I hear Liam behind me.

"What the hell?"

"What's up?" I ask, my eyes flying up to the rearview mirror. Liam's reflection is white as a ghost; his eyes open wide. "Liam?"

"It's Harry…he…10-1," he stammers.

It takes me a moment to clue in. 10-1. Dad alert. "Where?"

"I don't know. He didn't say."

"Ask him." I pull into Marya's driveway and twist in my seat. "Anything?"

"Not yet."

"Okay. Do not get out. No matter what," I tell the boys. I grab my phone, get out, and hit the locks.

I find the front door unlocked when I test it. Reaching down I slip my gun from my ankle holster and ease the door open.

"Mom?" A white-faced Theo is standing in the

hallway, eyes fixed on the gun in my hand. Behind him I can see Marya sit up and twist around in the couch.

"What's wrong?" she addresses Theo, who looks frozen on the spot.

"Where's Harry?"

I see her startle when she hears my voice and her eyes zoom in on me. "Dylan? Guys? What's going on?"

"Sweetheart, where's Harry?" I walk into the living room, just as she gets to her feet.

"Probably downstairs, why?"

It's only when I walk up to her and her eyes get big that I remember the gun in my hand. I quickly tuck it in the back of my waistband.

"He's not," Theo says from behind me, and I turn around to find him looking concerned. "I didn't want to wake you, Mom. He just went across the street to David's. I watched him all the way until he got inside, I swear."

"That's okay, he's—" Marya starts but I cut her off.

"Jeremy was released."

"Wait, what?"

"Not now, babe." I feel bad about being short with her, but I need to find Harry. "Theo, come with me, yeah?" I grab the boy by the arm in passing and pull him behind me. "Which house is David's?" He points to a raised bungalow, with blue siding a couple of doors down, on the other side of the road. "I need you to get the other boys inside, lock the door, and set the alarm. Can you do that?" I push the button on my car keys to open the doors.

"He answered." Liam shows me the screen on his phone as soon as he gets out of the truck.

10-7

"What was 10-7 again?"

"Hiding."

"I need to know where he is, keep trying, okay? I need you guys to go inside with Theo, if he answers, send me a message, yeah?"

I already have my phone out and am dialing Damian, even as I'm crossing the road to David's house.

"Berger's been spotted near Marya's place," I snap. "Her youngest is out there. I need help." I don't even wait for an answer, raising my hand to knock on the door.

"Yes?"

A woman opens the door and looks at me with some reservation. I can't blame her, if my face shows any of the emotion I'm feeling right now, it's bound to be scary.

"Is Harry here?"

"Who is asking?" She looks over my shoulder at Marya's house.

I flip my badge open. "Special Agent Dylan Barnes, FBI. Ma'am this is urgent. Is Harry Berger with you?"

She shakes her head, looking increasingly worried. "No, the boys went down the road to play in the park.

Why? What's going on?"

"Ma'am, if they show up here, do not let them leave, and call me right away." I dig a card from my wallet and shove it at her before jogging in the direction she points me.

There's no one in the damn park.

The small neighborhood park has the road on one side and the open mountainside behind it. I scan the road, and then the brush. No one.

"Harry!" I yell, while pulling my phone out of my pocket. I type in a quick message.

Dylan: Where are you?

I watch as the check mark appears next to my message, but there's no response.

Dylan: Harry? I can't help you if you don't answer me.

Again the check mark appears, but then I see the dots beside his name move.

Harry: Is he gone?

"Harry!" I yell again, just as a patrol car pulls up to the curb. I swing back to scan the mountainside when I see something move halfway up the rise. "Stay here," I tell the officer who joins me. "Keep an eye out while I go up there. We're looking for a man in his forties, six one, blond hair."

My eyes stay focused on the two boys slowly making their way down as I jog up to meet them. Harry runs the last stretch and throws himself against me.

"Is he gone?"

CHAPTER 26

MARYA

My legs almost give out from relief when I see Dylan come walking down the street, holding on to Harry with one hand, and David with the other. By the time they come walking up the path to the front door, relief has been replaced with anger.

"Harry, go inside." Dylan gives my guilty-looking son a little shove in my direction. "I'll be right back. Just dropping David off at home," he tells me, and all I manage is a stiff nod.

I step to the side to let Harry—who's dragging his heels—inside, where he's immediately questioned by his brothers.

"Guys," I close the door and turn around. "Do me a favor, and hang out in the basement for a bit." There isn't a single protest as the boys move toward the stairs. "Not you, Harry." My youngest, who clearly thought he could sneak off with the others, looks crestfallen.

"I'm sorry, Mom," he apologizes. "But we—"

"What is it, Harry? Are you sorry or are you making excuses? I've told you before, sorry is not an apology if it's followed by *but*." I lean my crutches against the side of the couch before dropping down. I've lost ten years off my life in the past ten minutes. "Sit down, so I don't have to crane my neck to talk to you."

With tears tracking down his cheeks, he wisely sits in the chair across from me, and my hard shield of anger starts cracking. I'm about to start lecturing him when Dylan comes in the door, followed by Damian, who hangs back.

"Tell us exactly what happened," Dylan's voice is much calmer than mine was as he passes by me and crouches down in front of my son.

Accompanied by sniffles, Harry starts recounting how he and David went to throw a Frisbee in the park. When he had to climb the hillside to retrieve it, he saw his father get out of a car at the far end of the block, and dart down the small alleyway four houses down from us.

My eyes are immediately drawn to the sliding doors off the kitchen, that open up to a decent backyard, beyond which is a gully that runs all along the back. It fills up with spring runoff or when we've had a bad rainstorm, but most of the time it's dry.

The men look at each other and I know some silent communication has taken place when Damian disappears out the front door.

"Why didn't you call your mom?"

Harry's eyes dart to me. "I thought I'd be in trouble."

"So you know you did something wrong," I point out. "First you sneak out without telling me, getting your big brother to do your bidding, and then you thought it would be a good idea to play in the park?"

"But I was just—"

"Being stupid," Dylan interrupts, and Harry's face dissolves. It's one thing being told off by your mother, but he hero-worships Dylan, so coming from him it hurts. I almost intervene, but this is about safety. "Remember those boys who went missing?" he continues and I wince. "They didn't mean for anything to happen to them, but it did. Just last week, you had to hide under your mom's car after you took off when you weren't supposed to and got yourself into trouble. Yet today you do it again, putting yourself in a position where you're not safe. You figure that's smart?"

"N-no."

Dylan gives my boy's shoulder a little shove with his fist. "You want to know what *was* smart, though? Hiding and sending that message."

Typical Harry, he grabs onto the positive and hangs on for dear life. Smiling through his tears at the compliment, he explains, "I didn't want Mom or Theo to come looking with him around, so I sent the message to Liam."

"See?" Dylan grins, ruffling his hair. "Smart. Now you've gotta try and be smart all the time." Then he leans in and stage-whispers in Harry's ear, "I'm thinking your mom could use a hug right about now."

Harry doesn't waste a minute and launches himself at me. He buries his head against me and I look up at Dylan, whose face is serious as he tilts his head to the door. I nod in response. I assume Damian, and whoever else is out there, is looking. I can understand Dylan wants to be out there too.

"I'll lock the door behind me," he says before slipping outside.

I snuggle Harry for a minute before I grab his shoulders and move him back a little. "You think maybe you should go downstairs and apologize to Theo?"

The reluctant, "Okay," tells me he'd rather not, but he knows better than to argue at this point and heads down to the basement.

I hoist myself up and walk into the kitchen, making sure the sliding door is still locked. I peer into the thick brush threatening to overgrow the back fence, but can't see any movement. After a few minutes I give up trying, and set out to make a fresh pot of coffee.

I'm pouring some fresh brew in a travel mug—the only thing I'm able to carry with my crutches without spilling—when I hear yelling outside, followed by a sharp crack.

Gunshot.

Instinct has me drop down, spilling coffee all over, when I hear footsteps running up the stairs.

"Mom?"

"Stay down there!" I yell out, hearing Theo's worried voice. "All of you stay in the basement. I'm fine!"

Or as fine as I can be with my back pressed against the cupboard and my ass sitting in a hot puddle.

Five minutes is a long time when you can't stop your mind from conjuring up images of the horrible ways your boyfriend could be bleeding to death in your backyard. So long that, when I finally hear a key in the lock, I'm light-headed and my chest hurts from my heart pounding hard.

"Marya?"

The "here," I'm trying to formulate comes out in a sob, and Dylan's on his knees in front of me in a nanosecond.

"Shit. Are you hurt?" His hands run over my body until he feels the puddle on the floor. "Let's get you cleaned up," he says with a sympathetic look on his face.

"It's coffee," I snap, shoving his shoulder. Immediately followed by, "Did anyone get hurt?"

"I wish," he mumbles before adding at normal volume, "Found the idiot hiding in a culvert behind your neighbor's yard. He didn't want to come out and we didn't want to crawl in the mud after him. Damian fired off a warning shot, which got his ass moving. He's in custody and being transported to the station."

He gets to his feet and helps me up as well, brushing the back of his fingers down my cheek before leaning in for a bruising kiss. If not for his arms holding me steady, I surely would've ended up back on my ass.

"Can it be over now?" I ask in a small voice when he lifts his mouth, and tucks me under his chin.

"Fuck, I hope so. I'm about ready to pack you all up and move to Alaska."

"Can we go dogsledding?"

Both our heads turn in the direction of the stairs to find four pairs of eyes on us.

"We're not moving to Alaska," I tell Harry.

"I wouldn't mind dogsledding," Theo says with a shrug.

"We're not moving to Alaska," I repeat.

"That would be really cool, though," Max contributes with a cheeky grin on his face.

"Forget about Alaska."

"I'd go."

My eyes shoot to Liam, who shrugs, grinning sheepishly when the others start snickering. Hope blossoms in my chest—almost painfully—when I take in his playful blue eyes among the brown ones.

Blinking against the burn, I let go of Dylan and wag a finger at the boys.

"No Alaska."

DYLAN

"You'd better have a real good fucking explanation!"

Detective Tony Ramirez doesn't flinch when I come charging up to his desk at the DPD station. He simply turns his chair, stretches his legs, and folds his arms over his chest.

"Take it easy, Barnes," his partner, Keith Blackfoot, suggests.

It wasn't until after I left Marya and the boys at her place that I realized how badly this could've ended, which meant by the time I got to the station, I was worked up again.

"Have a seat." Ramirez indicates a chair across the desk from him and waits until I sit down. "I followed Berger and his two sleezeball lawyers to the DoubleTree Hilton, watched them park the car, and walk into the lobby. I kept an eye on the door and their vehicle the whole time."

"And yet, Berger ended up behind Marya's house."

"Regrettably, yes. He must've gone straight out the back. There's just one of me, Barnes."

It's a natural enough reaction to want to blame someone, but the truth is, there's nothing I would've done any differently myself.

"How'd he get from the hotel to Marya's?"

"Uber," Blackfoot answers. "I just got off the phone with the driver. He confirms picking up Berger behind the hotel and dropping him off on Lawrence Avenue."

"The lawyers?"

"Still at the DoubleTree, as far as I know," Tony confirms.

"Wouldn't they be on their way back here?" I suggest.

"You'd think so, but as it turns out, our boy in there—" He nudges his head in the direction of the holding cells. "Doesn't want them around. He's been yelling he wants to talk for the past fifteen minutes."

"So what's the hold up?"

"Yeager's on his way."

———

"So talk."

I'm wedged into the small room with Blackfoot and Ramirez, watching and listening as Yeager barks at Berger. Like last time, Damian's in there, as is Joe Benedetti, who has taken up his spot leaning against the wall.

"Before I talk, I need your guarantee my daughter is safe," Berger fires back. His eyes nervously dart from one to the other.

Damian flips through the file in front of him. "Amelia?"

My mind immediately pulls up the image of the little girl I saw on the mantel at Sylvia Berger's house.

"Yes. You need to get her out of there. She's not safe."

"Why would you say that?" Yeager wants to know and Berger's eyes flit back to him.

"If you don't get her safe—"

He swallows the rest of his words when Yeager gets out of his chair and leans with his fists on the table. "Let's talk about why you were caught hiding behind your ex-wife's house, violating the protective order yet again."

"Please," Berger pleads. "I'm trying to protect my daughter."

"I think we get that," Damian jumps in. "What we'd like to know is what, if anything, that has to do with Ms. Berger and her children."

"Everything!" he bursts out, agitated.

"You're going to have to give us more than that, Jeremy," Yeager picks up. "Why do you feel your daughter is in danger?"

"Please, just make sure."

"You're not telling us anything that would justify the Montrose PD to go knocking on the door, Jeremy," Yeager pushes. "There needs to be cause. Is there anything we need to know about your wife? We can call her, see if—"

"No—not her!"

The chair topples over when Berger surges to his feet. Joe immediately pushes off from the wall, closing in on the agitated man from behind.

"You need to calm down, Jeremy," he says in a cautioning tone. "Or we'll be forced to shackle you."

"She…she's been brainwashed. Talk to Alba. She's Amelia's nanny. Please…"

I've heard that name before. Sylvia mentioned the nanny when her father ordered her to check on the little girl. There'd been something off about that whole scene. Keswick being the pompous asshole he is, I thought at the time he was just flexing his muscle for our benefit, but maybe...

"*Shit,*" I hiss, remembering the way Keswick possessively snatched Amelia's picture from my hands.

"What?" Keith wants to know.

"I need to talk to Roosberg. For the life of me I can't see the connection with Marya and the boys, but Berger may be right, the little girl might be in trouble."

"It's possible," Luna concurs over the phone. "It crossed my mind at the time that the interaction between father and daughter seemed weird. Uncomfortable, even."

"Exactly."

"Still doesn't explain why, if he's so worried about his daughter, he's in Durango, harassing his ex-wife and the kids."

"I know, but I don't think he'll talk unless the girl is safe."

Luna promises to start looking into Connor Keswick when the door to the interrogation room opens and Berger is being led out by Joe.

"I gotta go."

Damian steps into the hallway, catches my eye, and with a nudge of his head tells me to follow. I walk into the conference room where Yeager and Benedetti look to be in a heated standoff.

"We've got a boy to find, we don't have time to indulge this asshole," Yeager barks.

"He's not talking unless we do," Joe counters. "Local PD can't do shit without an official report filed. You guys can as part of this investigation."

"It's a waste of time, he's just stalling." It's clear Yeager is frustrated with the lack of progress after he drove here from Farmington—for the second time in as many days—hoping to get ahead in his search for Thomas.

"Actually," I interrupt and launch into my observations during our interview in Montrose.

"You think he's abusing his granddaughter?" Yeager sounds incredulous.

"I think it may be possible."

"Let's suppose that's the case," Damian puts forward. "It makes him a child molester...a pedophile."

His words hang in the conference room and you can almost hear everyone thinking.

"Do we have anything on him?" Yeager asks in general.

"Roosberg is digging," I volunteer.

"We should all get digging. Fucking lay the man bare. Talk to the damn nanny, to the daughter, but we better play this by the book, because that asshole has the means and the connections to slip through our fingers."

"What about Berger?" Joe inquires.

"Let him simmer."

CHAPTER 27

MARYA

"It looks good."

Can't say I agree, looking down at the ten-inch incision down the front of my knee, but I'll take his word for it. Not like I had award-winning knees to start with.

"Battle scars," Mom jokes beside me.

I have a few of those, what's one more?

It's been a week and a half since surgery, and even this follow-up visit with the surgeon is a welcome distraction from my couch and Netflix. It doesn't help I've not really seen Dylan since Sunday, and that was for a brief moment when he kissed me goodbye at the crack of dawn.

Beth and Clint showed up mid-afternoon to pick up Max, while Kerry was there with her little one. Mom insisted they stick around for coffee. It didn't take much to convince Beth at least, who claimed to be in need of some quality baby-time with Dante, and Mom used the opportunity to pick Clint's brain about upgrades she envisions being done to *my* house. Something I would normally have argued about with her, but I was too busy trying to wrap my head around the workings of Kerry's online store.

We have talked a few times, though, so I know there's been a potential new development in the case. He wasn't able to share specifics, but he did say time was of the essence and they were working almost around the clock.

I miss him being around. Selfishly miss waking up to his body wrapped around mine, but then I remember he's out there busting his ass—trying to find that poor boy—and I feel guilty because my kids are safe under my roof, while Thomas' parents have to wonder if they'll ever see their son again. I've just had a brief taste of that kind of agony, so I can only imagine the torture they've lived these past eleven days.

"I'd like to see you again in a month," Dr. Andrews announces, pulling me from my thoughts. "I've adjusted the brace for some movement of the knee, but I need you to talk to reception and have them set you up an appointment for physical therapy in the next few days. No driving until I see you in November." He catches the grimace on my face and chuckles. "Slow and easy wins the race in this case, Marya. Push too hard and you won't like how far back that could set you."

"Slow and easy isn't a pace she's accustomed to, Dr. Andrews," Mom decides to share.

"I get that impression, and it's Frank." He smiles at my mother.

"I'll make sure she's careful…Frank," she adds as an afterthought.

"Umm, I'm in the room, guys," I remind them. "Forty-one and quite capable of following instructions."

I wait at reception to get my appointments, while Mom and Dr. Andrews stand in the doorway of his office, undoubtedly chuckling at my expense.

"November twenty-seventh for Dr. Andrews, and the earliest I could get you into the PT clinic here at the hospital is next Tuesday at ten thirty. Will that work for you?"

"That's fine," I tell the girl behind the counter when she hands over two appointment cards. "I'm sure it'll be the highlight of my week."

"Ignore her," Mom says, hooking an arm in mine, her eyes on the receptionist. "She's out of sorts because she has to put up with my driving."

Mom is still grinning when she helps me into the passenger seat of my Jeep, which is easier to get in and out.

"It wasn't that funny," I point out when she gets behind the wheel.

"What?" She turns to me, genuinely confused and wearing a healthy blush on her cheeks I suddenly realize is not from the cold wind outside.

"No way," I blurt out, shifting sideways in my seat.

Mom lifts her eyebrows high and blinks a few times. "What?" she repeats, but she's not throwing me off.

"Oh my God, I just witnessed my mother flirting," I mumble at no one in particular. "I didn't even know that was possible."

"I'm not dead yet," she snaps, putting my Jeep in gear and backing out of the parking spot. "He's a nice man."

He's also probably ten, maybe even fifteen years younger than her, but far be it from me to point that out. I'm in love with a guy eight years my junior. Plus, Dr. Andrews—Frank—*is* a nice man.

I glance at her profile. Her hair is gray now, her skin no longer so smooth, and her chin is softer than it used to be, but my mother is still a beautiful woman. Clear eyes that are always kind, a full mouth permanently tilted up, and a warm heart underneath her sometimes abrasive nature.

I realize, looking at her, that I'm seeing myself in twenty-five or so years, and it's not a bad thing. Not at all.

"He is, Mom. And he's also a damn lucky man you noticed that."

Her eyes flit to me and a soft smile plays on her lips as she grabs my hand for a quick squeeze. "What do you want for dinner?" Never big on letting the occasional sweet moment linger too long, Mom gets practical.

"I wouldn't mind some soup. It's the kind of day for it, kinda chilly."

"Potato soup and grilled cheese?" she suggests.

"Yes, that sounds good."

"Let me stop at the City Market to pick up a few things. You can wait in the car, I won't be long."

She's just disappeared inside when my phone rings in my purse. I smile when I see Dylan's name.

"Hey."

"How did it go?"

"He seemed pleased with the healing. Adjusted the brace so I can actually bend my knee a little, and has me start PT next week. But…no driving, no standing for long periods of time, for at least another four weeks, until I see him again."

"Slow and easy, Sweetheart." I hear the smile in his voice.

"Not you too," I moan. "Mom and Frank are already on my case."

"Frank?"

"Dr. Andrews."

"I see."

A pregnant silence follows, and I have to bite my lip not to start laughing when it occurs to me he might be jealous. After all, Dr. Andrews is a handsome man and age-wise is stuck somewhere between Mom and me.

"I only know his name is Frank because he made it a point to share that with my mother."

"Your mother?"

"Yeah, apparently you're not the only guy who has a thing for older women," I tease him.

"I don't have a thing for older women," he disagrees. "I have a thing for *you*. You happen to be older, that's all."

If I wasn't already gone for him, that would've surely done the trick. "Okay, you need to stop being perfect. My heart can't handle it."

"How's that?" he asks, clearly amused.

"You've already filled it to the brim. It'll burst."

"It'll stretch," he says, his tone gentle.

My eyes stare unseeing as I focus on the sound of his voice. "What if it can't?"

"It will. Mine does every time I get to hear your voice."

A deep sigh escapes me at his words. *Gah*…this man. "You're doing it again," I accuse him but he just chuckles.

"Want me to stop?"

"Fuck, no."

The last thing I hear is his hearty laugh as he ends the call.

It's only when Mom returns with the groceries that I realize I never asked how his day was going.

Me: I never asked you how your day was.

Dylan: Infinitely better after talking to you.

Me: Anytime you want to talk, I'm here

Dylan: I know and it keeps me going.

DYLAN

I'm still staring at the screen when Damian comes out of his office.

"Luna back yet?"

"On her way," I tell him.

We've spent all week trying to find anything that might connect Keswick to the boys' disappearances. It's like shooting blindfolded, hoping something we try will hit target. The IP addresses connected to *SoccerLord*, the boys' league, a dark-colored van—anything.

The table in the conference room is littered with printouts of any information we could pull to compare. Some of it publicly available, some of it obtained through questionable means in our desperation to find Thomas.

Damian drove to Montrose, to see if he could talk to the nanny, but found only Sylvia at home. According to her, Alba had to leave for Honduras for a family emergency. The only contact information she was able to provide us with was an email address and a cell phone number. The phone just rings unanswered and there's been no response to the email Damian sent.

First thing this morning, we finally managed to connect with Keswick's VP at Contechs, who was able to tell me the man left for Texas on Sunday, personally overseeing the final stages of the new plant installations. He's not expected back until after the grand opening November first.

Damian sent Luna back to Montrose shortly after. With Sylvia's father a few states away, she was going to try to convince the woman to come in and bring Amelia.

"Benedetti is waiting. As soon as she gets here, we're heading over to the station. See if the asshole will talk now."

Berger has refused to talk to anyone, including his lawyers, just reiterating that unless his daughter is safe, we won't get anything out of him. Hopefully that'll change soon.

***

"What convinced her?" I ask Luna.

We're watching through the one-way mirror as Berger is led into the room, drops to his knees, and hugs the doll-faced little girl who runs at him. I can't see Sylvia's face, but her back is ramrod straight in the seat beside Damian.

"All I did was tell her I could keep her and her daughter safe. The woman is afraid of her own shadow. Just the promise of taking her away from Montrose was enough to have her pack a bag for her and Amelia."

"If she was so scared of her father, why did she stay?"

"Keswick carries a lot of influence in Montrose.

Plays golf with the mayor, belongs to the local Rotary Club, as does the chief of police, the district attorney, and the local sheriff. He's a generous contributor to a variety of local charities and is one of the biggest employers in the area. Her mother died young, and by the time Sylvia was twelve, he took her everywhere: fundraisers, charity events, Rotary events, dinner gatherings, Christmas parties. She was expected to fill the slot her mother left." We watch as Berger sits down at the table with his daughter in his lap, and reaches a hand across to his wife.

"In bed?" I ask.

"She didn't specify, and I didn't want to ask with the little girl in the car. When she met him—" Luna lifts her chin at Berger. "She thought he would be the way out, but all he saw was his meal ticket and couldn't wait to get close to her father."

"From one abuser to another."

"Of sorts," Luna agrees. "She admits Jeremy was occasionally rough with her—would shake her—but that it had been her father who'd wanted her to file the complaint against him. Insurance, he'd called it."

In the room Damian gets to his feet and turns to the mirror, tilting his head to the door.

"That's my cue," Luna says, before slipping out the door. A few seconds later, I see her enter the interrogation room and lead Sylvia and her daughter out, leaving Berger, Joe, and Damian inside.

"Ready to talk?" I hear Damian ask.

"Will you keep her safe?"

"Yes."

Jeremy nods and then stares down at his hands wringing on the table in front of him. "I work... worked for my father-in-law." He snorts and shakes his head. "More like a glorified gopher he liked to order around. Anyway, a few months ago I was in his office and found some...he had pictures..." His voice drifts off.

"Pictures?"

"Kids, boys mostly. Some were just snapshots. Others were...sick. A few showed a bunch of kids going through what looked like drills on a soccer field. My son was in those pictures."

"When you say you found those pictures, where exactly? On his computer? In his desk?"

Jeremy's eyes dart up. He looks at Damian, then at Joe, before returning his gaze to his clasped hands and answering in a low voice, "In his safe."

It's a pretty safe bet why Jeremy was going through the safe, something he eventually admits to Damian.

"He had my son's pictures, so I confronted him." He puffs up his chest. "I have to look out for my boy." My toes curl in my boots. The man's never looked after any of his boys. Marya did that. He more than likely tried using those pictures to blackmail Keswick.

"What happened?" Joe prompts him and I can see Berger deflating.

"He started talking about Amelia, how with her sixth birthday coming up, she's almost old enough to have a sleepover at her grandpa's house. Said maybe he'd take her for a trip to Disneyland, just the two of them." At least Jeremy has the decency to look about as sick as I feel listening to this. "Then he suggested that of course, if I were to bring Liam for regular visits, he might be too busy for Amelia."

The fucker was trading one kid for another. A boy has been brutalized and killed. Another is missing. I see red when I push into the hallway and almost rip the door to the interrogation room off its hinges when I barge in.

"Barnes…"

I barely hear Joe as I pull the fucking weasel from his seat, back him against the wall, and press my forearm against his throat.

"Is that when you approached Marya? You were going to deliver your son into the hands of a predator? What kind of sorry fucking excuse of a man are you?"

I feel the other two men crowd in behind me, ready to pull me off.

"Dylan, keep your head," Damian warns, his hand on my shoulder.

"You have the blood of those boys on your hands," I growl, my face inches from his, before I back up.

He grabs for his throat, gasping for air. Then he glances up and meets my eyes, almost like he's looking for understanding, but he'll get none from me. Not ever.

"She's my princess."

Damian sent me home, told me not to show my face back in the office for at least twelve hours. Instead I end up sitting in Marya's driveway, leaning my forehead on my steering wheel, weighed down by the new information uncovered this afternoon.

How am I supposed to explain that the man she shares three boys with was willing to hand one of them over to a pedophile, in order to guard the safety of his daughter?

We have no concrete evidence, just the testimony of a guy who was heading the suspect list himself. The only person who might be able to verify his claims would be Sylvia Berger. Damian planned to head over to the Arrow's Edge compound—where Luna had taken Sylvia and her daughter—to question her.

A tap on the window startles me. Marya is standing on the other side and steps back when I open the door.

"You shouldn't be out here," I grunt, getting out of the truck.

"I waited for you to come in, but you were taking so long I figured I'd come get you."

"That leg should be up." I point at her brace.

"Come inside then."

She turns and hobbles on her crutches to the front door. I follow without argument. Inside she directs me to the fridge to get myself a beer, while she installs herself on the couch.

I haven't even kissed her yet, but instead of calling me on it, she seems to sense I have my reasons.

"I'm here," she says when I start to sit in the chair

across from her. A small smile plays on her lips and she pulls up a challenging eyebrow. I drop down beside her instead. "The boys are in bed, so I'm all ears."

I take a deep tug of the beer—in need of some liquid encouragement—set it down on the table and turn my body to her. Ripping off the bandage is best, so I give it to her straight. Her expression goes from shock to anger, then disgust, before morphing back to shock.

Then it's her turn to shock me.

"Is that why you hesitated coming in? Why you haven't touched me yet? Because I've gotta tell you, this news would be a whole easier to take in if you weren't sitting on the other side of the couch."

The words are barely from her mouth when I scoot over and haul her in my arms, dropping my forehead to her shoulder. "I'm so fucking sorry," I mumble in her hair as her hand slides around the back of my head, holding me close.

"Don't apologize for something you carry no responsibility for."

"Telling you this shit goes against every one of my instincts. I should be shielding you and the boys, but I also didn't want you finding this shit out from some other source."

She lifts my face in both her hands and presses a gentle kiss on my mouth, her gorgeous eyes soothing.

But it's her words warm me from the inside out.

"And that's just part of why I love you."

CHAPTER 28

MARYA

Dylan is still sleeping when my alarm buzzes. I quickly shut it off, but still he grunts and tightens his arm around my waist. I wait until I feel the tension leave his body, and his breathing evens out, before I roll myself out of his hold.

Sitting on the edge of the bed, I quickly fasten the brace on my leg and make my way over to the bathroom. I manage to pull on some lounge pants and a shirt before I carefully head downstairs.

I left my crutches in the living room last night, letting Dylan carry me upstairs. We didn't do much more than kiss and grope a little before he started dropping off. He clearly needed sleep more than a release, so I snuggled close, stroking my hand over his back until finally I drifted off too.

I'm determined to let him sleep as long as I can, and

from what he told me last night, he's not supposed to be back to the office until ten or so. He looked ready to drop last night, carrying the weight of the world. There's not much I can do to relieve that load, but I sure as hell can make sure he's well-rested.

I go through the motions getting lunches ready for the kids. As usual, Theo is the first one to surface.

"Dylan here?" is the first thing out of his mouth.

"Morning to you too, love. Yes, Dylan is still sleeping, so I'd appreciate it if you guys were a little more quiet than you usually are."

"He in your room?" he asks, looking at the empty living room.

"He is," I confirm, keeping an eye on my son while I pour myself a coffee. It's not the first time he's spent the night, but on previous occasions he was up and either downstairs or out of the house by the time the kids got up. "You good with that?" I lean my back against the counter to take the load off my bad leg and take a sip of my coffee.

Theo shrugs. "Fine by me. He's a good guy," he says in a casual way, far too mature for his thirteen years. My oldest has thrown up as my protector in the past years and asking his opinion is my way of acknowledging his self-appointed role, while at the same time letting him know he can relax now.

"Yes, he is. I like him, Theo...a lot."

"No duh, Mom. You wouldn't let him be around us otherwise. It's cool."

"Love you lots, Theodor Berger. I think I need a

hug."

I love the small awkward grin he's trying to hide as he rounds the counter with an aw-shucks look on his face, walking straight into my arms. "Love ya too, Mom," he mumbles, his head in my neck.

When he straightens I notice I'm looking up at him. My boy is growing up.

"Do me a solid and go wake your brothers. Tell them if they can keep it down up there, I'll make you guys quick bacon and egg muffins to getcha going."

Sure enough, all three boys are back downstairs ten minutes later with a minimum of noise. I already have half a dozen of the egg sandwiches stacked on a platter and the boys make short work of them.

I'm by the door saying goodbye. Harry is always easy with his affection and hugs me, Theo gives me a peck on the cheek, but Liam has always been more reserved. Still, when he passes me last, I pull him in a tight hug. "Love you so much, Bub," I whisper in his ear.

Hesitantly I feel his arms come around me. "Love you too, Mom."

My eyes are watery as I wrap my arms around myself and watch them heading out for the bus stop.

"Do I smell bacon?" I hear from behind me to find Dylan perched on the bottom step of the stairs, his hair standing in every direction.

"Shit. We were trying to be quiet," I grumble, closing the front door. "I wanted you to sleep in."

"I did," he says, walking toward me. "I normally

get up around six, it's close to eight now, so technically I slept in." He wraps me up in his arms and my head automatically tilts back. Without hesitation, he covers my mouth with his.

I drop my crutches and grab onto his shoulders, but he goes a step farther, bends through his knees, and with his hands under my ass, lifts me up. With our mouths fused, he carries me right back upstairs.

"Sexy," he rumbles, a smirk on his face when he has me naked—except for my knee brace—on my back in bed.

"I can take it off," I offer, reaching for the straps, but he grabs my hands and presses them to the mattress, his hips settling between mine.

"Don't. I'm living a dream, I have the *Bionic Woman* naked in my bed." His cock lies hot and heavy against the inside of my thigh and I squirm underneath him.

"My bed, if you want to get technical," I tease a little breathlessly.

"I'd love to get technical with you," he returns, his eyes focused and heated. "In fact, I've fucking missed getting technical with you."

"I missed you too," I confess, freeing my hands and curving them around his neck.

He doesn't need much encouragement and takes my mouth again. "Can't wait for the day I can take my time with you," he mumbles between kisses. "I'm gonna need at least a full weekend to make a dent in this need I have for you."

I get restless underneath him, lifting my hips looking for the connection I crave. The next moment he gives me what I want as I feel his shaft filling me.

"Dylan…"

"Right here, Sweetheart."

His pace is torturously slow and I move my hands to his firm ass, flexing under my palms as he strokes me deep. My fingers dig in, encouraging him to move faster, but he never does. Just thrusts strong and thorough, rolling his hips deep every time he roots himself inside me, grinding on that sensitive bundle of nerves.

My mouth opens and my head rolls to the side, but with his elbows in the mattress, he uses a hand to ease it back. "Watch me love you, Marya."

He builds me slow, loves me fully, and with his eyes on mine, his hands bracing my face, he wills me over the edge. I come without sound because the surge of waves pounding my body steals my breath. I'm still pulsing with the force of my climax when Dylan finds his and lets me carry his full weight as we recover.

"There's more to me than missionary, Sweetheart, but I don't want to hurt you," he mumbles in my neck, making me laugh. He pushes up on his elbows, smiling in my face.

I laugh for a good while, feeling mellow and happy. "Your missionary is stellar, honey, but I can't say I don't look forward to discovering what else you have in store for me."

"Love hearing you laugh. Can't wait for a chance to clear this dark cloud over our heads, so I can make you laugh more."

DYLAN

"What did I miss?" I ask when I walk into the office a little after ten.

"Damian and Luna made out like a bandit last night with Sylvia," Jasper informs me. "She wasn't just a stand-in for her mother at parties and events. She was more than that, at least until she was about fifteen and developed. He's a child molester. Yeager had a federal magistrate sign a search warrant for Keswick's homes."

I plop down in my chair, running a hand through my hair. "Jesus." I know we all suspected it, but it's sickening to find out it's true. "He's got more than one home?"

"House in Montrose, a place in Farmington, and a new condo in Austin. He likes to be comfortable when he visits his plants apparently."

"Local FBI executing the warrants?"

"Yes. The Grand Junction agents are on their way to Montrose. We're coordinating information from here."

"What about Keswick himself?"

"Waiting to hear from Yeager's office. Local agents are supposed to pick him up this morning. The moment they have him, the warrant will be executed."

At that moment, the phone rings and I reach for it.

"La Plata County FBI office, Special Agent Barnes speaking."

There's a hesitation on the other side before I hear Toni's familiar voice. "Uhh...Dylan, it's Toni. Yeager asked me to call. He's on his way to Austin. Keswick's been picked up for questioning."

They wouldn't arrest him for child molestation right off the bat, or he'll lawyer up right away. With Thomas still out there, the last thing we want is for him to clam up. I don't expect he'll be volunteering any information, but he may let something drop unwittingly, that might give us some direction.

"Thank you," I tell her politely, despite my residual anger with her.

I go to hang up when I hear her. "Dylan? Look, I'm sorry. I—"

"Toni, we've got work to do, and to be honest, I don't want to hear it." I look up to find Jasper observing me, one eyebrow raised. "Not the right time," I add a little less abrasive.

"Of course. You're right. We'll call in as soon as we have something to report," she says.

"You're in on the search warrant?"

"Yeager said all hands on deck."

"Right. Keep us in the loop."

"Will do."

I end the call, get up to pour myself a coffee, and try to ignore Jasper's pointed stare. It's still there when I sit back down, though.

"What?"

"You've got some serious control, brother. Don't think I'd have it in me to stay professional if I were in your shoes."

I shake my head, mostly to hide the fact his words sounded like a compliment I tuck away safely, but I feel a little lighter when I pull some of Keswick's records toward me. We still have to find a connection between him and the soccer league or the *Fortnite* chat.

I think we all feel in our gut it's him, but you can't charge a man without some evidence.

At least with Keswick held at the FBI offices in Austin, he can't hurt anyone.

We work in silence for a few hours, but it's difficult to concentrate when we're waiting for information to start coming in from the searches. When Luna and Damian walk in around noon, after working deep into the early morning hours, I update them on this morning's developments.

This time, when the phone rings, Damian answers and puts it on speakerphone.

"Agent Parker, I have you on speakerphone."

"Okay, so we just completed our preliminary search of the Montrose house. No sign of the boy, so far nothing to indicate either of them were ever there, but we have a forensics team going through the house. We were able to get in the safe in the office, but the images mentioned in the warrant weren't in there."

"Not really a surprise," Luna remarks. "Stands to

reason he would've gotten rid of those immediately after discovering Berger had seen them."

No one is surprised by it, but it would've been the proverbial smoking gun we are all hoping for.

"Anything else?" Damian asks.

"Maybe. He had a box of single use pouches of lube in the bottom of his bathroom cupboard. There was also a supply of needles and what looks to be a few ampoules of Ketalar in that box."

"Ketamine, it's used by vets," Jasper shares.

"Not just that," Parker clarifies. "It's a relaxant with hallucinogenic properties, so it's popular on the black market. Known under a variety of names: Ket, Vitamin K, or Special K and whatever else. Injected it takes just twenty or thirty seconds to take effect."

"Jesus, it's a rape kit," Luna blurts out.

"It could be," Parker shares. "But in the hands of the right lawyer, it could simply be a bad habit and a proclivity for anal sex."

He makes a good point. We still need to find a connection to the boys to show that find in a more sinister light.

"I'll need pictures of the labels," Jasper advises.

"I'll send them."

"That it?"

"Lots of paperwork to go through, mostly relating to Contechs. If we find anything, we'll let you know," Parker promises.

Over the next few hours, we receive similar calls from the team in Farmington and in Austin, and try to fit together the pieces. Luna is standing by the large whiteboard in the conference room, adding information as it comes in. The visual overview helps to keep the large picture when we get too focused on details.

I'd rather be out in the field, physically contributing, than in here getting overwhelmed with the minutiae of this case to the point where I can't think anymore. I also haven't eaten since the quick bagel Marya made me this morning, and I'm getting light-headed. I need some air, maybe give her a quick call.

"I'm gonna pick up some food, can I get anyone anything?"

Damian looks up from his laptop. "Just call for a couple of pizzas. Get them delivered."

Shit. So much for fresh air and a little hit of Marya's voice.

I place an order and am about to turn back to comparing lists of phone numbers when my cell rings.

"Hey, Sweetheart," I tell Marya whose name shows on my display.

"It...it's Liam." I hear her blow out a shaky breath, and I surge to my feet, attracting the attention of the others. "Theo called from school. Said he and Harry were about to get on the bus, but Liam never came out of class. He's also not answering his phone. I tried too."

"They on the bus now?"

"Yes, Mom is waiting by the bus stop."

"Did you call the school? Talk to the teacher?"

"I called you first."

"Good, that's good. Look, Liam may just have missed the bus or was kept after class. Call the school. See if you find out more from his teacher."

"Okay." I hate the panic in her voice; so different from the relaxed and laughing Marya I left this morning.

"I'll head over to the school now, just in case. You stay right there."

"What if—"

"Sweetheart, don't go there. Berger is still in DPD custody and our main suspect is held at the FBI office in Austin. Call the school, I'm on my way there."

All eyes are on me when I hang up, concern on their faces.

"What are you thinking?" Damian asks, reading me well.

What am I thinking? I let those boys go this morning, believing everything I told Marya just now, that with a team of FBI agents on Keswick and Berger behind bars, the kids would be safe. I should've known better.

"I'm thinking the link we've been looking for between Keswick and the boys is still out there."

"*Fuck*." Damian curses. "Jas, get on the line with Austin. See if there's anything useful they're getting from Keswick."

I don't wait, grabbing my jacket and heading out the door. Luna comes jogging out after me.

"I'm coming with you."

CHAPTER 29

LIAM

It's dark in here.

It takes my eyes a moment to get used to the dim light.

The floor is cold underneath my cheek, but when I try to sit up, I discover my hands are tied behind my back. My head starts spinning and I'm about to puke, so I lie back down.

I don't know where I am, or how I got here, but I know I'm in trouble.

The last thing I remember is Mr. Gruber, my PE teacher, asking me to put away the balls and cones we'd used during class on the sports field behind the school. Outside equipment goes into the storage shed at the edge of the field, next to the parking lot. I can remember walking in, but nothing else.

I look around me, wondering if maybe I was still in

the shed, but this place is bigger, and almost empty. There aren't any windows; just a small crack of light showing under what I think is a door on the far side. It also doesn't smell like the shed; like fresh cut grass and leather. This place stinks, like the locker room after someone takes a dump. Sweat, piss, and shit. It makes me gag.

I try sitting up again, my eyes focused on a pile of blankets or something in one of the corners. It's not easy without the use of my hands, but I manage. This time the spinning is not so bad, and I'm able to lift myself and lean my shoulders against the wall.

The pile of blankets looks like it's moving.

I try to pull on whatever I have tied around my wrists, but it cuts into my skin so I stop. It feels like one of those plastic straps. It's on tight; my fingers are tingling.

The blankets move again. Is someone under there?

"Hey," I try, my voice a little raspy, but it sounds loud in the room.

I watch as the pile shifts and a head pops up. I can't make out the face.

"Who are you?" The question is whispered, but I can tell it's a kid.

"Liam. What is this place? Who are you?" I automatically start whispering as well. I don't want whoever stuck us in here to come back.

"Thomas, and I don't know."

"You're the kid that went missing. Everyone is looking for you." He doesn't say anything, but I hear

him sniffle. "Hey," I try again, scooting closer to him. "They'll find us. My mom's boyfriend works for the FBI. Dylan will find us."

I manage to get close enough to see him curled in a ball, his head the only thing visible in the pile of blankets.

"How long have I been here?" he finally asks, opening his eyes on me.

"A while. Two weeks or so." He closes his eyes again. "Do you remember anything?" He doesn't answer so I try again. "Hey, did they hurt you? Have you tried getting out? Thomas?"

Nothing. He's not even moving anymore.

I sit next to him, leaning my head back against the wall, pulling my knees up. The moment I do I feel something poking into my stomach.

My phone. We're not supposed to have a phone in class, but I just turn it off. It's small enough it fits in the little pocket inside my sports shorts, and I feel better having it on me.

"Thomas," I hiss trying to get his attention, but the only response I get is him turning his face in the other direction.

I twist my arms behind me to try and reach for the phone with one of my hands, but I can't reach far enough that way. Then I try to move my hands under my ass. My brothers sometimes tease me for my freakishly long arms, but for once I'm glad for them.

It's a struggle to work my lower body through, because the backs of my wrists are tied together, but I *finally end up with my bound hands in front.*

I drop the phone twice before I manage to turn it on. The moment I do, though, it starts pinging with messages and missed calls coming in.

"Shut it off," Thomas sits up, the blankets falling away.

I notice he's not wearing a shirt while I try to work the little button on the side to lower the volume. It's not easy when your thumbs are pointing in the wrong direction but I get it done. Flipping it open, I manage to dial the shortcut for Dylan, but it doesn't even ring. I notice it doesn't have any bars.

"Shit."

"What?"

"There's no signal."

"Try sending a text."

"How is that going to help?"

"Dad says they don't need as strong a signal."

I move my thumb awkwardly over the keypad trying to type out a message. I'm concentrating so hard I don't hear the footsteps until they're right outside the door. I'm just able to hit send when the door slams open and a bright light blinds me.

DYLAN

"Fuck!"

I pound my fist on the steering wheel.

"Cool it," Luna snaps beside me. "You're not doing anyone a favor if you don't keep your wits about you."

We're in the school parking lot after a frustrating fifteen minutes with the principal and Liam's PE teacher. They'd stayed behind after Marya called and alerted them to the fact Liam was missing. Everyone else was already gone.

The idiot teacher had left Liam unattended on the sports field to store the equipment and hadn't checked to make sure he'd come in after. He'd just assumed the boy had come and gone when he found the locker room and showers empty. A quick look in his locker showed his regular clothes and backpack still there.

The only helpful thing the man had been able to share, when we asked if he'd noticed anything, was the dark blue van that pulled up at the edge of the field toward the end of the period. He'd assumed it was a parent picking up one of the kids in his class, stopping to check out the action on the field. He added defensively it wasn't that unusual.

"Now what?" my voice croaks. I'm sick at the thought of having to face Marya to tell her Liam had been taken.

"Now we touch base with the office."

She calls in on speakerphone so I hear Damian answer. In brief highlights she outlines the information.

"What was the last time anyone saw him?" Damian asks.

"Around two forty-five is when Gruber went inside with the rest of the kids."

"Almost an hour by now."

"Anything helpful from the searches?"

"We haven't been able to get hold of the team in Farmington yet, but we did talk to the agent in charge in Austin. The condo didn't yield anything useful and Keswick was not exactly forthcoming, but they did get a DNA sample from him. It's being flown to the lab in Quantico."

"That won't help us find Liam," I bite off, impatient with the now useless information. Even if it didn't take at least forty-eight hours to get results, it's clear Keswick didn't take Liam, so it's a moot point.

"What about his phone? Did you find that in his locker?" Jasper's voice pipes up. "I've tried using the tracker, but it's not showing up."

Shit. I'd been so pissed with the teacher, I hadn't even thought about it. I reach into the back seat, pull the backpack I stuffed his clothes into on my lap, and start pulling everything out.

"No phone," I answer. "We know it's turned off, but he must have it on him."

"Or it was disabled," Luna adds.

"Hang on one sec," Damian interrupts. "Farmington on the other line."

We hear a click when we're put on hold. Luna reaches over and puts her hand on the fist I have clenched in Liam's clothes. "We'll get him. We'll get both of them."

I just wish I could feel her confidence.

"That was Linden. They found evidence at the Farmington residence to indicate Seth was there at some point. One of his sneakers was found in the walk-in closet of the master bedroom. Looks like they may have hit on his playroom. You don't wanna know what else they uncovered."

I try to ignore Damian's last words. "We're heading to Farmington," I announce, already starting the car.

"You're jumping the gun," Damian cautions.

"I'm following my gut." I'm pulling out of the parking lot and beside me Luna clips in her seat belt. At least she seems on board.

"What if you're wrong?" he asks.

"Can't sit on my hands, Boss."

I focus on driving and barely hear the rest of the conversation between Luna and the office. It's not until we're coming up on Aztec that she breaks the silence in the vehicle.

"Do you even know where to look?"

"No, but I'm hoping it'll come to me," I admit.

"Jasper will keep trying to find the signal on his phone."

I nod. I know he will, I just hope to God when he does it won't be too late for Liam. I'll never be able to face Marya again. I should never have let down my guard.

As if conjured up by my thoughts, my phone in the center console starts ringing, Marya's name on the screen.

"Are you gonna answer that?" Luna asks, her glare burning me when I let it ring a few times. When I don't move, she picks it up and identifies herself.

"Hey, Marya, yes, he's behind the wheel. Hang on, I'll put you on speaker."

"Dylan?"

Goddammit. She sounds like she's barely holding it together.

"Right here, Sweetheart."

"Anything?"

"Is your mom there, Marya?"

"Yes, and Kerry's on her way. Dylan? Did you find him?" Damian must've alerted his wife at some point, and I'm grateful to know Marya will have some support.

"Not yet. We have a few ideas we're running down." I can't bring myself to tell her we have good reason to believe he was taken.

"O-okay," she mumbles.

"Hang in there. I won't stop until I find him."

Luna looks at me sharply but I mean every word. I will not stop until I find her boy. I just fucking hope he's alive when I do.

"I know. I should let you get to it."

I know I don't deserve the faith she puts in me, but I'll be damned if I won't do everything to live up to it. "I'll call you right away when I have news."

Luna ends the call and still has the phone in her hand when a message comes in.

"What's that?"

"Shit. Pull over."

I don't hesitate and do as she asks, stopping on the shoulder of the road. We're somewhere between

Durango and Aztec along the 550. I take the phone from her hand and look at the message.

Liam: 10-3 Thomas tied up dark no window only do

"10-3? Stop transmitting?" Luna asks, confused.

"No. The boys made up their own codes. 10-3 is SOS. He's with Thomas."

"Right and tied up in the dark. No window, only... door?"

"I'm guessing," I mutter, already calling into the office. "Jas? Run the tracker, Liam just sent a message. I'll forward it to you."

"Fuck," I hear Jasper curse, never a good sign. "Shit man, the signal flashed on the map a few times and then disappeared again."

"Where," I snap.

"South of Farmington. Between the San Juan River and Highway 64."

I put the Expedition back in drive and dust flies up behind me as I peel away from the shoulder. "What is near?"

I hear him curse again. "The Contechs plant."

"How far from his house?"

"Ten minutes, tops."

"Call—"

"Already on it, brother. Damian's got them on the phone. What's your ETA?"

"Half a goddamn hour."

MARYA

I'm staring blindly at the TV Mom turned on as distraction for the boys. I'm wedged between them on the couch. They haven't left my side since they walked in, pale-faced and quiet. I'm sure I look the same.

I can hear the quiet whispers from the kitchen where Kerry and Mom have withdrawn. I shut down after talking to Dylan, mentally hanging onto his promise he'd bring my baby home. I replay his words over and over in my head like a mantra—a prayer—I'm afraid to stop.

I barely register the doorbell ringing and Mom opening the door. It's not until Clint sits down on the coffee table in front of me I can pull myself together.

"Hey, little lady," he murmurs in his deep Southern drawl. "How 'bout I take these youngsters with me? Get them out of the house for a bit?"

"I don't know."

"Beth's waitin' with some grub and Max is eager to show them the tree house."

"Tree house?" Harry's voice pipes up and I turn to him, only now noticing my arm is tight around his shoulders. Same on the other side, holding Theo firmly against me.

I guess it wasn't so much them not leaving my side; it's been me not letting them go. It's almost painful to lift my arms, but I do and the small sigh of relief coming from my oldest doesn't escape me.

"Big ole tree house. I built Max one when he was little and we still lived in Cedar Tree. Then when we looked for a house in Durango, we made sure we had plenty of trees big enough on the property to build him another. Max helped build this one. It's big enough for a sleepover, if y'all bring your pillows."

"Cool." Harry is already on board.

"What do you think, Bub?" I ask Theo, sensing his struggle. I'm pretty sure I've freaked them out more than they already were when they got home, but I also know my oldest feels he needs to be here for me.

"I dunno."

"Listen." I turn to him and take his face in my hands. "I want you to go with Clint and look after your brother. I'm okay. Grandma's here, and so is Kerry. We'll be okay until Dylan brings home Liam." I read the disbelief in his eyes, grab his shoulders and gently shake him. "He *will* bring him home." This time he nods, albeit reluctantly. "Get your stuff, guys. Sounds like you're sleeping in a tree tonight."

The moment they disappear upstairs to grab their things, Clint grabs my hands. "I'm bunking up in the tree with them. As for Dylan, that boy won't rest until he's got your son home. You can believe that to your soul."

I nod, pressing my lips together and swallowing hard. I manage to smile at the boys when they come downstairs and hug me goodbye.

The moment the door closes and I feel two pairs of arms sandwich me; I totally lose my shit.

CHAPTER 30

LIAM

I almost cry when I hear my phone hit the far wall. I'm sure it's in pieces.

All could I see was his outline, but I know it's a man. He yelled a curse word, I heard him drop something, and then he charged at me, pulling the phone from my hand and flinging it.

I'm blinking, trying to get a better look at him, when he turns and shines the flashlight back on me, and I know I'm in trouble.

Reaching out, he grabs me by the hair, and starts pulling me toward the door. It stings so bad; it feels like he's pulling the skin off my head. I scream, but I don't stop struggling against his hold.

The next moment I'm dropped and my head hits the floor. I catch a glimpse of Thomas hanging onto the man's neck and roll to my knees, making a dive for his legs. He wobbles, but doesn't go down.

I hear a loud smack and a cry, and next I'm flying through the air, hitting the floor hard enough to knock the breath out of me.

I'm gasping for breath, blink a few times, and see Thomas lying in a crumpled heap only feet away looking back at me. He has no clothes on at all.

His gaze moves up and his eyes go big a second before I sense him looming over me.

"I don't fucking get paid enough to deal with you little bitches."

I recognize the voice at the same moment my head is lifted off the floor by the hair and slammed back down.

The last thing I hear is a woman's voice.

"FBI! Back away!"

DYLAN

"How far out are you?"

Toni's voice comes over the Expedition's sound system, whispering.

"A few minutes, why?"

"I'm on the south side of the property, there's an old structure I noticed on the satellite images I wanted to check out. Dylan, the blue van is parked in the trees on the riverside."

"Jesus, are you alone?"

"Yes," her voice sounds small. "I...they were gone by the time I got back to the office. I'm sure they're searching the plant. I just wanted to help…"

"Stay put. I'm turning into the lot now."

"Follow the drive past the main parking lot, it turns into a dirt road that runs right to the river. You'll… I've gotta go."

The line goes dead.

"That doesn't sound good," Luna comments beside me, pulling her weapon and checking the chamber. Then she adds, "That doesn't look good either," pointing at the decrepit small warehouse where I can just see a figure slip through a side door.

I immediately veer the vehicle toward the building, more worried about speed than stealth. We both unclip our seat belts before I slam on the brakes.

Luna is out of the Expedition seconds before I am, and I trail her into the dark building. The moment I hear yelling coming from a hallway to my left, I switch direction and pick up the pace, following the sound. Luna's steps are right behind me.

At the end of the hallway I can see Toni standing in a door opening, from her stance it's clear she has her gun drawn and pointed.

"Put him down," she says, her voice shaking. Her words send a chill down my spine.

"Fuck you!"

I know in an instant who's inside that room.

"We've got your six, Agent Linden," I say in as calm a voice as possible.

When Luna slips to the other side of her, Toni barely moves her stance. Her voice may be shaking, but her training is solid.

"Peter Grunsberg!" I yell out, hoping to startle him before I slip by Toni into the room, tucking my gun away and holding up my hands. The only light in the room is whatever is coming in from the hallway, and from a flashlight lying on the floor behind him; the stench is overwhelming.

My eyes immediately latch on Liam's limp body held up with an arm around his throat, his feet dangling off the ground. I suck in a breath as blood boils hot through my veins like lava. Then I catch movement behind the tall man, and my eyes focus on the naked shape of a young boy, slowly crawling toward the heavy flashlight.

"Peter," I quickly draw the man's attention. "You need to let Liam go." I try to move a step closer, lifting my hands higher.

"Stop right there," he growls. "All it takes is a little more pressure."

I sneak a glance at the little boy who's now close enough to touch the flashlight. I don't want him to move.

"Peter, let's find a way to resol—"

I don't get a chance to finish before the boy grabs the flashlight and with both hands swings it in the side of the man's knee.

"Ahhh!"

I dive forward the moment I see him topple and his arm releases Liam. I'm only partly aware of Luna and Toni surging into the room behind me, struggling Peter Grunsberg to the ground, since my focus is Marya's boy. Theirs is on Grunsberg.

I watch Liam's legs crumple under him the moment his feet touch the ground, but I manage to cushion the rest of his body as he falls heavily on top of me. I sit up and pull him up to lean against my chest. My hand immediately comes up to cradle his head, but I instantly pull back when I encounter sticky wetness.

"Luna! We need EMT!"

I turn my head in the direction of a tangle of limbs on the floor where Luna and Toni are working on subduing the large man. The moment they have him in cuffs, Luna pulls out her phone, while Toni takes off her jacket and carefully drapes it over Thomas, talking to him softly.

"Ambulance is en route," Luna says, grabbing the flashlight and walking over to shine it on Liam's head. The boy hasn't moved yet. "He's got a good-sized laceration above his ear. Is he stirring at all?"

The words have barely left her mouth when he groans.

"Is he okay?" Thomas asks, standing a few feet away, Toni's jacket wrapped tightly around him, his spindly bare legs sticking out.

"Thanks to you, kiddo." I look him straight in the eye. "You have no idea how happy I am to meet you face-to-face, Thomas."

He nods, lowering his eyes.

"Let's go," Toni says, gently putting her arm around his shoulders. "I have a pair of sweats in my car that shouldn't be too big."

Not long after the Farmington FBI agents arrive on

scene, two ambulances drive up. Peter Grunsberg is limping from the blow to his knee and quickly looked over before he is carted off to the FBI offices.

Both Liam and Thomas are being loaded in the back of an ambulance. Since Thomas won't let go of Toni's hand, she ends up in the ambulance with him. Luna and I stand behind the ambulance holding Liam.

"Get on the horn with Damian. Tell him to get Marya over to the Beaumont Hospital. I'll call her from the road."

With that I climb in, directing an encouraging smile at a groggy, but awake Liam.

MARYA

It was Mom's idea to stay active. Had it been up to me, I would've been in a ball on the couch, sucking my thumb.

There is no way to describe the depth of my fear, the paralyzing sense of helplessness, but she was right that doing something made me feel marginally better.

My house is cleaner than it's been in a long time, Mom and Kerry doing most of the hard work, while I did the laundry they brought down. Now we're in the kitchen, prepping meals for the weekend with what food there is in the fridge. Thanks to Mom, we have quite a bit.

But awareness of time passing pushes back to the surface and the overwhelming fear squeezes the air from my lungs.

"It's getting dark out," I choke out, dropping the knife on the cutting board as I stare at the waning light outside the kitchen window. The thought of my baby out in the dark, scared out of his mind, has a sob burst free. Where is he? Is he hurt?

"Don't, honey," Mom advises. "Don't let your mind go there. They will find him."

"One boy is dead, the other missing for two weeks now, Mom. How can I not let my mind go there? I thought I could imagine what those parents were going through. I was so wrong. This agony is beyond any imagination, and it's been hours for me, not weeks. I don't think I could survive."

"You can and you will. Your boys count on it."

With that, I lose another battle with my tears and drop my head on my arms; the sound of more sniffles joining mine tells me I'm not the only one. Strong arms fold around me from behind and I turn to bury my face in my mother's neck. I inhale her familiar scent for some comfort as she holds me tight against her.

What I wish for are Dylan's strong arms, his quiet confidence, but he's not here. He's out there somewhere, looking for my boy.

It takes me a moment to recognize my ringtone, but Kerry beats me to it, checking the screen before handing it over.

"It's Dylan," she whispers and suddenly I'm afraid to answer. What if…

"Answer the phone, Marya. He wouldn't call you

with bad news."

She's right. I quickly answer the call.

"Dylan…"

"I have him, Sweetheart. Liam's going to be fine."

"He's found him," I announce, tears coursing down my face and the other women don't fare much better. Then I clue into something Dylan said. "He's hurt?"

"He has a cut on his head, and since he was out of it for a bit, we're on our way to the hospital so he can get checked out."

"I can be there in fifteen minutes." I'm jump started into mom-action when he stops me.

"Not Mercy. The boys are being taken to Beaumont in Farmington. Damian is making arrangements to get you here as soon as possible."

The information takes a moment to process. "Thomas?"

"They were together. Not sure what that kid went through these past weeks, but he's a big part of why I'm looking at your son's blue eyes right now."

I choke down a sob. "Can I talk to him?"

There's some rustling and then I hear him.

"Mom?" His voice is soft and a bit drowsy, but it's the most beautiful sound ever.

"Baby. I love you so much. I'm on my way, okay?"

"'Kay."

More rustling and then Dylan is back.

"Pack an overnight bag for yourself and bring him some clothes, Sweetheart. Just in case. Damian should be there soon. We're rolling up on the hospital so I better go."

"Look after him, please."

"Won't leave his side. I promise."

"I love you."

"Love you too, Marya. Now go pack. I'll see you soon."

I've just updated Mom and Kerry when the doorbell rings.

"Kerry, would you get that?" Mom says, taking charge. "I'll run up and pack a few things."

"Marya..." Damian's deep voice sounds from the doorway as he crosses the distance in a few long strides and folds me in a tight hug. "He's going to be fine."

His arms feel solid and I'm not afraid to lean into him heavily while I try to regain my equilibrium. "Where did they find him?" I finally ask when he releases me.

"I've got the vehicle out front, let's get on the road and I'll fill you in."

"I'm coming. Dante will be fine with your sister," Kerry announces, challenging Damian with a look.

"So am I," Mom seconds, coming down the stairs with a bag.

It's not until after we pack into his SUV, and I quickly call my boys at Beth's house to tell them their brother is found, that Damian tells us what he knows.

"It was actually Agent Linden who found the boys. She contacted Dylan, who was only minutes away, and along with Luna they were able to overpower the suspect."

"How did she know?"

"Good instincts. They were in a small abandoned warehouse on property that belongs to a company called Contechs, a manufacturer of electronic components. The company belongs to Connor Keswick, who is Jeremy Berger's father-in-law."

"Jeremy?"

"No. Although your ex-husband has plenty to answer for, he was not involved with the abduction of the boys or Seth's murder."

"So it was Keswick," Kerry contributes from the back seat she shares with Mom.

Damian glances up at her reflection in the rearview mirror. "Not exactly. We're still working on tying all the pieces together, although it should be easier now that we know all the players."

"Who took the boys then?" I ask, meeting his quick glance my way.

"Peter Grunsberg."

There's something familiar about the name. I've heard it before, but I can't quite place it.

"Who is that?" Mom voices my question but before Damian has a chance to answer it comes to me.

"Coach?"

CHAPTER 31

MARYA

I'm still reeling with the knowledge Liam's soccer coach is a predator when Damian pulls up in front of the hospital to let us out.

The first person I see, when the nurse shows Mom and Kerry the waiting room and I follow her on my crutches into the ER, is Toni Linden. She appears deep in conversation with a couple standing outside one of the rooms in the long hallway.

The already dissipating anger I've felt toward the agent melts away completely as I watch her wrap the clearly distraught woman in a hug. These must be Thomas' parents. Trying not to intrude, I follow the nurse and slip as best I can past them, but when I throw a glance over my shoulder I catch her peek at me.

I recognize the apology in her eyes as if she'd

spoken the words and simply I nod my acceptance. It's all I have time to give her; my son is waiting for me.

The nurse holds open the door to an image that burns itself into my soul. Dylan leaning forward on a stool, pulled close to the head of the hospital bed that holds my son. His large hand is covering Liam's chest, and his head is resting on the pillow next to my boy's bandaged one.

Liam appears to be asleep, but Dylan's head lifts up the moment he hears the door click shut behind me.

"Sweetheart," he murmurs, before carefully removing his hand from Liam's chest and getting to his feet.

With one hand he takes my crutches, while the other arm pulls me tight against him. My nose is pressed against the hollow of his throat and my hands clutch his shirt at the small of his back. My nose stings and I have a lump in my throat, but I refuse to give in to tears. I've shed enough of them the past hours.

"Was he..." I let the word trail, afraid to finish my question, but Dylan hears it anyway.

"No."

I slump against him. "Oh God, thank you."

"Mom?"

Dylan takes a step back and we both turn to the bed. "Hey, baby." I hobble to Liam's side and try to smile, even as my eyes take in the large bandage wrapped around his head and the crusted blood not quite wiped from his neck and behind his ear. It's a good thing life with three boys includes plenty of encounters with blood; otherwise I might've lost it again.

I feel Dylan's hand settle on my lower back and feel the instant comfort it provides.

"The doc will be here soon. Liam just got back from a scan maybe fifteen minutes before you got here. Why don't you have a seat?"

"I got stitches," Liam says, as I'm gently pushed down on the stool.

"Twelve of them," Dylan says behind me and Liam grins up at him.

"Did I break the record, Mom?"

I roll my eyes. Everything with my boys is a competition. Who's taller, who's stronger, who has the scariest injuries and the biggest scars—and we haven't quite hit puberty yet.

Lord have mercy.

"Probably, Bub," I answer with a sigh. Dylan starts chuckling behind me.

The door opens and a doctor walks in and stops at the opposite side of the bed. "Hey, Liam. Mrs. Berger?"

"It's Ms.," I clarify.

"I'll just wait outside," Dylan says, but I grab him by the hand and hold on.

"Stay."

"Your son has a nice size cut on his head we already cleaned and closed, but aside from that, a concussion, and a doozy of a headache, there's no additional injury. We'll keep an eye on him overnight and see how things are tomorrow."

"Can he have visitors?"

"As soon as we have him moved up to a room. A nurse will be in shortly, I believe there's some insurance stuff to be filled out, and as soon as that's done he can be on his way."

True to his word, the same nurse who showed me here comes in with a clipboard and I quickly fill out the questionnaire.

"I'm moving him to the third floor, room 312. Give us twenty minutes to transfer care and get him settled in?"

"You head to the waiting room," Dylan suggests. "I'll be right behind you. I'm just going walk him to the elevator."

I kiss Liam, who wraps an arm around my neck— something he hasn't done in a long time and has me swallow a lump—and watch as Dylan helps the nurse navigate his hospital bed through the door.

The waiting room is full of familiar faces: Mom, Kerry, Damian, Luna, and Toni with her arm firmly around the shoulders of Mrs. McKinley. They look up as one when I walk in.

"Twelve stitches and a concussion," I immediately inform Mom who half-rises from her chair. "He'll be fine. They're just moving him up to a room and we can go see him."

"Where's Dylan?" Damian wants to know.

"Right here," his deep voice sounds right behind

me, as I feel the pressure of his hand on my lower back. "You should sit down," he adds for my benefit, and I let him guide me to a vacant chair beside my mother. Then he turns to Thomas' mom and crouches down in front of her, grabbing her hand as he speaks to her in a gentle tone. "I don't know how much your son is willing to share about what happened, but I need you to know—if not for his actions—things may well have ended much differently. He's a fighter, and you should be very proud of him."

"Thank you." The words are barely audible, but the grateful look she shoots him with eyes brimming with tears is clear.

Moments later her husband comes in to get her.

"Thank you," Toni echoes, getting to her feet, but her eyes are on Dylan. "Her son didn't want her in the room when the doctor came in to examine him. She can guess, though. What you said, I'm sure it helped."

The implication of what she says fills me with some form of survivor's guilt as I realize how lucky Liam was.

"I've got her," Luna says, following Toni—who claims to need some air—out of the room.

DYLAN

"Jesus," Damian runs a hand through his hair, looking shaken.

It's coming on to midnight, and we're standing in the parking lot, Kerry already tucked inside the running SUV.

Luna left for Yeager's office with Toni earlier, where apparently they're waiting to interview Grunsberg until the boss gets there. He's flying back from Austin. She left the Expedition for me.

Jasper had called around the time Marya went up with Lydia and Kerry to see her boy. The team in Montrose found the connection in the paperwork they took out of Keswick's house there, something that had easily been overlooked initially, simply because so much time had passed.

They found a copy of a birth certificate listing one Katherine Grunsberg as the mother of Peter James Grunsberg, born eight years prior to Katherine's marriage to Connor Keswick. From what they pulled together from the family papers, Sylvia was born three years after that. The last mention of Peter was a letter from a boarding school in Vermont Keswick donated a whack of money to, confirming the then fourteen-year-old's arrival. Sylvia would've been just three years old and wouldn't necessarily have remembered him.

We have to wait to get information from Grunsberg himself, since it's doubtful Keswick will talk, but it's clear their paths crossed again at some point. The only witnesses able to perhaps shed a little light are the two boys.

While I was getting some missing details from Liam—mostly about what happened in that windowless room—Damian had the difficult task of interviewing Thomas. Something that clearly affected him.

"Tough," I mumble sympathetically.

Damian snorts in response. "Nowhere near what his poor parents are faced with."

"For sure."

"The kid never left that room. The first week he never saw who had taken him. All he remembers is playing a game of *Fortnight* with *SoccerLord* the night before he was taken. The guy asked him to meet in the back parking lot at the soccer fields. Said to wait by a navy blue van, because he had some special edition game the kid could borrow. He doesn't remember much else until waking up in that room." He shoves his hands in his pockets and turns to look at his wife, who appears to have dozed off, her head resting against the window. "He had a bucket in the room with him, and didn't know if it was night or day. He remembers looking forward to the door opening that first week, because that meant a bottle of water and a couple of granola bars would be tossed in the room. He said he'd feel sleepy after and would doze off. Then one time he woke up while he was…" Damian swallows hard and I know it costs him. I look away and give him a minute, my own fists clenched in my pockets. "Anyway." He clears his throat. "He remembers trying to fight, recognizing Grunsberg, who easily overpowered him, muttering something about not being able to wait his turn. That's all that was ever said to him when the man returned. He never got his clothes back."

I don't trust myself to say anything, so I don't. I just swallow hard.

"Liam?" he asks, and I shake my head.

"Was spared that."

"Good."

"Yeah."

"I'm gonna drive my wife home, but first I'm gonna swing by Bella's to pick up our son. I feel the need to have him close tonight."

"I hear you, Boss."

His hand claps on my shoulder. "You did good today. Go be with your family, Barnes, and don't wait too long to make that official. Time is as precious as it is fleeting, so grab the fuck on."

***

I turn to look at Marya, who is yawning in the passenger seat. Grabbing her hand, I give it a squeeze and earn an exhausted smile.

Liam was released forty-five minutes ago, after a very uncomfortable night in his room.

The nurse ended up wheeling in a recliner we told Lydia to take, Marya crawled in bed with her son—something the nurses frowned at but didn't interfere with—and I sat on the floor by the door, my back against the wall. I dozed off occasionally, but every time I did, staff would come in to check on Liam. They might as well have put in a revolving door. It's quieter at Marya's place with all four boys running around.

A quick glance in the rearview mirror shows both Liam and Lydia asleep. Good, because I'm not sure we'll get much of a chance at Marya's.

Before we left the hospital, I made a call to my mother to see how the boys fared in the tree house last night, and to give her a heads-up we'd be on our way home soon. From what I gather, the kids are bouncing to see their brother. I have no doubt they'll be waiting at Marya's when we get there.

"I...uhh...do you...*shit*,"Marya uncharacteristically stammers.

"Spit it out, Sweetheart."

She huffs and blows a stray strand of hair out of her face. "Are you just dropping us off?"

"Wasn't planning to."

"Oh."

"Did you think I was gonna throw you out and be on my merry way?" I turn to her with an eyebrow raised.

"I wasn't sure." She throws a quick glance over her shoulder, and finding the back seat occupants still safely sleeping, she leans in a little closer. "Things haven't exactly been moving along a traditional path thus far. It's hard to know what to expect. It's like we've lived a lifetime in the past couple of months, and at the same time I feel like maybe we've missed some steps."

I turn our hands palm to palm and slip my fingers between hers. "What do you want?" I ask bluntly.

She stays quiet, so I try again. "Today, next week, next month—what is it you want?" When she still hesitates, I continue, "Okay, I'll tell you what I want. Today I don't want to leave you or the boys, so unless you don't want me to, I'll stick around."

"I want you to."

I grin at her. "See? We're getting somewhere. Now, aside from something popping up that requires my presence at the office, I'd like to hang around tomorrow as well."

"Fine by me." Her grin matches mine.

"Excellent. Then tomorrow night, seeing as it's technically a school night, Max and I should head back to my place. Not because I want to," I add quickly, "but because I think it's better to give the kids a chance to get used to the fact we're becoming an *us*. Next weekend we can be back here, if you'll have us."

Her fingers squeeze mine but before she can respond, Lydia answers from the back seat, making us both laugh.

"Ohhh, she'll have you."

CHAPTER 32

DYLAN

"Hey."

"Hi, is this a good time? I can call back—"

"It's always a good time for you, Sweetheart," I tell Marya, get up from my chair, and walk into the hallway, away from my team's prying eyes.

The truth is, we've been swamped, and although I've talked to her every day, I haven't seen much of her.

The feedback from both Keswick's and Grunsberg's interviews had been sparse, since neither was particularly forthcoming, so we've been digging hard.

Monday we received the search warrant for Grunsberg's house in Durango, as well as his office at the office furniture outlet he's managed the last six months since moving here from Grand Junction. The guy has a wife and two young daughters for fuck's sake.

The wife looked shell-shocked when we arrived on her doorstep Monday afternoon. It was clear she already knew her husband was in FBI custody, but she'd been clueless the navy blue van belonging to her was used in the abduction of children. The same van she used to take their own daughters to daycare in.

She'd been equally clueless about her husband's connection with Connor Keswick, who she only knew as the father of her college friend, Sylvia, well before she even met Peter Grunsberg. It's turned out to be a tangled web for fucking sure.

The only thing we found in the house was his PS4 in the basement rec room, but we hit the jackpot when we later searched his office at the store. In a locked drawer in his desk, we discovered a digital camera storing not only the soccer tryout pictures Berger had alluded to, but also pictures of Seth, Thomas, and a total of five more young boys. I'll never be able to get those images out of my mind.

From what we were able to collect from Grunsberg's home and office, along with the evidence found in the Montrose and Farmington searches, the picture was getting clearer.

As of yesterday, three of those unknown boys have been identified. The first one we matched was a boy who disappeared in June of 2013 on a school trip to Arches National Park in Utah. He was never found.

The other two disappeared from the Grand Junction area. One was found wandering along the Colorado River near Palisade, nine days after he went missing in 2017, and the third boy was gone for two weeks just last year before he turned up sitting on his own front step. Both boys claimed not to remember what happened and both showed evidence of having been sexually assaulted. The cases were never connected.

They are now.

The similarities in the cases we uncovered are undeniable. All the kids fit the same general physical description, were between nine and twelve, and were avid gamers. I bet we'll find the same is true for the kids in the remaining two pictures, once we identify those.

God only knows how many similar cases there are. How many of these kids are still missing.

There's enough to make a case against Peter Grunsberg, but any case against Keswick is purely circumstantial.

Last night, all information we uncovered was handed over to Yeager. He planned to interview Grunsberg again today, confronting him with some of the evidence. So far most of what we found makes for a solid case against Peter—including the semen found on Seth's body which turned out to be his—but there isn't really anything concrete to tie in Keswick.

That's what I'm hanging around the office for, a call from Damian who's sitting in on the interview in Farmington. Hopefully with some good news.

"It's just that…were you and Max are still planning to be here for dinner?"

Marya's voice draws me from my thoughts and I take a quick look at my watch. It's already five thirty.

"Absolutely," I tell her, realizing I'm wasting time at the office when I could—should—be spending time with her.

I've been eating and breathing this investigation, and as much as I'd like to wrap this case up in a tidy package, so there can be some closure for God knows how many parents out there, I can't lose sight of my own family. The one we've only just started building.

Time for me to adjust my priorities and head home.

If anything new comes up, there's always the phone.

"I just need to swing by my folks to pick up Max, and run home to pack our bags. Is six thirty okay?"

"Six thirty is perfect."

"Anything you want me to pick up?"

"Mom did groceries, so we've got food bulging out of the fridge. But…"

I can hear the sound of a sliding door and I'm guessing she stepped on the back deck.

"But what?"

"Do we need condoms?"

Immediately my cock stirs to life, pressing against the fly of my jeans at the promise of sliding inside her bare. "Clean as of my last annual checkup and there's been only you, so you tell me."

Her hissed breath before she answers has the hair

stand up on my arms.

"I'm on the pill and I'm clean. There…there hasn't been anyone in years."

The small hesitation only highlights how fucking lucky I am she let me in. "How likely is it we can get the boys to bed right after dinner?"

"Not," she answers on a snicker, "but the anticipation will be sweet while we watch *Aquaman*. I promised the boys we'd rent it."

"You one of those women with a thing for Momoa?"

Another snicker.

"Maybe. But think, once the credits roll, all that lustful attention will divert to you."

She laughs heartily at my involuntary growl.

"Did you pack clean underwear and socks, Kiddo?" I ask Max, as he comes barreling down the stairs.

"I couldn't find any clean ones."

Shit. I haven't even thought about doing laundry lately. "Hang tight, I'll go grab the basket. We'll just have to do it at Marya's."

"Dad?" Max pipes up when I carry down an overflowing basket with dirty laundry.

"Yeah, Max."

"Wouldn't it be easier if we just moved into their house?"

From the mouths of babes.

Still, it's only been a couple of months we've become more than just acquaintances. Although, technically, I've known Marya for a few years. Sure, from a distance mostly, but I've always been well aware of her, waiting for an opportunity.

"It would and it's the direction we're moving in, but a lot has happened in the past few weeks, and I think maybe everyone needs a little breather before we make that official."

My easy-going son shrugs his shoulders. "It's a pain, Dad. I have three beds, one here, one at Grammy's, and now one at Marya's, and sometimes I don't know which one I'll be sleeping in."

He's right. Of everyone, Max has been shuffled around a lot and has taken it all in stride, so I never really thought to take that into consideration, but I should. I ruffle his hair.

"Good point, kid. Maybe we should all sit down this weekend and talk about it."

I look around our modest house and although comfortably familiar, it's never really represented home to me. In truth, I much prefer Marya's rambling house, more so because she's there.

My phone rings in my pocket. The office.

"Gotta take this call, Max. Grab my keys and start hauling stuff to the truck, okay?"

"Can I start it?" he asks, a big grin on his face.

"Over my dead body."

"That can be arranged," the smart-ass quips with a grin, before snagging the keys from the table and making for the door.

I quickly answer the call. "Barnes."

"You sitting down?" Jasper asks.

"Sure," I lie.

"Grunsberg is singing."

"No shit?"

"Nope. Got scared when Yeager shoved the pictures from his camera in his face. Told him he's going down for all charges related to these cases and any other one we can find. Grunsberg was quick to implicate Connor Keswick. Confirmed he was sexually molested during the entire time living in Keswick's house. According to him, he continued being a victim at boarding school until his senior year when he became predator instead of prey."

"Jesus."

"Oh, it gets better. He stayed in the New England states until he happened to read an article that mentioned his stepfather's company, Contechs, had nailed a major international contract seven years ago. He came back to Colorado, threatened Keswick with exposure for a payoff, who turned around and offered him a better deal."

"Let me guess, Keswick foots the bills while Grunsberg finds the next victim to feed their sick sexual proclivity. Both reap the so-called rewards."

"Bingo. We may never know how many victims they've left out there, but apparently the law had come a little too close when he was questioned about the boy that went missing from the school trip to the park. Grunsberg was the school bus driver. Keswick got nervous and thought his stepson should get married.

Less likely to stand out as a potential suspect when you've got a wife and kids."

"His daughter's college friend."

"He remembered her family was from Grand Junction."

"Right in his wheelhouse. She clearly didn't have a clue what she was getting into."

"From the way he tells it, she didn't even know he was connected to the Keswick family. She and Sylvia lost touch.

A long entangled history but all the pieces are starting to connect.

"Did he talk about what happened to Seth?"

"According to Grunsberg, Keswick killed him when the poor kid came to just while he was being assaulted. When asked why his DNA was all over the boy, he confessed he'd been so worked up he masturbated on his body. Frustrated, he'd abducted Thomas shortly after, but Keswick kept postponing their plans, and Grunsberg finally decided to keep the boy for himself and find a 'fresh' one for his stepfather."

"Liam," I conclude.

"Yes."

"Christ, I've seen the worst of the worst in this job and I can usually distance myself, but this one will leave a shadow I'll never be able to shake."

"I hear you, brother. One last thing; this morning Luna saw Sylvia at the Arrow's Edge compound and asked her about Alba, the nanny. Turns out it was

Keswick who told her about the family emergency. She never spoke with Alba directly."

"Are you thinking what I'm thinking? The nanny knew something or saw something?"

"Another thing we won't know for sure unless and until a body turns up."

MARYA

I'm in the kitchen when Dylan lets himself and Max in the front door. His eyes immediately zoom in on me, and the heat they radiate has my nipples tighten and a charge shoot straight down between my legs.

It's going to be a long night.

"Are the boys downstairs?" Max asks, yanking me back to reality.

"Try saying hello first, Kiddo," Dylan rumbles.

"Sorry." Max detours from the top of the basement stairs to the kitchen, where he wraps his arms around my waist. "Hey, Marya."

I hug him close for a minute and press a kiss to his head. "I've missed you, Max. Head on downstairs, the boys have been anxiously awaiting your arrival. Oh," I call after him. "And tell them dinner in five minutes."

"Make that fifteen, kid!" Dylan yells downstairs before stalking over to me.

I don't even get a chance to say hi before his mouth slams down on mine, his tongue claiming. Large hands lift me up under my arms and plant my ass on the counter, right next to the plates I'd already pulled down. All I've been able to do is curl my fingers in his shirt, pulling him impossibly closer. His hips wedge between my legs, pressing the wide ridge of his hard shaft against my heat.

Fuck. How are we ever going to manage to stay dressed until the boys go to bed?

"God, I missed you," he mumbles against my lips, when he finally lets me up for air.

Any uncertainties about where we stand after only talking a few times this past week fly right out the window. There is no doubt this man wants to be here—with me.

"I love you, Dylan," I whisper back. "A week is too long."

He suddenly takes a step back, looking at me intently. "For real? Because Max and I want to move in."

It takes my mind a moment to process, but my body is already on board, judging by the butterflies bouncing around my stomach.

"Max?" I finally ask.

"Kid told me it didn't make sense to move back and forth all the time. I happen to agree with that."

I tilt my head to the side and look at him from under my lashes. "So moving in here would be a convenience?"

"Fuck, yeah," Dylan says, as he smirks. "I even brought our laundry." He grins even wider when my mouth falls open.

"You're serious?" I snap. I'm all for combining our households, but not so I can be a convenient housekeeper.

I'm pissed and slide off the counter, trying to push him out of the way, but he cages me in with his solid arms. All I can do is turn my head away when he leans close enough I feel his breath against my ear.

"Serious as a heart attack, Sweetheart. I love you, love your boys—and Max fucking loves everyone—and I want to come home to you every day." I feel myself melting as his lips kiss that soft spot behind my ear. "And for the record, I'm happy to take on everyone's laundry, just don't ask me to fold shit."

"Tease," I grumble, ineffectively punching his shoulder. When I turn my head, his face is inches from mine, a warm smile in his eyes.

"What do you say, Marya?"

"We need to work out logistics. I want the boys all to have their own space."

"Agreed."

"We have to consolidate rules, chores, that kind of stuff. It should be the same for all of them."

"Of course."

"If there's anything we disagree on, we talk to each other first."

"Always."

He brushes hair from my face and leaves his hand against my cheek, bending in for a kiss.

I take in a deep breath before I lay out my last condition.

"And my boys have to be on board."

I know this might be the one thing holding us back from making such a big move, but it's important to me. They've been through a lot of stuff they had no control over, they deserve to have a voice in this.

"Wouldn't have it any other way."

I should've known that would be his response. He's a fantastic father, not only great with his son, but with my boys as well. Of course he would have their best interests at heart.

"In that case—yes. I say yes."

He lets out a loud, *"All right,"* lifting me off my feet and swinging me around.

"Can we eat already?" Harry's voice interrupts, just as our lips touch for a celebratory kiss.

With a groan Dylan sets me down on my feet and I turn to my youngest. "Yes, call up your brothers."

Brothers.

The word slips out without thinking, but I guess that's what the four of them will be. I look at Dylan and he winks.

"Why don't you ever make pot roast, Dad?"

He turns to Max. "Because I wouldn't know where to start. But your dad grills a good steak and pretty damn juicy hamburgers."

"Mom's burns our burgers," Theo volunteers, and I shoot him a dirty glare.

"I do not. I just like them a little crispy."

The guys collectively snort. I groan when I realize I'll be dramatically outnumbered in a house with five men.

Dylan just grins. "Your mom can do the fancy cooking, I'll man the grill."

"Sweet," Liam says, shoving back his chair.

"Scrape plates before you put them in the dishwasher," I remind him, like I have to remind the boys every night. "Liam has dish duty tonight. You're on tomorrow, Max."

I'm testing the waters, but he simply says, "Sure."

"Can we watch *Aquaman* now?"

I quickly look at Dylan before I answer Harry, and receive a slight nod. "Actually, guys, we're having a family meeting first."

Theo groans and is echoed by Liam in the kitchen. Harry looks curious and Max grins at his dad.

"About what?" my firstborn demands to know.

"Something we all need to be present for, so let's give your brother a minute to finish up so he can join us, okay?"

"Hurry up, Liam," Harry eggs him on.

He's done in record time, and I'm pretty sure I'll need to check the dishwasher filter for the remnants of dinner before it gets clogged up again.

"Here's the scoop," I start, feeling a little nervous. "Dylan and I are together."

"Duh," Theo shares, earning him a scolding look from yours truly.

"We'd like to be together all the time," I forge on.

"In fact, we'd like for all of us to be together all the time."

"You want us to move?" This from Harry who looks a little worried.

"No," Dylan answers for me. "You'd stay right here, but Max and I, we'd like to move in with you guys."

"I'm taking the basement," Theo announces matter-of-factly. "Max can have my room."

"Wait, but—" I'm interrupted by Harry.

"Cool, but we'll need an extra beanbag downstairs."

"I'm sure something can be—" This time it's Max who cuts me off.

"I have a gaming chair in my room."

"Sweet," Liam says, pushing away from the table again and starting an exodus.

"Hey, guys, hold up," I call out before they all disburse. "So what do you think?"

"Sounds good to me," Theo says, shrugging his shoulders before he saunters into the living room, grabs the remote, and drops down on the couch.

"I think it's awesome," Harry shares, following his older brother and sitting down beside him.

"It was my idea, so…" is Max's contribution as he too disappears into the living room.

Liam is the last one and my biggest concern.

"Liam?" I prompt him gently. "We want you to be honest, honey, if this is—"

"I'm okay with it," he finally says.

"You sure?" Dylan asks. "Your mom is right, we

want you to be straight. That's why we're asking you."

"Of course I'm sure," he answers, moving away to join his brothers when he looks back over his shoulder and grins at Dylan. "You're our 10-CODE."

I feel arms surround me from behind as blink against my emotions and try to swallow down the basketball-sized lump in my throat. Before I can turn and burrow my face in his chest, Harry calls out.

"Mom?"

"Yeah, Bub."

"We're gonna need a much bigger couch."

EPILOGUE

DYLAN

"Oh my God, Dylan. I'm so close."

Marya squirms under me, working hard for the maximum contact I'm holding back.

We woke up this morning to an empty house. A rare treat.

All four boys are having a sleepover at my folks. It was Clint's idea, claiming it would be the last chance to sleep in the tree house before the snow predicted for Christmas this coming weekend hits. We made sure the kids were outfitted with long johns and down sleeping bags, and Clint had a small space heater he hooked up to keep the worst of the chill off. Overnight temperatures were expected to be slightly below freezing, but the kids had all been excited at the prospect.

It was Marya who was up at the crack of dawn

calling Ma to see if they'd all survived. They had and were waiting for the pancakes she'd been in the middle of cooking. Then this afternoon, they're taking the boys on the Polar Express, a Christmas-themed ride aboard the Durango & Silverton train. By the time they get home tonight, I expect they'll be well and worn out.

I found her in the kitchen, prepping a pot of coffee. It didn't take me long to coax her onto our new massive sectional sofa that can comfortably hold all six of us.

What started as some relatively innocent making out, quickly turned into a passionate tangle of naked limbs without her brace hampering our movements. She just got rid of it last week.

It's still uncomfortable for her to be on her knees, so I have her standing bent forward over the side of the couch. I keep her down with my hand between her shoulder blades, but she pushes her fucking amazing round ass back on my cock.

"Stop torturing me," she moans when I pull almost all the way out.

"Prolonging the pleasure, baby," I mumble when I bend over her and gently bite her shoulder, making her wiggle even more.

"You're mean."

"Not mean, Sweetheart, selfish—maybe. So far I've only been able to enjoy this side of you from a distance, I've looked forward to taking my time getting familiar with it."

Without losing our minimal connection, I use my hands, teeth, and tongue to do just that; get very intimately acquainted, until I can't hold back myself.

"Yessss!"

Marya's head whips back when I grab onto her hips and pull her back on me as I power inside her. I try to pace myself, but I soon lose myself to a frantic rhythm. Nothing but the sound of skin slapping, her moans, and my unintelligible grunts as I feel the first ripple of her orgasm massage my cock. I follow seconds after.

There's nothing like the feel of her wet heat clamping down on me skin to skin.

"This one's from Grammy and Grampa for you."

Max hands a similar box to the one he just opened, to a slightly awkward Liam.

As expected, Harry was already calling them by those monikers the first family dinner we had at my folks' house. By the time Clint was done putting up a wall and updating the little bathroom in the basement for Theo, he was calling them Grammy and Grampa.

The only holdout so far has been Liam. Already a little unsure of himself—plus having had his trust betrayed by two important people in his life; his father and his coach—it's not easy for him to let new people in.

The child psychologist he's been seeing after his ordeal has made communication easier for Liam.

Having Max around seems to have helped as well, maybe because he's no longer alone in the middle of the pack.

He still seems to feel a little unsure around my folks, though.

Throwing a hesitant smile in their general direction, he starts ripping the paper from the box, only to stop when he sees the Nike logo.

"Cool!" Max cries out, enthusiastically waving his own red Cristiano Ronaldo CR7 Nike soccer cleats in the air. "You got the same ones I did!"

Marya and my eyes meet across the room. We both noticed the blush creeping up Liam's neck. I shake my head slightly when she makes a move to get up. I think we should let him react however he's going to, and then deal with it. I send Marya an encouraging smile and see her settle back in beside Theo.

"Well, open it up," Harry urges his brother.

Liam's jaw is working, but he continues to open his present, pulling out the lime green pair of the same cleats. His head is bent.

"Liam?" Marya's worried voice is gentle.

His head comes up, his eyes welling with tears as he looks at Ma and Clint. "You gave me the same ones as Max."

"Well..." Clint drawls. "Seein' as two of our grandsons are soccer stars, I reckon they both oughta have the same cleats the great Ronaldo wears."

"But I'm not really—"

"Bull hickey," Clint cuts in, making Theo snort.

"Never had kids, but Dylan here is the best son a man could want. Met Max when he was just a wee tyke, about yay high—" He holds his hand about ten inches off the floor, causing a round of giggles from the peanut gallery. "All he did was flush remote controls down the toilet and decorate the house with his Grammy's underwear, but he's my grandboy nonetheless. Already love your mom like a daughter, so how can you be anything else but grandkids too?"

I hear Ma sniffle, and by the looks of it, Marya is barely holding it together as well. To be honest, I'm pretty moved too, and I realize Liam is not the only one who's been hesitant letting someone in. Heck, I've known Clint almost nine years, and although the man looks after my mom like it's his reason for being, and has been the only father I've known, I've never called him anything but by his name.

Before I can do anything to rectify that, Liam gets up and walks over to him, throwing his arms around the burly man's neck.

"Thanks, Grampa."

I see he's moved by the kid's gesture, and slaps him awkwardly on the back, mumbling, "Shucks."

"You too, Grammy." Liam does the same thing with my mother who just nods, hugging him back.

"Oh, for Pete's sake," Lydia, who's been unnaturally quiet so far, blurts out. "Would you knock it off? Y'all are ruining my makeup." She dabs furiously at her eyes, only making the damage worse from what I can see.

"Grab another tissue, Lydia, 'cause I've got more," I say, turning to Clint.

"Ahh, Son, don't make me lose my street cred with these youngsters now."

"You'll earn it back. Almost nine years and I haven't given you the respect a real father deserves. That changes today. How's Pop sound?"

"Good," he forces out, nodding his head furiously. "Sounds real good."

MARYA

I know it's just a civil service, but I couldn't resist wearing a pretty dress. I don't often get that chance.

The soft pastel print boho dress was the 'something new' Kerry found and bought for me. The dress leaves my shoulders bare and the short poofy sleeves just cover part of my upper arms. The blousy bodice is cinched in at the waist with a wide corset-like belt in the same powder blue from the print, which takes care of the 'something blue.' The skirt hits just below the knee and is full and roomy.

Mom and Kerry are fussing with my hair, even though I told them I wanted it down. I ended up compromising and let them pin up the front with a few loose curls framing my face.

I put my foot down on the deep plum lipstick, though. Knowing Dylan, we'll both be wearing it the first chance he gets at my mouth. Clear lip gloss is as far as I'm willing to go.

Luckily, Kerry has a light hand with makeup, because I prefer a natural look.

My only concession to my surroundings is the 'something borrowed' biker boots on my feet. They're actually Luna's and as it turns out we have the same size feet.

The 'something old' my mom took care of when she wrapped the pearl necklace her grandmother had left her around my wrist.

"Are you ready?"

Theo sticks his head into Ouray's office, temporarily turned into my dressing room. A little unconventional with the large Arrow's Edge insignia on the wall behind his desk, and the massive old barn wood table surrounded by a mismatched collection of chairs under the picture window.

It had been Luna's idea, when she heard we were planning a quiet civil union in the La Plata County Clerk's office on the same day as the MC's annual spring barbecue, to combine the two and have Ouray officiate. I was about to pass when I caught the big smile on Dylan's face. Turns out, my husband-to-be is a bit of a motorcycle fanatic. I learn something new every day.

Just over a month ago—when Dylan and I were at the bank to open savings accounts for the boys and the manager addressed me as Mrs. Berger—I told him I was sick of people calling me by that name.

We were walking out of the building when he turned to me and asked whether I'd have an issue if people called me Mrs. Barnes.

It was that practical. We were standing on the sidewalk, he stopped and turned to me and simply said, "Be my wife."

I didn't hesitate.

Back in January, Jeremy had been given the choice either to face the charge of aiding and abetting in the commitment of a crime, or enter a plea that would mean reduced time and included signing off on his parental rights to all his children.

After everything that happened, I shouldn't be surprised he didn't waste time signing away his kids to save his own hide. Typical.

Today I'm getting a name I can wear with pride, and someday if my boys bring it up, they may choose to go with a different name as well. That's up to them.

"I'm ready, Bub," I tell my son with a smile.

Five minutes later, my three boys walk me down the aisle running right down the center of the clubhouse main room. I know either side is full with our family and friends, but all I can see is a grinning Dylan in front of the large window, his pop and son standing in for him, all in black jeans and white dress shirts, while on my side Kerry and Mom are waiting in pretty summer dresses.

"Be happy, Mom," Theo says, kissing my cheek.

Harry is next and as he always does, he wraps his arms around my waist, crushing the pretty flowers Luna and Ouray's son Ahiga picked for me. "Oopsies," he grins up at me sheepishly. "Love you,

Mom. I'll pick you more later."

"Okay, buddy."

"Are you happy?" I turn to Liam, who whispered his question.

"So happy, baby. I have the five best men to love and they all love me back. How could I not be?"

He nods his face serious. "I'm happy too, Mom."

I'd kept it together all the way up the aisle. Not anymore.

Those innocuous words are a meaningful statement coming from Liam.

"Hand over your mom, Kiddo. She's losing it."

Liam untangles himself from my bone-crushing hug, takes my hand, and offers it to a still grinning Dylan.

"Stop laughing," I hiss, trying to get my happy tears under control.

"Not laughing, I'm just deliriously happy." He leans down, his mouth by my ear. "Sweet dress, and I really dig those boots, Sweetheart."

"All right, I ain't got all day. Let's get this show on the road," Ouray grumbles, but he does it with a grin. "We'll keep this short and to the point. We've got a pig and cold beer waitin'."

Loud cheers go up around us. I turn around and find a sea of familiar smiling faces, but Ouray quickly calls the place to order.

He's right; the official part is short and sweet, aside from a moment of hilarity when he called Dylan, Bullseye. An inside joke I'll have to get to the bottom of.

As I had anticipated, my husband doesn't just kiss me; he devours my mouth to loud cheers and whistles.

It took no time at all for the clubhouse to empty out into the large yard, where picnic tables were set up with a ridiculous amount of food, a whole pig was roasting over a big outdoor grill, and the first cold beers were being drawn from one of the kegs.

"What are the odds we can get out of here soon?"

I turn to smile at Dylan. "Sorry to disappoint, honey, but we'll just be going home with the kids."

He leans closer. "Wrong. The boys are having their first tree house sleepover of the season. They're going home with Ma and Pop."

I immediately get to my feet and grab his hand.

"In that case, as soon as we say goodbye."

THE END

ACKNOWLEDGMENTS

As always I have a laundry list of people to thank for bringing my books to you.

My family for putting up with my headphones and monosyllabic answers when I'm buried deep in my fantasy world.

My incredible editorial team; Karen Hrdlicka and Joanne Thompson. They are with me from the time these stories are barely in the concept phase and are still there well after the book is released.

I am so grateful for my fabulous team of beta readers. Every new book I produce, they take the time to read—often on short notice—and give me feedback in between rounds of editing.

The awesome CP Smith, who puts on the finishing touches on my written words with her stellar formatting, turning the novel into a visually pleasing paperback.

I would be lost without Buoni Amici Press—Debra Presley and Drue Hoffman—who keep me on track and work hard behind the scenes to make sure you, my readers, know about my books. Their knowledge of the industry is an incredible asset.

Keeper of my sanity is Stephanie Phillips of SBR Media, my agent. She provides me with constant encouragement, never losing faith in me even when I have none left.

All of the bloggers who take time out of their schedule to help me bring my stories to you. Some of them have been there since my very first release.

And as always, my gratitude to you—my readers. Your enthusiasm for my books—your love for my characters, you reviews, your kind words—is what drives me to write the next one.

Love you all.

ABOUT THE AUTHOR

Freya Barker inspires with her stories about 'real' people, perhaps less than perfect, each struggling to find their own slice of happy, but just as deserving of romance, thrills and chills, and some hot, sizzling sex in their lives.

Recipient of the RomCon "Reader's Choice" Award for best first book, "Slim To None," Freya has hit the ground running. She loves nothing more than to meet and mingle with her readers, whether it be online or in person at one of the signings she attends.

Freya spins story after story with an endless supply of bruised and dented characters, vying for attention!